TO THE BEAT
OF A SAVAGE DRUM

TO THE BEAT
OF A SAVAGE DRUM

AJ HERRON

Paperback ISBN: 978-1-909154-91-9

eBook ISBN: 978-1-909154-93-3

A CIP catalogue record for this book is available from
the National Library.

Although set within a real historical context, this book is a work of
fiction. With a few notable exceptions, the characters are of the
author's imagination and are used fictitiously.

Cover Design by Tess Purcell

To the memory of Ger McGann,

Re-enactor,

27th (Inniskilling) Regiment of Foot

AUTHOR'S NOTE

This is not the story of the Battle of Waterloo, nor is it an analysis of what happened on that day. Rather, it is the story of a young man who enlists as a drummer in the 27th Regiment of Foot, the Inniskillings, and ultimately finds himself participating in that epic confrontation. I have used the events leading up to Waterloo, and the battle itself, as a setting in which to place drummers from their initial recruitment into the army to the moment they find themselves in the line marching courageously towards the enemy, beating time for their musket-bearing comrades. I have tried to be historically accurate in my depiction of the life of the common soldier in the early nineteenth century, and in presenting the battle scenes at Waterloo, to allow James Burns to tell the drummer's story in an authentic voice. The earlier events that I have described, prior to the 27th arriving in Ghent, are entirely fictional as are most of the book's characters. For ease of reading, military slang of the period is kept to a minimum and, where used, is explained in context. Drum signals are referred to using capitalisation as are some military terms and units; French place-names are not italicised. All mistakes are mine.

This book is written as a tribute to the brave drummers of all armies who, as unarmed non-combatants, marched into battle with their comrades, and whose drums were silenced.

Being the narrative of James Anthony Burns,
27th Regiment of Foot, the Inniskillings

1

'The drum is a savage instrument, boy, and it's the soldier's job to be savage.'

It's a lifetime since I heard those words. Yet I hear them still, as if Drum Major Edward Hicks of the 27th Regiment of Foot, the Inniskillings, had uttered them just seconds ago. The Drum Major's large, round, whiskered face was seasoned after twenty years of service in the army, most of it abroad. He towered over me, a giant of a man, broad-shouldered and long-armed, his strength making me gasp as he pulled me by the shirt towards him on that first day of drum school. My youthful bravado disintegrated as he held me close enough to see the stitching of his immaculate, braided uniform and smell the polish of his crossed, white belts.

'Why are you here, lad?' he demanded.

'Because I want to be a drummer, Sir.'

'A drum brings out the savage in a man,' he said. 'Can you be that kind of drummer?'

'Yes, Sir,' I said, trying to keep the tremor out of my voice.

'Well, let's see if you can, then,' he said, letting go of my shirt.

And that was it. Drum Major Hicks's first words to me, as I recall them. Not a long exchange, I'll allow, and of little significance at the time but those words would see me all the way from that initial encounter in the army depot in Enniskillen, County Fermanagh, to the rolling, fertile countryside around Mont St Jean, just south of the village of Waterloo. Is there a single moment in biological time that marks the end of carefree youth or is it a combination of accumulated experiences built up over time that, inexorably, dislodge us from that state of innocence? Even now, looking back after a full and eventful life, I cannot settle upon a fixed answer. But such a time came for me when I made a momentous decision that marked the end of my early life. Although it was impossible to know then, that decision culminated in my participation in an event beyond all human comprehension, an event that I was fortunate enough to survive when so many of my comrades did not.

Perhaps I should begin with that bright, spring morning, when the frost was still white on the long, stiff grass. I was checking the snares I had carefully set the previous evening, as was my custom. Years of patient stalking along the familiar hedgerows had given me the wits of a poacher and the eye of a hunter so returning home empty-handed was not a frequent occurrence for me. But when I beheld my last snare still untouched at a gap in the hedgerow that had never before failed me, I tasted bitter disappointment. I remember being on my knees in the grass beside the empty snare, feeling utterly dejected, wondering how I'd find something for the pot for dinner, when I heard the sound of approaching drums. I'm not fully sure what went through my head at that precise moment on that particular day for I had heard it many times before, but my heart suddenly soared at the intrusion.

In an instant, I abandoned the futile hunt for game and raced off across the open fields towards the crossroads where the alehouse, known to the locals as The White Star, stood. From there, I would have a better view of the oncoming soldiers. As the beating of the drums grew louder, I recall the sense of excitement that welled up within me as I anticipated their passing. Looking back, perhaps it was the shame at my age of going home to my mother with my game bag empty that finally tipped me into doing what I did. As I hurried to get to the crossroads before the soldiers arrived, it never dawned on me that my life was about to change forever.

What I'm about to tell you happened at the beginning of 1813. By then, Napoleon had put his disastrous campaign in Russia behind him and was secure again in Paris. His *Grande Armée* lay in tatters after their long-delayed, arduous withdrawal from Moscow, annihilated as much by the extreme cold as by the merciless Cossacks who pursued them. Once back in Paris, though, he had immediately engaged himself in raising yet another army. The reaction across Europe was instant as recruitment fever gripped every kingdom, duchy and province. It reached Ireland, too, coming into my little corner of

Fermanagh nestled between two lakes. So, parties of 27th Inniskillings, such as the one that neared me, became a regular sight as they routinely set out from the depot in the town, scouring ever further afield for men to press into the army, to replace those who had recently been sent to Sicily. These press gangs could be gone for days at a time on the hunt.

The column that was approaching The White Star had already had some success by the looks of it as a number of shabbily dressed, barefoot males shuffled along in disorderly contrast to the disciplined movements of the escorting soldiers. They must have been picked up some distance away as the local men who worked on the nearby estates and farms were exempt from the army. The fertile land around Lough Erne demanded large numbers of labourers to keep the grain stores and the hay barns full in order to supply the needs of a rapidly expanding military force.

The soldiers, led by a captain on a horse, crunched their way along the gravel lane towards the alehouse, marching to the steady beat of two drummers who accompanied them. One of the drummers looked just a year or two older than me, his long arms sprouting out of his sleeves as he played. The other was a veteran, one of those who had survived years of life in the army, growing grey and wizened before their time, beating out their memories of past campaigns with every tap of the drumstick. As the party reached The White Star, the officer raised his hand. 'Column, Ha-alt,' he ordered. A small group of men came out of the inn, pewter mugs in their hands, drawn by the arrival of the military. A few other straggling travellers on the road paused also and joined the gathering. That was exactly what the captain wanted, an audience. As every recruitment party knew well, where you had onlookers, there was always the possibility of another catch, an unwary traveller, perhaps, whose brain had been softened with drink, and I spotted a few likelies among them. I pushed through the small cluster of curious bystanders to get a better view.

The red coat and buff collar and cuffs of the 27th Regiment was a familiar sight to me from my earliest memories, as was the sound of the drum that dictated the routine of the soldier's day. Usually, when I'd see a file of soldiers marching by, I'd find myself staring at the hands of the drummer, transfixed by his dexterity as he controlled every movement they made with the sound of his instrument. I liked the glamour of the uniform, of course, but it was the drumming, always the drumming, that most attracted me, reeling me in like a fat salmon on a line. And until that moment, I'd always pulled myself free of the hook and headed off home to my mother. She had lately started to talk of me taking up an apprenticeship with a weaver in the town but I didn't want to hear. Somehow the more she talked about my prospects employed in that craft, the more I realised that a life at the loom was not for me even though she had her heart set on it.

The thought of enlisting must have been lurking somewhere at the back of my mind long before then and I had probably been holding off entertaining it out of respect for my mother's wishes and not wanting to be a disappointment to her. Whatever it was, on that occasion, the drums triggered something deep within me as I stood there and I stopped fighting it. I became a creature of the moment and allowed myself to be led astray.

2

The recruiting party was still on the hunt. The older drummer switched to the fife and the marching beat transformed into a lively, dancing tune. With just two instruments, the bandsmen created a merry atmosphere at the crossroads with the low sun sparkling in the blue sky and the growing crowd enjoying the music. A few of the drinkers started to sing, swaying gently to the rhythm, knowing they were safe from the clutches of the army. The soldiers were relaxed, slouching on their long muskets, glad of the break from the hard road but they made sure to keep the gaggle of new recruits carefully bunched in their midst. The sergeant, a big stalk of a man, propped his pike against the whitewashed wall and entered the tavern. A minute later, he came out balancing a tray of small glasses each full to the brim with whiskey. He distributed them among the soldiers first and then to the men accompanying them. There was a bit of hurrahing and cheering as they all drained the whiskey and toasted the life of a soldier. Then the drums beat out a long and stirring crescendo. After the last echo died away, there was a sudden silence.

The sergeant stepped forward and, waving his seven

foot pike at the motley gaggle of potential recruits, shouted 'Who will join with these here proper gentlemen who are about to take the King's Oath to protect us against the likes of Napoleon Bonaparte, the greatest scoundrel Europe has ever seen?' There was a bit of coughing and shuffling but nobody answered.

'Who will join these brave gents?' the sergeant repeated, taking off his shako, the stovepipe hat with the badge of the 27th on it. He wiped his brow. It was clear that he had spent a considerable length of time overseas as his face was tanned by the sun except for a long, white streak of a scar on his pock-marked cheek. The drums then began a low, steady roll as the sergeant looked around at the flushed faces of the onlookers, more in hope than in expectation. In an area where the odd bout of fisticuffs outside a local tavern was the only kind of free, public entertainment, any display that the army musicians provided was a welcome distraction. But nobody moved. It was clear that there would be no willing takers in the crowd for the sergeant's open invitation.

For a few moments more, the sound of the drums continued to roll over our heads, demanding a response. This time, at last, I surrendered to the inner urge I had long denied. Without realising fully what I was doing, I slowly began to mimic the young drummer's actions as if I, too, had drumsticks. I began to speed up, trying to match the rhythm of his rapid wrist movements, imagining that it was I who was creating the bewitching sounds. He noticed what I was doing and nodded over at me, his strokes continuing all the while. He smiled as he did so, and I tried to keep with him, much to his amusement. The roll quickly built to an almighty climax until, with arms suspended over his head, he delayed for a few seconds before finishing with a last dramatic flourish. There was a sudden silence but my hands still moved, as if they belonged to another. Eventually, realising what I was doing, I stopped. I remember breathing heavily with the excitement of the moment. The captain drew his sword and held it aloft, the sun catching the blade, blinding me for an instant.

'Come now,' he shouted, his face red under his officer's burnished helmet, his cajoling words ringing around his audience. 'There must be a man among you who wants a different life to that of the field and the forge, who wants money in his pocket and three square meals a day. Enlist now in the King's service. I see some fine specimens of manhood here who are a perfect fit for the 27th Regiment of Foot. Come, my fine sirs, sign your name, join the Inniskillings, and let's drink to the King's health.'

The sergeant held a bottle of whiskey aloft and bawled: 'Will any brave man toast with us?'

A few men twitched uncertainly, enticed by the captain's encouragement and the bottle of whiskey, but wary at the same time. The young drummer nudged the officer and whispered in his ear. Then they both looked over in my direction.

'You, lad! Come forward,' the officer shouted.

I remained motionless.

'Yes, you! Step forward, young sir.'

Quickly, the crowd parted and I stood alone. The captain beckoned me towards him. It was a strange moment for me to be the centre of attention but, for some reason, I didn't care. It was as if I simply couldn't help it, as if someone were pushing me forward. I found myself in front of the officer. He pointed at the drum that the veteran had placed on the ground. As I stood there rooted to the spot, suddenly incapable of movement, the young drummer picked it up and placed the belt over my head. He then settled the drum at my side. I was tall for my age, with a slight frame, but the ungainly bulk of the instrument hung comfortably at my side. He angled it better, and I felt it nestle against my thigh. In that instant, I felt complete. It was as if a piece of myself had been missing until that drum was given to me. He stepped back and held out his sticks.

'If you want to drum,' he said, simply, 'then play a real one.'

I turned the sticks round in my hands, enjoying the feel of them, their length unnatural in my grasp. They were like two delicate, extended fingers and I had no idea what I should do with them to make the drum sing. The crowd went silent.

The fife started a slow tune. The veteran drummer nodded his head, encouraging me on. I closed my eyes and turned away from him, listening to the notes he was playing, concentrating on the pattern, allowing the melody to wash over me. Then, nervously at first, I began to make small movements with my wrists. I touched the drum. It wasn't much of a beat but it produced a sound and it felt good. A tingle went through me such as I had never known before. I did it again. And again! Then the other hand. Again! And again! Then both hands together, slowly, steadily, over and over, feeling the calfskin top of the drum vibrate, like it was alive, responding to my touch. Then one hand after the other, gently, tentatively, getting the feel of the instrument. It was like gradually immersing myself in a deep pool in the river, enjoying the lapping water and the cool feel of it against my skin.

Another drum quietly joined in, keeping with me at first, leading me on. I knew it was the younger drummer. As we tapped together, I tried to match the tempo he was laying down, easy at first. My hands grew lighter as the drumbeats became firmer. My confidence was soaring. I struck the calfskin harder, feeling for a rhythm, my rhythm, and I began to believe that I could play. The other drum upped the tempo, beating faster, and I tried to keep with it, wanting to make the magic last. But, all too soon, my wrists started to hurt. My fingers grew stiff and my hands lost their power of movement. They felt like claws. Then there was just one drum playing, and it wasn't mine. One stick dropped from my claw-hand to the ground, followed by the other one. I opened my eyes and looked around. Everyone was staring at me, including the captain and the entire party of redcoats. The younger drummer beamed as he continued to play, his hands only a blur at that stage. Then he paused suddenly, sticks crossed and held aloft, before finishing with a loud, dramatic roll. He was still smiling when the last sound died away.

'Hurrah for the lad,' the captain shouted.

That day, when the drum bewitched me, I was just short of fifteen years of age.

3

'What is your name?' the officer enquired, sizing me up.

'James Anthony Burns,' I replied, perkily.

'Well then, James Anthony Burns, the regiment is in need of a drummer and you look like the very man. Would you be willing to enlist?'

I took one quick glance down at the exquisite drum before answering the officer unhesitatingly.

'Yes, Sir.'

'Good lad,' the officer replied approvingly. 'I'm Captain Grant, and this,' he added, pointing to the soldier beside him, 'is Sergeant Curley. He'll be your company sergeant, if you are accepted, of course.'

The tough-looking sergeant shook my hand. 'Pleased to make your acquaintance,' he said with an effort at a smile that made his scar move. His remaining teeth were stained brown. He stared at me for a moment, then wiped the neck of his glass on his sleeve, poured a measure of whiskey into it, and offered it to me.

'To the King's health,' he toasted. Impetuously, I swallowed the spirit in one go. The raw alcohol made me gag, much to everyone's amusement. Although it wasn't my first time taking drink, I was far from used to it. When

I had recovered sufficiently, Curley took out a new shilling coin from his pocket, spat on both sides, rubbed it on his tunic and showed it to me.

'You can keep this now, lad, and you'll get a lot more if the surgeon finds you're fit enough for the regiment,' he said. A shilling was more than a day's pay to me then, and the thought of the bounty I'd get when I signed up would ease my mother's disappointment, or so I hoped, as I quickly pocketed the coin. Captain Grant seemed satisfied.

'Have you kin?' he asked.

I nodded. 'Yes, Sir. My mother lives near here.'

'Then, go bid farewell to her,' Grant said. 'Accompany him closely, Sergeant. And mind you bring him back with you. We'll stay here awhile and keep our new recruits whiskey-happy until you return.'

Curley strode beside me as we set out from the alehouse. Anxiety gripped me as we took to the narrow, winding lane that led towards my house, a good ten-minute walk away. Striding effortlessly along beside me, the sergeant struck up conversation almost immediately, asking me many questions about myself, how I passed my time and what I knew about army life. I told him little that would satisfy his curiosity, for I felt he was after something. When he asked who my father was, I remained silent. There was nothing much I could tell him anyway as I knew practically nothing about my father beyond his name, but I had begun to be wary. When I didn't answer, his next question came in a sly manner.

'Your mother, her name wouldn't be Kate, by any chance? Would it?'

My expression must have given me away as I saw him smile and nod. The whiskey had loosened my senses and I realised that, without saying a word, I had told him what he had wanted to know. 'So you're Anthony Burns's son,' he said, almost to himself. From then on, I tried to stay one step ahead of him so that I wouldn't have to look at him but he stepped in closer to me, almost on my shoulder, as if he thought I was going to run away.

'You've lived in the depot before,' Curley said. It was a statement, not a question. I stayed silent, not wanting to betray myself again but he continued as if I had replied. 'Then you know, soldiers is soldiers. You'll get used to them. Just like your mother did.'

I didn't like how he smiled when he said that, and I knew he was trying to rise me but I had begun to think about my enlisting and how she would react when I arrived home with a redcoat sergeant. I didn't regret my decision, though. What young man would at that age? And I certainly didn't consider the enormity of the hole I would leave in her life when I departed. Thankfully, Curley said nothing else until we reached our humble destination.

The little cabin that was my home stood in the corner of a field. The vegetable patch in front of it barely gave my mother and me enough food to last through the winter so she did small bits of lace needlework for other folk by rushlight in the evenings. She was always good with her hands. Through sheer hard work, and being thrifty by nature, she had managed each year both to pay the rent, doing needlework for the landlord's wife in part-payment, and also to put something by. She often told me that she intended this small fund for me so that I could aspire to make something of myself – she had already insisted on me learning how to read and write, skills that I put little value on then.

Walking in with Sergeant Curley, as I did that day, broke her heart more than I ever realised, not just because she had never intended for me to enlist as a common soldier but because she had built all of her hopes upon me making a success of my life in the weaving trade. It wasn't because she held anything against the army as such. After all, it was the army that had given her a husband but she grew to hate the fact that the army had also taken him away from her, leaving her practically destitute. Things had been onerous for her in the depot, as a young widow trying to live alone with an infant, until she came by this little house and managed, at last, to live a life separate from the military. I don't know if she then began to avoid other people or if they did the avoiding but I never saw her mix much with anybody after leaving. In the evenings, when the darkness had drawn in around the tiny cottage, she would sit close by the meagre fire and talk to me for a while. 'Always remember,' she would say to me in that sad voice of hers, 'you're no product of a wren's nest, James. You're the son of a brave man. You were born right.' Then she'd creep into that lonely world of hers and leave me to my own thoughts.

People who knew her when she was younger used to say that she brought the sunshine with her wherever she went but I never saw that in her. She was on the other side of happiness by then. She wouldn't talk to me about my father either. It was as if she couldn't bring herself to share him with me. All she ever told me was his name, Anthony James Burns. Whatever else there was about him she kept wrapped up in herself, burdening herself with a sadness that blocked out everything around her, including me. I was hoping that she would at least come round to tolerating the notion of me enlisting, even if she fell short of fully approving. Maybe that's why I had been holding off. Whatever my flawed thinking was at the time, I soon found out that she hadn't changed her mind one little bit. In fact, I was surprised by the vehemence of her reaction when I told her. She took a step back, put her hand, palm side, to her mouth and just looked at me, as though I had betrayed her.

'James,' she cried, the pain visible on her face, 'don't do this to me. Don't break my heart. Not you as well.' Tears sprang into her eyes and she became agitated in her movements. She pleaded with me not to go, crying out in her desperation, reminding me of her hopes for my future and why she wanted things to be different for me. I couldn't say, even now, that she was angry with me. She was simply devastated. All I could do was stand in front of her uncomprehendingly, shaken by the depth of her response. In my youthful ignorance, I couldn't understand why she wasn't glad for me, for not accepting that I must follow in my father's footsteps. She railed and railed, while I stood and listened. Her final, despairing objection was: 'But you're still too young to enlist.' And I, being unwittingly cruel, replied: 'Not as a drummer.' Defeated, she slumped into the chair she usually occupied beside the hearth.

'It was always going to come to this, James,' she said,

finally, quietly conceding. 'I left the depot so that you wouldn't become a barrack rat, like the other boys who lacked a regular upbringing.' I knew what she meant. My mother hadn't wanted me to scour out an existence hanging round the soldiers, feeding off scraps, listening to filth of every kind, smoking, swearing and drinking like a hardened veteran by the age of ten, and so she had quit the depot as soon as she got the chance. She wanted me to have a life that was better in every way to what she saw around her in the army. I still remember the look of infinite sadness on her face as she spoke to me.

'I always knew that red rag would come knocking on the door some day to get you,' she said. 'I prayed every night I'd have time to give you a different life before that happened. I was hoping for too much.'

What could I say in response? The damage had been done and I couldn't turn back, even if I had wanted to. All the time she was speaking to me, Curley had stayed by the door. I had almost forgotten he was with me until she turned to him.

'Look out for him, Sergeant,' she pleaded. 'He's all I've got left.'

'Of course, Ma'am,' Curley replied, and I saw the sly wink he made at her. 'Or may I again call you Kate? You've been a soldier's woman before. Is there anything else I can do for you, now that I'm here?'

She looked at him sharply, and a flash of recognition crossed her face. The question hung between them for a moment, as if she suddenly lacked the energy to speak. Then she shook her head and said curtly: 'Get out, Nathan.'

17

A mean look crossed Curley's face at that. 'I'll just wait outside for the lad while he gets his things. Make it a quick farewell, Kate. He's not yours anymore. He belongs to the regiment.'

'In that case, the regiment has now taken everything from me,' she said, her voice little more than a whisper. 'I've nothing left.'

I didn't get the real nature of this exchange at the time but I knew there was more to it than the words at the surface.

She didn't put up any further argument against my decision when Curley had withdrawn. She scolded me a little for what I had done, more in sorrow than in anger, warning me not to become like the sergeant or his type but to be my own man, no matter what. But I was only half-listening, wanting to be away. Then, out of the blue, her voice hard in a way I'd never heard before, she said: 'Your father left too, you know, just as you're doing now. I followed him to Flanders, when the regiment was part of the Duke of York's Army. He marched off with the battalion one morning, promising he'd be back to take care of me, as I had told him I was expecting you. But he never did come back. All he left me with was shame.'

Of course, I didn't want to hear any of that. I wanted to placate her, to convince her I knew best. 'But I'm only going as far as the depot in Enniskillen,' I pleaded. 'I'll be near you.'

'For how long?' she snapped. 'They always send the Inniskillings away, to the hardest places they can find. And when you leave with the regiment, as you surely will one day, don't think I'll be sitting here alone, waiting to hear that you've died with a bayonet in your gut or succumbed to some wasting disease far away just because you want to wear a red coat like your father did. No, I won't be coming to the depot, James Burns, for I want no part of this. You've made your choice. Now go! Leave me!' And she hushed up. I couldn't believe what she had just said. I saw no reason for her to feel shame because of my father. Wasn't he a brave man who had died an honourable death in battle?

I tried to embrace her but she would have none of it. She had withdrawn inside herself again, locked away in her own thoughts. She sat on the chair, rocking herself back and forward, and brushed me away with her hand. I wanted to ask her why she was so bitter about my father, and to assure her that I'd be in good hands, but there was no point. With a heavy heart, I walked out of that house with my few possessions under my arm, unable to explain to her that it was the drum that I wanted, not the red coat. I was blind to the fact that they were one and the same thing. Curley guided me by the elbow and I didn't resist. I can still see the silent tears falling on her cheeks as I stole a last glance at her from the doorway.

She was right. I had broken her heart again, as my father's death must have done years earlier. But I was just a lad, too young to know the misery of loss and the full impact of the hurt I caused her. As I see it now, of all the regrets in my life, that one is still the biggest. That was how I left my home, such as it was, me and my big dreams of the drum, and didn't look back. With the selfishness of youth, I never conceded that my mother had dreamed of other things for me, dreams that she nurtured through my early childhood years in the depot, dreams that I crushed when I walked out that door leaving her with her secrets.

Writing about it now, after all these years, I can see that she must have been plain worn out with the hard life she'd had, following my father on campaign, riding on the battalion's baggage carts with a few other permitted womenfolk, always watching out for him, wondering if he was still alive, if he had lost an arm or a leg, or had died in agony on some scrap of parched earth with nobody to hold his hand. I suppose it wasn't much of an existence for her coming home to a town where some looked down on her for the life she had led with the army, for giving birth to a missing man's child, and then for keeping herself to herself. At least, when she had been a camp follower, she had the company of the other soldiers' women who lived her kind of life, and who'd share what little they had with her when times were tough. When she came back after my father's death, she had picked herself up and got on with it in her own determined way. She tried to keep me free of all ties, as if my liberty was a compensation for the shackles that bound her.

I now understand my mother's feelings about the army. Serving in the King's ranks brings out the brute in the most decent of men. My mother always knew that, and she didn't want that for me. No, the army was something I chose for myself. And maybe, at the back of my mind, I enlisted thinking that my father would have been proud to stand beside me, had he lived.

How different to my innocent dream of the drum it all turned out, for I have seen soldiers do the most cruel things when that blind, unstoppable, rage comes upon them and they find themselves facing unimaginable horrors. Worse than that, I, myself, know what that rage is like for I, too, have succumbed to it, and have blood on my hands.

4

They were all the worse for drink when we got back to the alehouse, even Captain Grant. But the soldiers were still canny enough to keep the pressed men within their circle so that none of them should slink off with the King's shilling in his pocket and a belly full of whiskey at the army's expense. A lost man would cost the recruiting party dear since the bounty they hoped to share would be greatly reduced.

Curley downed a last few tots before helping Grant back into the saddle. The column then formed up again and, with the drums tapping a beat, moved off unsteadily. The soldiers were relaxed now, singing and joking with each other. Every now and then, they'd jostle the intending recruits along, laughing at their shuffling progress, trying to get them to march. They were all in good humour. Curley seemed determined to keep step beside me as if he thought I was going to try to run back home but I had no intention of doing that. Strutting along with the file of redcoats had awakened my earliest memories and I felt at ease in their company. The nearer we got to Enniskillen, the more my sense of excitement grew. Curley kept up a constant chatter, telling the men how lucky they were to have escaped the drudgery of toil on the land and the frustration of the cold, marriage bed in exchange for the carefree life of the soldier.

Up ahead, Grant had little or nothing to say. From the lolling roll of his helmet, it looked as if he had nodded off. He gave no direction at all to his mount. It just kept up a steady gait as if it knew it didn't have too far to go. We passed a shebeen on the road and the party paused to top up again. Curley procured jugs of cheap beer and passed them around, telling the new recruits that there was a brewery right beside the depot in Enniskillen and that they would have plenty of time to sample the quality of its products when they were in uniform. At that age, I had yet to develop a soldier's want for drink so the sergeant's words, and his beer, meant little to me. But it was obvious that Curley intended to keep the new men in a befuddled state of mind until we reached the town. Eventually we moved on, more a rabble than a column.

By the time we reached Enniskillen and passed along Brook Street, they were all the worse for wear and needed the support of the escorting soldiers. Curley shouted an order and the soldiers smartened up as they marched across the bridge, taking the salute from the redcoats standing guard there. The drummers loudly announced our arrival on Barrack Street but nobody paid us much heed. The sight of military coming and going was a daily occurrence and there was nothing notably different about our party. A ragged beggar suddenly shouted at us from the shelter of a doorway: 'Ye poor sods, ye'll soon be worse off than me.' I waved at him and he raised his hand back at me. I held his stare until we had passed him by.

It's strange, but the image of that outcast in the doorway has stayed with me, probably because his was the last voice I heard before leaving my youthful freedom behind.

The sentries saluted as we passed under the arch and entered the home depot of the 27th Regiment of Foot, the Inniskillings, or, as they were more frequently called, the Skins. Although I hadn't been there for quite a while, nothing had changed. Nothing ever does in an army depot. It's built of blocks of stone, enclosing you within its solid and unchanging grimness, a permanent presence. In this drab, military world, the only splashes of colour were the red tunics of the sentries on duty and the contrasting dark-blue uniforms of the artillerymen who busied themselves around a couple of 6-pounder cannon. Away to one side, outside the stables, two officers' chargers snorted and stamped as white-shirted grooms brushed their glistening coats.

Captain Grant roused himself as we entered the cobbled square. He motioned to the drummers and they gave a final roll. In the abrupt silence that followed, the captain slid down from his horse. An orderly ran over, saluted smartly, and led the animal off. The pressed men, new to the depot, huddled together, still feeling the effects of the drink they had consumed, and wondered what was coming next. I stood a little apart from them, looking around at the once familiar buildings, conscious of distant, childhood memories. The redcoats made a loose circle around us, clearly pleased that they had got us back to the depot without mishap. Someone tipped my shoulder. I turned. It was the younger drummer. He grinned at me, gave me the thumbs up and, with a cheery 'See you later,' headed off with the older drummer.

'Sergeant,' Grant drawled, when he had steadied himself on the ground. 'You will see to these men. They are at the mercy of your tender care now,' and he strolled off towards the officers' quarters, his helmet under his arm. Curley saluted at his back and turned to us. 'With me, you new men,' he bawled, and briskly we were led off in a gaggle across the square to a low-roofed building at the end of the main block, our escort in close attendance. He paused at the door and turned to us as the two sentries there presented arms.

'Welcome to the surgeon's examination room, boys,' Curley announced. 'Let's see what Mr Mostyn makes of you. He'll decide if you're fit for the ranks. Stand up straight when you're talking to him. You're not farm boys any more. You're going to be soldiers.'

We entered a large room, dark and cool due to the small size of the windows. There wasn't much by way of furniture apart from a table and chair, a book-lined cabinet by the wall and two long benches. A low platform covered with a horsehair mattress served as an examination bed as we waited. Time seemed to drag. In the silence, thoughts crowded in upon me, giving rise to doubts about my fitness for the army. I recall thinking that, just because I had decided to enlist, I was going to be accepted as a matter of course. Suddenly, I wasn't so sure of that. What if they wouldn't have me? How could I go home a failure? One doubt opened the door to another and soon I had a dozen reasons why I could be rejected. To distract myself, I looked around to see how the other men were doing.

Apart from me, I saw that the recruitment trawl had netted sixteen possibles, as they were called, and most looked as if they were regretting the rashness of their decision. The room was such a dismally depressing place that it stifled all conversation. An air of nervous apprehension hung over the men as the alcohol had largely passed through their systems and the reality of their situation was hitting them hard. Those who had elected to remain standing were mooching about awkwardly and staring at the ground. One glanced ruefully at the door as if contemplating a sudden burst for freedom but that would have been futile. There were redcoat sentries outside, armed and vigilant. To me, the pressed men looked as if they would be better suited to being in a field at harvest time rather than there, waiting for the surgeon to enter, with their awkward country stance and their 'what have I done?' expressions. The only consolation they had was the thought of the bounty that would be paid if they passed the medical. It would be worth a small fortune to them. As for me, I felt quite smug, content with my decision, and the place had no mystery for me. I had no intention of turning back. I had put myself in for it and that was that.

One of the men gave me a friendly wave. I recognised him as a local farmer who lived some distance from our cottage. He reached out a hand as if relieved to see someone he knew. I couldn't think of his name at first but he knew who I was.

'You're James Burns, aren't you?' he said. 'My name's Francie Doherty.' I took the proffered hand. It was rough and calloused, that of a man used to hard work. I remembered that his family were peasant farmers who leased out small parcels of land in the next parish whenever they could. I knew Francie was a married man so I was surprised to see him there. He must have guessed what I was thinking.

'I have to do this,' he explained, a slight tremor in his voice. 'My lease was up and the middleman put the squeeze on me. He refused to give me a new term. Someone must have offered him more. There was nothing else forthcoming so what choice do I have? My brothers have barely enough for their own needs without taking in four extra mouths to feed so it's the regiment for me. I don't want Tess and the little ones to starve. I never told her what I was doing. I hope she forgives me.' Francie smiled wryly at me but he clearly wasn't a happy man. He looked as if he had carried a bag of troubles with him to the bridge and had then forgotten to drop them in the river.

Curley eyed us with disdain and I knew what he was thinking. All we meant to him was the additional bounty he would share with Captain Grant and the rest of the recruiting party. He had probably already worked out the amount he was going to get if we all passed the medical. He didn't care about anyone's personal circumstances. His gaze held mine for a few moments. Then I quickly looked away, unsure of the slight change in his expression as he caught my eye. I didn't move for fear I was provoking him. I felt him staring and I wondered about his interest in me.

All jesting and camaraderie in the group had long been banished by then and a heavy silence had taken deep root.

Francie and I were the only ones who continued to converse, and we confined ourselves to speaking in hushed tones. Suddenly, warm tears sprang into my eyes, taking me by surprise but I coughed and wiped my face in my sleeve to conceal them. I don't think any of the others noticed; they were all too wrapped up with problems of their own to pay attention to my little breakdown. It was the same for all of us in the room at that moment, I suppose. Leave-taking and homesickness have no respect for age. Every man in that room was burdened in some way.

5

Suddenly, Curley was shouting. 'All stand for assistant surgeon Mostyn.' A smallish, pot-bellied man entered the room, his whiskers neatly trimmed. He took us all in with one sweeping glance.

'Scraping the bottom again, I see, Sergeant?' he said. He didn't care if we either heard or understood. Curley just shook his head.

'Getting harder and harder out there, Mr Mostyn,' he replied. 'Most likelies are tied to the land or apprenticed off to the weavers. Or just plain too crocked for service. This is the best we could get. We'll work on them till they can take their place in the line, never fear.'

'Young, too,' Mostyn said, nodding in my direction. 'Will the magistrate pass him?'

Curley grinned.

'He's keen on the drum, that one is, so there shouldn't be a problem with His Honour.'

'Then let's see to them,' said the assistant surgeon. Curley lined us up for inspection. I was shoved to the end, probably because I was the youngest. Mostyn instructed us to unclothe ourselves. I didn't like doing so in front of the men but I had to. So I stood shivering, waiting my turn. As the assistant surgeon worked his way along the line, there was much poking, prodding and feeling of limbs, examining of teeth and checking of heads for sores and lice. He measured our height and arm length and finally had us take turns in a weighing chair. During my examination, Curley jibed at me, passing comments. This amused the others, and I wasn't much bothered at first but, when he made a crude remark about my manhood, Mostyn barked at him to be silent. The sergeant flushed at this but I was secretly pleased that he was put in his place.

When the assistant surgeon had finished his examinations, he quickly wrote up his report. He then called each of us by name and announced his findings. Two of the men were rejected out of hand, one for having a slight limp that he had tried to disguise, and the other for having a weak chest that caused him to breathe with a rasping noise. The two rejects cheered up instantly at the news as, having sobered up again, they realised they were free to go. I heard the one with the limp whisper to the other on the way out that he had been turned down elsewhere many times before but that it was always worth his while coming back for the shilling. One by one, the rest were all pronounced fit for service in the army pending the magistrate's approval. A few men put their heads down in their hands, whether in relief or in despair I couldn't tell. Nobody was jubilant. Mostyn turned to me last of all and, as he hesitated before speaking, I thought he was going to reject me along with the first two. But I needn't have worried, he passed me without any bother.

'You've still a bit to grow, lad,' Mostyn said, 'and you need muscling up if you want to be a calfskin fiddler, but you'll do. You know you're not guaranteed the drum but I'm sure you'll get a trial and if you show any flair at all for it, you'll do well. Drummers get paid more than the rank and file, so you'll be coming out ahead straightaway. Good luck with the magistrate when you see him.' He turned to Curley. 'That's all, Sergeant. I can do no more for now. Until they are sick or shot, or get the pox, which is more likely, then I'll see them again.'

We filed back out into the square. The early spring sun had dropped behind the depot walls having done nothing to remove the chill from the air. A couple of young redcoats sidled over to stand near us, bayonets fixed on their muskets. I knew they were keeping watch on us but they said nothing. They didn't have to. The point of a bayonet makes a great argument all on its own and they weren't about to risk losing anyone at that late stage. Curley lined us up again to await the arrival of the magistrate. Already I was learning that sitting around waiting was a big part of army life.

Soon, the sound of approaching drums accompanied by the tramp of many feet drew our attention. We looked towards the arch. It wasn't long before mounted officers entered the square at the head of a long column marching in close order. Accompanying them were two drummers dictating the marching time. The soldiers had a spring in their step now that they knew they were home, and were being observed by all in the depot. They filed into the square and first wheeled around its perimeter. Then they marched to the centre where they deployed from close column into line, the drums communicating the orders shouted by the captain in charge from his position at the rear. Another column arrived hard on their heels with drums beating loudly, closely followed by a third. The officer timed his orders so that each rank in turn slotted into line with admirable precision. When the three companies had formed up exactly behind each other in the middle of the square, a sharp, final command brought a roll of the drums and a stamp of booted feet on cobbles. Then absolute silence reigned. The colours, the flags representing the regiment, flapped in the breeze as they were carried to the front. A redcoat escort formed around them and, with an ensign in charge, the colour party marched away. We watched in admiration at the men's rigid discipline.

'Very pretty, very pretty,' muttered Curley, sarcastically, for us all to hear, 'but can they do that when the air is full of shot and men are having their heads blown off?' He spat noisily. As I got to know Curley better, I learned that this kind of cynical comment was typical of the man. But he had spoilt the moment for us.

We listened as the men were name-checked against the muster roll by a sergeant major. Finally the senior officer, Major Roland de Villiers, as one of our guards told us, dismissed the men. The companies broke rank and quickly dispersed, relieved that their long day's march was over. The Non-Commissioned Officers, the NCOs, also scattered with their platoons while the officers headed off to their much more comfortable quarters. A corporal approached Curley, taking off his shako and mopping his brow as he drew near. He looked hot and bothered in his tunic, his face beetroot red above the light buff collar.

'Belcoo and back,' he complained, 'and on a day like this, too.' He loosened his heavy knapsack and let it fall to the ground. 'God, but that's an uncomfortable weight.'

Curley laughed. 'Think that was hard, Shanley? You're lucky you weren't in Spain. Now, that was tough.'

'It's those blasted drums,' said the corporal, 'they never let up. Speaking of Spain, de Villiers decided we should come back the Light Infantry way, walk three, run three, for twelve miles. Said that's how the 95th Rifles did it at Talavera. It's fine for the major, he has a horse to do the walking for him. My feet are so blistered I'll never get my boots off.'

Curley didn't bother replying but instead pursed his lip as if he had grown tired of listening to the corporal's complaining.

'More cannon fodder for the Skins, I see,' Shanley said, sitting down on the steps. Then he spotted me. 'Ah, a nipper,' he laughed. 'He'll fall over his own musket.'

'I want to be a drummer,' I rejoined, goaded into answering. Curley's hand was a blur. He back-slapped me hard across the side of the face, sending me flying. I never saw it coming but Francie Doherty was just as quick. He caught me before I hit the cobblestones, breaking my fall. Infuriated, I got up quickly. Curley stuck out his chest and planted himself in front of me.

'Don't ever talk back to an NCO like that,' he snarled. 'If you were signed up, I'd put you on punishment detail for a week to teach you a lesson.'

Blinded by anger and the indignity of being struck, I started to square up to him but I could feel Francie's strength as he restrained me from behind. And he was right. If I had fought back, Curley would have beaten me to a pulp, and then used that as an excuse to have me thrown out of the 27th before I'd even joined. I shrank back a little and let my body relax but Francie didn't let me go until he felt the fight go out of me. Curley stepped back knowing he had me licked. I knew what he was at, using me as a means of imposing his superior rank and position on the new men. All the same, I was amazed at the anger that boiled within me. I'd done my share of street scrapping, of course, with lads my own age or a bit older, but I had never been hit like that by a grown man. Francie dragged me back into line beside him, half-blocking Curley's view of me.

'Curb it, James,' he hissed in my ear. 'He'll do you.'

One of the redcoats moved closer to me, his musket sloped across his chest, ready to club me if I offered any kind of resistance but Curley must have realised there was no more entertainment to be got from me. He turned his back and resumed his conversation with Shanley, saying he'd done well enough out of the day with only two turned down by Mostyn. Francie stayed close to me, as did the redcoat. Maybe that was just as well as I was still seething with anger at what the sergeant had done. Two other NCOs came over with jugs of beer that were passed around among us. I watched as they all drank straight from the jugs, the beer dribbling down onto their chins. Although I was unused to idleness, I didn't mind waiting as it allowed time for my anger to evaporate. I leaned back against the cold stone wall and stared at nothing in particular. A couple of the new men began to converse quietly as the beer loosened their tongues again and they rediscovered their previous good form.

'Maybe the magistrate isn't coming,' Phipps, one of them, suggested.

'The magistrate will be here when he's good and ready,' muttered Curley. 'You just give the right answers when he asks the questions and you'll be fine.'

'I don't mind waiting a lot longer if you keep the beer coming,' joked Phipps.

Another recruit, whose name I didn't hear, replied, 'if we keep drinking, we'll likely see two magistrates, neither one steady.' And they all guffawed again.

With that, as if on cue, the magistrate himself clipped into the depot, mounted on a frisky, grey mare. I recognised him at once, having seen him many times when I'd been dawdling about the streets near the courthouse in Enniskillen. He was the one who usually attended the sessions. A stable orderly took his horse and two soldiers escorted him to the administrative block. He disappeared inside.

'He won't be long with the major,' Curley said. 'He'll be out soon. Let's go!' He led us across to a different entrance in the same building. We went down a short corridor and halted outside a door. Our escort stayed with us. Again we waited in line, Curley walking up and down, glaring at each of us in turn.

'When you speak to the magistrate,' he warned, 'call him Your Honour. Make sure to tell him what he wants to hear. We don't want to lose any more of you.'

After that, he paced up and down the line, a dark scowl on his face. This time, the wait seemed much longer than it actually was. I began to think I'd never get to enlist.

6

A clatter of footsteps on the corridor announced the imminent arrival of the magistrate. Out of the corner of my eye, I recognised Captain Grant beside him. Curley smartened up, saluted, and opened the door for them. The magistrate ignored him as he entered the room beyond but Grant motioned for the first man in line to follow him. The door closed behind them. Minutes went by, then a voice from within shouted 'Next!' Curley pointed to the door. The next man entered. This happened with all of us in turn, the line slowly getting shorter, until eventually I was left standing with only Curley for company. I kept my eyes cast down, not wanting to look at him. He stood so close to me that I could hear his breathing but he said nothing. I willed the minutes to pass quickly until it was finally my turn. I entered, relieved to escape from the sergeant's surly presence at last but not knowing what to expect within.

The room stretched almost the width of the building, its high ceiling compensating for its narrowness. It was devoid of any comfort or ease. The desk at which the magistrate sat was under a window at the opposite end. He motioned me forward. The sound of my shoes accompanied me across the stone-flagged floor and, for the first time in my life, I found myself standing in front of a magistrate. The elderly gentleman leaned forward as he looked me up and down. I couldn't say that his expression was unkindly but I instinctively averted my gaze. With a reputation for being tough on those who appeared in the dock before him, whether it was for lifting a fat salmon from the Erne River or for brawling in the streets, I didn't want him to see the guilty look in my eyes. Both of these things I had done many times but, thankfully, had never been caught. However, at that moment, I felt like a felon who had been apprehended in the act.

The magistrate's hand was poised over a document, a long quill held loosely in his grasp. Captain Grant spoke up from the armchair he occupied. 'This is the Honourable Robert Meldon, Resident Magistrate, young man. He'll swear you in, if you're without impediment, that is.'

'I haven't seen you before, have I?' the magistrate asked.

'No,' I replied, hesitantly, then remembered to add 'Your Honour.'

'Name?'

'James,' I replied hoarsely.

'Do you have another name, perhaps?'

'Burns,' I added quickly. 'James Anthony Burns.'

Suddenly the quill was pointing at me, accusingly. 'Have you been fighting already, James Anthony Burns?'

'No, Your Honour,' I replied, flustered.

'Then how do you explain the marks on your face?'

The magistrate stared at me, waiting for me to reply.

'I fell off a horse, Your Honour,' I said in desperation, saying the first thing that came into my head. I had fallen into the age-old trap of diving headlong into lies and evasions when the truth would have been the more sensible course of action.

'Did you now?' mused the magistrate, leaning back. 'What horse might that have been?'

'A plough horse, Your Honour.'

'A plough horse, you say?'

I knew the magistrate didn't believe me. He was just leading me on. It was cruel sport but I had given him the means to enjoy it.

'Show me your hands.'

I held out my hands, still soiled from crawling through ditches checking my snares earlier in the day. 'There are no scratches on your hands. Did you not have sense enough to put them out to save yourself as you fell? Or were your hands tied behind your back, by chance? Is that the reason why it's only your face that is marked?'

Grant couldn't contain himself any longer. He snorted loudly, trying to stifle his amusement at my expense. I clammed up. I had spoken stupidly, my attempt at a lie fluttering like a red flag in the man's face. Who did I think I was fooling?

'Look, lad,' the magistrate said, 'if you're going to join the 27th, you're going to have to become a better liar than that, for this regiment has some of the best practitioners of the art of telling falsehoods as I've come across in my life. Captain Grant here will attest to this. I'll allow your answer as youthful inexperience but I would urge you to try to stay on the right side of the NCOs from now on. They are quick with their fists and the lash and very slow to forbearance, especially when the loss of two potential recruits lightens their pockets somewhat.'

The quill wagged at me warningly, then the magistrate's features seemed to soften and I think the beginnings of a smile crossed his face. Maybe I wasn't the first to feel the effects of Curley's malicious temper. The sergeant had needed to vent his anger on somebody, anybody, and it just happened to be me. Sermon over, the magistrate moved on.

'Now, let's start again, James Anthony Burns, shall we? What age are you?'

I hesitated. If I told him how many summers I had, maybe he'd refuse me.

'He's nigh sixteen,' Captain Grant interjected, giving me a severe glance by way of telling me not to contradict him. 'He qualifies as a "growing lad". Besides,' he added with a yawn, 'he seems to have a talent for the drum.'

Being an officer and a gentleman, there was no question of the magistrate not taking Grant's word as truth, however unlikely the story was. But in my case he must have had a slight doubt.

'So you're old enough to know your own mind then,' the magistrate said.

'Yes, Your Honour,' I agreed. 'I want to be a drummer.'

'You know that the regiment can't guarantee that position? They might select another.'

'Oh,' I said, my disappointment obvious.

'In this case, Mr Meldon, the Colonel has already

39

agreed to make an exception,' said Grant smoothly, putting a taper to his pipe again and puffing out a ball of smoke. 'We're down a drummer as we shipped a sick one home from the colonies and had to send a replacement. The poor man's in the hospital bay now. Mr Mostyn says there is nothing more that can be done for him except to pray, and that's not where a surgeon's primary skills lie. Anyway, we're in need of a drummer and young Burns here's seems to be the right man.'

The magistrate nodded, and wrote something. He then went on to ask me if I had any hidden illness, or if I was apprenticed or indentured to anybody, and whether I was joining up of my own free will or under some form of duress or coercion. I told him my mother had made no objection but that I lacked her blessing, and that my father had been a soldier in the 27th who had died before I was born. Beyond that I said little more for fear the magistrate would turn me down. A man who has the power to send someone to Botany Bay was not one to be trifled with so I was thrifty with my words. He seemed satisfied with all I had said.

'Life, or Limited Service of Seven Years?' he finally asked.

I didn't know what he meant by that so I found myself saying: 'Seven years, Your Honour.' The magistrate signed the document in front of him and then asked Grant to administer the oaths. I knew this was the final step in my acceptance. First, the captain read the Oath of Fidelity to me, a few words at a time, and I parroted them back with no thought to their meaning. He then did the same with the Oath of Allegiance and again I repeated every word. Thus, I swore the next seven years of my life away. In evidence of this, a piece of paper was pushed in front of me.

'Make your mark there,' Meldon said, indicating a space at the bottom of the document. I took the quill from his soft grasp.

'I can write my name, Your Honour,' I said.

A surprised look crossed the magistrate's face. I must have been the only one that day who was able to do so. I signed slowly but with no small amount of pride in my skill. When I had finished, he sprinkled powder on the wet ink of my name. Then, he said: 'The Inniskillings own you now, lad.'

Grant stood and opened a small chest at his feet. There was a chinking of coins as he counted. Then he held out a handful of shining guineas towards me. I had never seen so much money before.

'All yours, James Burns,' said the magistrate. 'Your signing-up bounty. Mind how you dispose of it or you won't have it for long. Before you know where you are, your new comrades in arms will have you in Mother Hogan's alehouse, a den of iniquity that I urge you to avoid. I hope you don't intend to become a bounty-jumper. If you do, you'll appear in front of me again, young man, and I'll give you a different seven years.' He chuckled at his own humour. I looked at him blankly.

'If you're planning on running away with the money,' he explained, seeing I didn't understand what he had meant. 'That's what a bounty-jumper does.'

'No, Your Honour, I'm not going to run away.'

'Then I wish you well in His Majesty's service,' he

said. 'I think you'll need all the luck you can get.'

'Right, Burns,' said Captain Grant, 'off you go to get sorted out with the others. By the way, there'll be deductions for your regimental necessaries and uniforms from your bounty. The sergeant will see to that before you drink it all. Now, out you go.' I was dismissed, a recruit in my father's regiment at last. The drum was within my grasp.

Even though I had just sworn two solemn oaths to the Crown, the words had little or no impact on my life for the whole of the seven years I spent in the army. However, as soon as I left that room, I was to immediately get my first lesson in what did impact on the life of the rank and file soldier – the demand for absolute, blind, and unquestioning obedience to military authority. From my then lowly position as a raw recruit, that meant everybody else who already wore a uniform, as I was about to learn.

7

The coins jingled comfortingly in my pocket as I left by the rear door but I had hardly taken a step when Curley suddenly appeared and pinned me roughly against the stone wall.

'Well, here's Private Newcombe at last,' he growled, calling me by the jibing name given to all new recruits. He pushed his scarred face into mine. 'With a pocket full of guineas too, I'll bet. Give them here, lad. Did the captain not tell you about your regimental necessaries, services and expenses? Stuff like that don't all grow on trees, you know. The regiment's got to be paid.'

'Yes, Sergeant, but I need to keep some of it,' I said. 'For my mother.'

'Naw,' Curley said, with a shake of his head, 'not a hope! With you, Burns, it's all forfeit. That'll teach you to be more respectful to your senior officers. I lost some of my bounty entitlement today because of two unserviceables. Bloody useless scum! I have to make it up somehow so I thank you for your contribution to my welfare. And if you breathe a word to Captain Grant, I'll make life hell for you. Remember, too, I know where you live. I wouldn't like to see your mother go for too long without the warm attentions of a man.' He laughed in my face as he said this. I can still feel the brute strength of the man as he leaned his heavy bulk in against me, pressing me back against the wall. I found it hard to breathe. 'Now hand it all over, unless you want to get hit again?' he threatened.

'Stay away from my mother,' I managed to wheeze but he laughed again.

'Then, give!'

Alas, the guineas that had just been given to me didn't jingle in my pocket for long. I had no choice but to hand my bounty over. Curley tapped my ragged breeches to make sure I had given him everything.

That put me in a vexed, sullen mood as he brought me over to my new home, a cold-looking barracks building with '3rd Company' painted on the door. He pushed me up the stairs to the top corridor, passing a number of large rooms known as messes, soldiers' living quarters, where they ate, slept and relaxed. Loud voices and boisterous activity emanated from them as we passed. We entered the last mess at the end of the corridor. It, too, was already occupied. From their uniforms and facings, they were all drummers except for a corporal who had his back to us, replenishing the fire. The corporal turned, saw Curley, and shouted: 'Atten-tion!'

The drummers all sprang upright.

Being an end room, it was larger than the others we had passed. Bunk berths, three high, lined one wall while a row of lockers, each with a name on it, stood against the other. Empty drum boxes were stacked in the corner. The single window let in just sufficient light for the size of the room. A long, narrow table occupied the centre space with benches on either side for seating. The table had already been set for the evening meal. The air stank of sweat, pipe smoke, boot-blackening and cooking fat, overpowering smells for anyone unused to the close confines of the soldiers' mess. Straightaway, I recognised the two drummers from the recruiting party. Both had been reclining on their berths when we entered but they now stood rigidly to attention with the others. Curley waited a few seconds before speaking, smirking at the impact his presence had made.

'Corporal Ward!'

'Sir!'

'You need to set an extra place. Add him to your mess for the time being. He's a mouthy lad. I don't expect him to last long.'

'Yes, Sir!'

'And make sure he gets a decent wash. He stinks.'

Giving me a final, hard look, Curley departed. I could feel the tension melt out of the room when he had gone and my new messmates welcomed me warmly. I didn't remember all of their names at first, and it took a little time to get used to their peculiarities but these men would become, in time, like brothers to me. Corporal Charlie Ward was our NCO, a breezy, easy-going sort of character in contrast to most others who gave free rein to their baser instincts. As an NCO, he was fortunate to have a small room to himself and so was accorded some degree of privacy unlike the rest of the drummers who shared the mess together. Reggie Cox, all freckles and gangly limbs, was the younger drummer from earlier on, who had spotted me at the alehouse crossroads and had played alongside me. Ignatius McNeilis, known to all as Nosey for his hooked proboscis, was the older drummer who had been with the recruiting party. He was the senior drummer in the battalion, and was sporting corporal's stripes. The Fox Maguire, so called because he had been a renowned poacher around Lisnaskea before being caught, had wisely chosen the army rather than seven years transportation to New South Wales. I never found out his first name. Sammy Crooks was a simple, fresh-faced lad who would have preferred to be working in a stable. He was much given to whistling while he drummed, according to Reggie. And that left Con Gallagher, the lad from Donegal, who had arrived barefoot in Enniskillen eight years previously and had forgotten to go home. These were my new messmates, the men I would share every waking moment with as long as I remained in the depot.

Introductions over, I was immediately reminded by McNeilis of a long-standing, military tradition.

'Y'know it's customary for a new recruit to be welcomed to his new quarters with a jug of beer. Courtesy of the Johnny Newcombe, of course.'

They all laughed at this but I knew it to be true. A new recruit depended on his messmates to help him during the settling-in process, as well as to teach him the ropes, so a couple of jugs of beer was a small price to pay for ensuring such a smooth introduction. I would have been quite happy to keep up the tradition but I was in no position to do as they expected. I let them have their fun with me first before telling them that I didn't even have a brass penny left out of my bounty thanks to the sergeant who had cleaned me out entirely. It was down to him that there'd be no welcome beer for the mess from me. They stared at me for a moment, not sure whether to believe me or not but I assured them it was the truth and offered to turn my pockets out.

To be fair to them, they immediately commiserated with me on my misfortune. Then Ward clapped me heartily on the back, saying: 'Not to worry, lad. Curley usually leaves enough for beer when he shakes down a Johnny Newcombe but obviously not in your case. You must have done something to cross him. I'd watch out if I were you. Right, lads,' he said, turning to the others, 'the tradition must be observed. Empty the pockets. A sixpence from everybody and we'll send out to the canteen. C'mon now.' He held out his hand. Coins were contributed and Gallagher was dispatched on the errand. While he was gone, McNeilis showed me my berth, a top bunk. The mattress smelled of stale sweat and dried straw but someone had straightened out the coarse army blanket and centred the pillow at its head.

'This will be your locker, Burns,' Ward called out, indicating where I could stow the few belongings I had brought with me. He erased the name 'O'Devir' from the door and chalked mine in its place as he talked.

'Won't O'Devir need it again?' I asked naively.

'Not where he's going, he won't,' replied Ward. 'Mostyn says he'll be lucky to see the morn so we'll say no more about him, poor lad.'

With that, Gallagher arrived back with jugs of frothy brown liquid. A cheer rose in the room, until Ward shushed them with the warning that the noise would bring

Curley back and then he'd want a share. A tin cup was thrust my way into which a slosh of foul-smelling concoction was poured. It had the colour and texture of bog water. They watched as I raised the tin cup to my lips and tried the brew. It tasted so vile that I retched. This amused them to no end. Then they all made throw-it-back motions with their hands, encouraging me to finish it. Rather than risk alienating my new companions, I did so. It was so sickly sweet that I wanted to spit it out. They all laughed at my discomfiture but there was friendship in their crude banter. Before long, the jugs were empty and The Fox Maguire was told to go on a repeat run. Gallagher slurped at the last few drops from the upturned jug before Maguire grabbed it from him and headed off. Of course, more trips to the canteen followed that one.

An hour or so later, a row of empty jugs confirmed that I had been well-bonded into the group. Clay pipes were lit and the room filled with smoke. Meanwhile, McNeilis and Crooks busied themselves at the table, preparing chunks of meat and vegetables for the iron, mess pot which was then hung over the fire. Corporal Ward took me aside and offered some advice about Curley.

'If the sergeant's taken a set against you, lad, you'd better watch out. Keep your head down, don't give him reason to notice you and you'll get along fine. We're all messmates together but Curley's three stripes means that he can do what he likes with you, so I'd be careful if I was you.' I thanked him for his words of caution and assured him I would act upon them. 'Right, that's it, then,' he said, changing the conversation, 'before we eat, let's get you cleaned up, Burns. The washroom's that way. Curley was right. You do stink.' I looked at him, wondering whether he was being serious. 'The army won't give you a nice new uniform with you in that state of dirt,' Nosey McNeilis laughed, as he paused his pot-stirring. 'Besides, we don't want to pick up any of your country vermin, do we? Here, take this with you.'

He poured warm water into a bucket. I went into the washroom and, for the second time that day, stripped off. Sammy Crooks came in, bundled up all I had taken off, and headed for the door.

'Hey, my clothes,' I objected.

'Fit only for burning,' he said. 'There's lye soap and a sponge on the shelf. Scrub yourself like you've never done before. You don't want Curley to come and help you, do you?' That thought was enough for me so I set to the task of scrubbing myself. It was a long time since I had given myself such a thorough going over. Then, as I dried myself off, Reggie arrived with a clean, white shirt and a pair of light-grey breeches.

'Until you get your own kit tomorrow,' he said. I thanked him. Feeling crisp and fresh in my borrowed attire, I returned to the mess to see that the table had been covered with a white linen cloth with the number "27" stitched in the corner and a place set for each man with a knife, fork, spoon and mug.

'You sit there,' Ward indicated. He put a tin plate in front of me.

'Is this mine?' I asked him.

'O'Devir's,' he said, curtly.

Everyone sat down as McNeilis proceeded to ladle

dollops of stew onto each plate from a large dish that had been placed in the centre of the table. A thick hunk of bread was dunked into mine and I was told that if I didn't eat quickly, Gallagher would help me. I was so famished by then that I ate quickly and was first to finish. It was getting late in the evening, dark enough for the rushlights to throw cheery shadows on the walls as the dying embers of the fire struggled to dispel the gathering cold in the room.

'It's nearly time, boys,' said Ward. With that, the drummers rose from the table and busied themselves with the clean-up. I went to stand up too but Ward pushed me back down.

'You sit back and observe us, Burns, for this is the only evening you'll get for free,' he said, as the others engaged in their separate clean-up tasks, doing everything in an orderly and efficient manner. In a short space of time, chores done, the drummers began to arrange their uniforms and instruments for morning parade which would be before dawn the next day. Corporal Ward suddenly glanced at his watch, cursed under his breath, and told Maguire and Gallagher it was nearly nine o'clock. The pair quickly donned their tunics, grabbed their drums and a few minutes later they were signalling the end of the day from the square below. There was a loud ringing of boots across the square as men hurried from the canteen area back to their messes. Shouted orders floated up to our room as the guard outside was changed and the night-watch took over. Then silence descended upon the depot.

By the time that The Fox Maguire and Con Gallagher

had returned, their duty done, I was utterly exhausted. After my long and eventful day, I didn't mind the rank odour that came off the mattress as I gratefully lay down and drifted off into a light slumber almost immediately. However, my first night's sleep wasn't very restful because I'm sure it wasn't long past midnight when I woke suddenly with the thought that I had eaten off a dying man's plate and had then occupied his bed. I shivered. Pulling the blanket up, I lay there for a while thinking that life was indeed strange with the way things come at you, and you accommodate to them, and march on. I had never slept away from home before, nor had I ever shared a room with five others – not that that bothered me too much. I thought momentarily of my mother and hoped she wasn't too lonely without me. Eventually, making peace with myself, I nodded off again.

In the months after that first night, there were times when I'd lie on the hard, straw mattress, listening to the breathing, snoring and coughing of my room-mates before dropping off to a heavy sleep. There was something strangely comforting about it all. Other nights, when we'd return to the depot after a tough day's drilling and marching, I was so tired that I'd sleep as soon as my head hit the pillow, and the inevitable symphony of undignified, nocturnal noises provided by the others rarely disturbed me. Occasionally, one of them would shout out in the darkness as some nightmare memory clawed its way out of the depths of their subconscious, and they would wake up trembling and sweating and mumbling incoherently. Then, realising where they were, they'd fall back into an uneasy sleep, while I would stay awake, wondering at the source of their anguish. However, I became so used to our barracks that, on the subsequent occasions when we'd sleep in the open under a hedge or a make-shift shelter of some kind, it was the all-enveloping silence of the countryside, broken only by the odd yap of a prowling fox, that I found unusual.

But that first night in my new quarters ended all too soon because, before I knew it, the urgent beating of drums suddenly snatched me from my slumber. My first day as a soldier was about to begin. And it was still dark.

8

As if the drums weren't enough, our NCO, Corporal Ward was pounding on the door. 'Up, lads, up! Do you want to sleep forever?'

I dropped to the cold floor, groggy from lack of sleep, wondering what time it was.

'Not you, Burns,' Ward added, entering the mess. 'You stay here until I return. Then I'll see to you.' He went off and I heard him shouting into the next room. A candle flickered into life, throwing faint light on the others as they noisily engaged in the morning routines of the soldier. Stumbling about in the gloomy light, they took turns at relieving themselves in the slop bucket, then washed, shaved and dressed for early parade, all done more or less in silence. Finally, they meticulously made their beds. When I asked why they were being so particular with everything, McNeilis said that the NCOs would be inspecting everyone's kit and berth when we had gone and, if all wasn't in good order, a sloppy soldier would be punished severely. I was impressed with their speed and efficiency given the dimness of the room and quickly followed their example, throwing on my borrowed clothes.

'Whose turn is it for the water?' McNeilis asked.

'Mine,' came a mumbled answer. I made out Sammy Crooks's shape in the gloom as he left the room carrying the water bucket.

'Hurry, lads,' urged Ward, a few minutes later, appearing again in the doorway. 'The duty NCO's in the corridor below already.' He stood aside to let Crooks, now laden with a full bucket, back into the room. Then, with a final quick examination of their beds, they grabbed their drums and disappeared out of the room in a hurry. I heard them pounding down the stairs and out into the square below. I crossed to the high window and stood on a chair to see out. In the faint light cast by flaming torches on the cobbles, I could discern the rows of soldiers assembling in lines for early morning parade.

Then the drums began to roll again, loud in the pre-dawn air but not loud enough to drown out the angry roar that came from behind me. 'Burns, you young scum! What the devil are you doing?' It was Sergeant Curley, his hulking frame just a shadow in the doorway.

'Corporal Ward told me to stay here until he came back, Sir,' I replied, jumping down off the chair. I couldn't see the expression on his face but his anger was palpable.

'Salute your senior officer, you little shit.'

I touched my fingertips to my forehead.

'That's another thing you'll have to learn to do properly,' he snarled. 'Do you know where the garrison well is?' Of course I knew from long ago but, in my panic, my mind had frozen. A heavy bucket of cold water caught me full in the chest, throwing me back hard against the wall, soaking the clothes that Reggie had loaned me. I hadn't seen the bucket in Curley's hands. 'Maybe that'll help you remember,' he roared, advancing towards me. He flung the empty bucket into the corner and raised his clenched fist. 'Or do you need this too?'

'I know where it is, Sergeant,' I said quickly, suddenly remembering. He paused, fist in mid air.

'Good! Then before your mates return, I want every bucket in the corridor filled with fresh water. As well as the one you just dropped.'

'But, Sergeant,' I said, shivering in my sopping clothes, 'the others would have filled their own mess buckets by now.'

'Well, I emptied them, didn't I? So if they're not full again to the brim by the time I come back to check, you'll have disobeyed my order, won't you? And that means a punishment detail. So best get cracking. And wipe this floor, it's like an unhealthy slop house in here. Which is your berth?'

I pointed.

'Then use this to mop up the wet.' He ripped my thin mattress off my berth, threw it to the floor and trod on it. To my amazement, he then proceeded to angrily toss every other mattress in the mess onto the floor as well.

'Tell your mates I did this because they failed to instruct an ignorant little shit like you that chairs are for sitting on, not for standing on while gawking out the window,' he snarled, before abruptly turning on his heel and stomping out.

Breathing a sigh of relief at his departure, I quickly retrieved my bedding from the pool of water on the floor.

I then replaced each of the other mattresses as best I could and arranged the blankets and pillows. The results were pathetic. I knew the others would be livid over this but what could I do? I then hurried out with the bucket, the cool morning air making me shiver in my wet clothes, found the well, and returned with a full bucket. Thinking that Curley was only rising me about the other buckets, I entered the mess next door. He hadn't exaggerated as the bucket was indeed empty. And so it continued with each room I entered. It took me the best part of an hour, traipsing back and forward to the depot well, winching each bucket down, filling it, and returning a full one to each mess, before I was done. Tired from all my exertions, I finally wiped up the wet floor as best I could, sweeping the water out into the corridor and spreading it to let the draught dry it off. My clothes had half-dried by that time but they looked crumpled and unsightly.

When the others returned, they flew into a rage at Curley's spiteful antics and immediately set to putting their berths to rights, cursing as they did so. Ward was angry about the spilt water, telling me that the surgeons disapproved of wet floors on the grounds that it reduced the quality of the air in a confined mess, making it unhealthy for breathing. Curley would have known that when he threw the water at me, he added. When I told them I had been the cause of all their inconvenience by standing on a chair, none of them saw fit to blame me.

'That's Curley for you, all right. It's in his nature. Watch your back, Burns,' said McNeilis, adding his warning to what Ward had said the previous evening. 'I've been around this regiment for a long time and he's always been a mean one. He's trying to turn us all against you.'

After that, breakfast was a rushed affair of bread, cheese and scraps of cold meat, washed down with watery beer. We weren't sitting long when the door suddenly opened and a giant of a man, immaculately uniformed, entered. Everyone jumped to their feet and stood to attention. I stood also. I recognised him as the sergeant major who had called the muster in the square.

'G'morning, Corporal! Drummers!' he said in greeting. 'Stand easy.'

Nobody moved.

'All sober here, and fit for duty?' he asked.

'Yes, Sergeant Major,' replied Ward.

'And one not properly attired, I see.'

'He's a Johnnie Newcombe, Sir,' explained Ward. 'Just enlisted yesterday afternoon. He hasn't been to the Quartermaster yet, Sir.'

'Well, you'd better get him fixed up quickly, then. We don't want him dying of a chill on his first day because he somehow managed to spill water all over himself and half the corridor now, do we? Imagine what he'd say to the surgeon. Name?' he demanded, meaning me.

'James Burns,' I said.

'There was an Anthony Burns in the regiment once. You anything to him?' The question took me by surprise.

'He was my father, Sir.'

'I see!' He gave me a hard look. 'Well, we'll soon see what kind of stuff you're made of. All right, Corporal, carry on.' He left, and everyone sat down.

'That's the Regimental Sergeant Major,' Ward

explained. 'McGreel is his name. He's gruff on the outside but he's a fair-minded man. You'll see him again in a while at drill. He'll be observing you. I didn't realise your father was in the regiment, Burns.'

'I never knew him,' I said quietly. 'He died in the Flanders campaign before I was born.'

The others stared at me for a moment but I said nothing else and they slowly took up the conversation again. As I ate, all I could think of was that the sergeant major must have known my father. I looked up. McNeilis caught my eye and nodded slightly. And perhaps because of what McGreel had said, I guessed.

'You knew him too,' I stated.

McNeilis's jaw moved before he spoke, as if he was struggling with his thoughts. 'Yes,' he said. 'He was in the 1st Battalion when I joined. I saw him once or twice before he was sent to the Low Countries but I never spoke to him. That's all I know.' He then abruptly changed the subject.

I began to wonder, with all the movement of soldiers in and out of the depot over the years, if there could be any others left in the regiment who could tell me about my father.

9

When we had finished breakfast, everyone wiped their tin plates and cups and stacked them away until they were needed for lunch. Again, I was surprised at how neat and organised they were. They busied themselves with cleaning their kit and equipment for a while. Ward inspected their berths and lockers carefully before declaring himself satisfied. As the drummers headed out, Ward shouted: 'Not you, Reggie Cox. You stay.'

Ward then examined my berth, which I thought was fairly well done with all the practice earlier, but the corporal's verdict was different. 'Not bad for a Johnny Newcombe, Burns, but it's not good enough either. Reggie, show him.'

Reggie quickly rearranged my mattress, pillow and blanket, showing me at the same time what I had to be particular with. He stood back when he had finished for Ward's verdict.

'That's how you do it, Burns,' said the corporal. 'You'd better learn fast. Otherwise the whole squad gets into trouble, as you've seen with Curley. The inspecting NCOs don't give chances. Now, time to get you fixed up with the Quartermaster. Cox, go with him.

In the square, drums sounded again and soldiers hurried to commence their daily chores. Reggie trotted across the cobbles with me. A queue had already formed at the Quartermaster's stores as some new recruits were there ahead of me, each accompanied by a messmate. Francie Doherty arrived, looking slightly the worse for wear but he perked up when he saw me and gave me a warm greeting. We chatted about our first night as enlisted men in the regiment. Gone was the tension of the previous day. Everyone looked forward to getting new clothes and, for some of us, it would be for the first time.

We filed in and were checked off against a list before being given our boots and uniforms for formal wear, fatigue dress for informal everyday wear, and our necessaries, the various other items of equipment that comprised the soldier's kit. Two newcomers, Phipps and Melly, remarked that they had been barefoot all their lives. I watched as those two men were handed their first pair of boots by the Quartermaster's assistant. They held them like precious objects, examining the shape of the soles and heels, tracing the stitching with their rough fingers and marvelling at the craftsmanship. They found it very difficult to adjust to the feel of the leather cramping their feet when they tried them on for size but they quickly forgot their discomfort when told that our next visit that afternoon would be to the armoury. There they'd be given their muskets, known affectionately to every redcoat as the 'Brown Bess'. While I too would be trained in the use of a firelock weapon, all I wanted to know was when I'd get my hands on a drum.

Some time later, I returned to our quarters with

Reggie, both of us heavily laden with my knapsack, greatcoat, blanket, drummer's tunic, shako, two shirts and two pairs of grey breeches, undergarments, sleeping attire, shoes, belts and much more. Without his help I'd have had to make several journeys back and forth.

The other drummers returned when their duty chores were completed and took great delight in watching me don my fatigues, the lighter clothing that was worn when carrying out general chores and routines around the depot. While the cap was woollen, I was surprised at how light the white shirt and grey trousers were, both being made of linen. The formal tunic, as with the soldier's red jacket, was reserved for parade or for when we left the depot. My drummer's tunic was different to that of the line soldier, being in reverse colours of light buff material, with ornate white lacing criss-crossing the breast and white chevrons adorning the sleeves. It was all quite exquisitely made, like on a hussar's dolman. My chest puffed out with pride as I buttoned it up for the first time, and donned my black shako with its white, decorative ropes at the front looping under the regimental badge and the tall white plume on the left. I couldn't wait to survey myself in the small mirror that had been issued to me for shaving purposes. The shako was uncomfortable, the collar of my tunic was too tight, the woollen under-garment was rough to the skin and the shoes pinched my feet terribly but none of this quelled my excitement.

'That'll all loosen up,' said Ward, coming in to inspect me. 'Anyway, who says a soldier's uniform should be comfortable? So long as you look right, you'll be fine.'

'Our shako is different,' observed Reggie. He turned

my new hat around and pointed. 'See, there's a brass drum badge on the back, that way everyone behind knows who we are.'

By mid-morning I found myself in my fatigues joining the other new recruits in a corner of the square. Sergeant Major McGreel arrived and, for the next two hours, he watched us with growing impatience as two red-faced, foul-mouthed drill sergeants tried to instil basic marching skills into us. Eventually, the session came to an end and he dismissed us in disgust, swearing at us for being such pathetic material for the regiment. I was separated from the other recruits and instructed to find the Drum School which turned out to be a drab room set back from the accommodation blocks. I knocked and entered timidly.

A loud voice greeted me. 'So you've decided to join us at last, Burns.'

I didn't know who he was when I went in but it wouldn't take long for me to become very familiar indeed with Drum Major Edward Hicks. His large frame was squeezed into a uniform resplendent with gold and silver lace, and with broad, white belts crossed on his chest. The feathered plume of his cocked hat hung at a jaunty angle as his voice boomed around the room.

'Come in, Burns. Meet your drum instructor, Corporal Ned Kennedy.'

The Drum Major stood beside a large, walnut desk, an older drummer beside him. Kennedy was a stark contrast to Hicks, not only by virtue of being a smallish man but also because of his slight stoop. Reggie had told me about Kennedy earlier, that he was a legend in the regiment, a veteran of thirty-two years distinguished service, now retired from active duty but still a fixture in the depot. He knew everything there was to know about military drumming. Even though his hands were stiffening, there was no better drummer than he. Then on half-pay, but still retaining his rank as Corporal, Kennedy was a regimental mascot. I stood in front of the Drum Major and Kennedy in my new fatigues, trying to look soldierly.

'Can you read, Burns?' Hicks snapped.

'Yes, Sir!'

'Can you read this?' he asked, stabbing with his finger at a thick book that lay open on the desk. It was like no book I had ever seen before. The writing was totally illegible, consisting of lines and dots and squiggles. He saw from my blank face that I couldn't make any sense of it but, of course, he would have known that already.

'If you can't read staff notation,' Hicks roared, 'then this book is of no damned use to you.' Laughing at his own humour, he flicked more pages to reinforce my ignorance. 'Then you'll have to learn on the job, Burns,' he announced, closing the book, 'just as we all did.' He leaned in closer to me, making sure by his imposing proximity that he had my full attention. It was this moment that has always remained in my memory, when he said that the drum brings out the savage in a man,

'Can you be that kind of drummer?' Hicks boomed, pulling me towards him by my shirt.

I answered, petrified. 'Yes, Sir,' little knowing how true this would turn out to be.

'Well, by God,' he said, 'you'd better find the savage within, or you'll be no bloody good to the regiment.'

He let go of my shirt and I shrank back, my legs

trembling at his vehemence.

'If you're going to be a drummer,' he added, his voice softening a little, 'you'll need this, Burns, won't you?'

And he removed a cloth cover from a brand-new, gleaming side drum.

10

My terror vanished in an instant, to be replaced with sheer, raw excitement. My own snare drum at last. What I beheld was a truly magnificent percussion instrument, with a thin cord stretched across the top to increase the vibrations when it was struck. It was painted buff with red rims, the regimental number and the crest, Enniskillen Castle, facing proudly to the front. The battle honours, the names of places where the 27th had fought, were all listed. Even then, it made impressive reading. The drum was tied tight with natural hemp cords and the sweet scent of the soft calfskin across the top was like perfume to me. Just as I was about to touch it, Drum Major Hicks snatched it away.

'But not quite yet,' he said, replacing the cloth cover over it. 'You don't think the army would give a valuable piece of regimental equipment such as this to a shitty little excuse of a recruit like you, do you? You've got to earn this drum, my boy. The hard way! That is your drum for now.' He pointed to a rather worn-out instrument sitting dejectedly in the corner. Kennedy had turned his face away from me but I knew from the shaking of his shoulders that he was laughing silently at me as he went to fetch the dilapidated drum.

'Learn your craft on that one, Burns, because when you get to play this new one, men's lives may depend on your skill. Corporal Kennedy will teach you, if you're fit to learn. Now, try it for size.'

The paintwork was long faded, the cords grey with age and the calfskin blackened in the centre from years of use, but I happily slung the drum round my neck. Would you believe it, that old instrument fitted me perfectly. My fingertips stroked the smooth, worn surface as I wondered how many of the campaigns listed on the new drum this old one had seen.

'Sticks!' said Kennedy, holding them out to me. I took them, twisted them awkwardly in my hands, and poised. The moment of truth had come. I tapped. Kennedy clucked in disgust. With a toss of his head, Hicks picked up the new drum and headed for the door. He had no intention of listening to my first, tentative efforts.

'He's all yours, Corporal,' he said, turning in the doorway. 'Bring out the savage in him.' I watched the Drum Major depart, trepidation growing in me now that the moment had come. When I turned back, Kennedy had slung on his own drum.

'Drum Major Hicks is a master of instruments,' he said, taking his sticks from his belt, 'but I'm a judge of hands and wrists. I'll know if you've got what it takes when I see you move. This is what I want from you.' Kennedy readied himself, poised, and then proceeded to give me a demonstration of what I can only describe as inspired and extraordinary drumming, the like of which I would not have believed possible. I stared at him in awe as he bent slightly over the drum, at the oversized, purple hands that were creating such wonderful rhythms from what is, in essence, a hollow, skin-tight barrel of air. Within the space of a few minutes, that man showed me just how much I had to learn to become a regimental drummer. When he finally finished his performance, with the room still reverberating to the sounds of his last roll, I firmed up on my purpose to become the best drummer the regiment would ever have. I wanted to be as good as Ned Kennedy. No, I wanted to be better than Ned Kennedy.

'That's the way I want you to play,' my drum instructor said, a smile crossing his wrinkled face. 'I see potential in your expression. Let's see if we can make you into a drummer worthy of the 27th.' And so, my first lesson started. Kennedy told me to listen carefully to the simple beat that he wanted me to imitate, then tap it out myself. Of course, I was impatient to learn and found it hard to confine myself to the light taps that he was demonstrating so when I beat harder and increased the tempo, Kennedy's hand moved like lightning, fetching me a sharp rap across the knuckles with his stick.

'Only tap what I show, lad, otherwise you'll need new knuckles within the week. You will start as we all did. Watch, listen and learn. Slow and easy at the start. You're no virtuoso yet.'

I shook my hand to ease the pain but he had certainly managed to get my full attention.

'Yes, Corporal,' I said, meekly. And so the lesson progressed. Kennedy was a good drum teacher, I'll give him that. He felt my shoulders and upper arms, and then twisted my wrists around. 'You've good joint movement,

Burns,' he said. 'With a bit of muscling up and a great deal of practice, you'll be fine. But you've a lot to memorise. I hope you've a head for it.'

He made me practise those few taps at first, mastering a very simple sequence. Then he threw me by asking how long I could keep going for. I naively bragged that I could keep going indefinitely.

'Show me,' he said.

I tapped for as long as I could but, within a minute or two, I had to stop, my hands and wrists aching and my coordination non-existent. Kennedy meanwhile had been looking at his fob watch all the while. He glared at me, a stony expression on his lined face.

'The men have barely marched as far at the bridge,' he said. 'They've another seventeen miles to go before they can bivouac for the night. Now who's going to drum for them if you decide you've had enough. Toughen up, boy. Drumming has to be like marching. You keep going because the men need you to.'

The lesson continued from a demonstration of single- to two-handed play, from single stroke rolls to double stroke rolls, and then to mixed sticks. Kennedy pushed me hard, showing me at what distance to hold my arms out from my body, even measuring my strikes with a ruler so that they would be exact for every beat. He told me that the best drumming comes from the movement of the wrists and not from the shoulders, although some drummers preferred to play that way.

'Always aim for the centre,' he added, 'that way you get the best sound.' He then showed me how he could tell the centre of the drumhead by sound. He blindfolded himself and told me to keep moving the drum around while he played. No matter how slight the shift I made, he unerringly adjusted the sticks to the centre of the calfskin. I was really impressed for I didn't hear any difference in the sound at all but he did. 'That comes with practice, lad,' he said, removing the blindfold. 'It's not enough to know your drum. You must love it. Every touch has to be a caress, no matter how hard you strike the calfskin.'

After that, I did exactly as Corporal Kennedy told me. I watched, listened and learned, absorbing each new rudiment as he introduced it, and then practised it over and over. Starting with the Regulatory Calls, the drum beats for the most basic functioning of the soldiers' day, I learned how to wake them up with Reveille, to assemble with Troop, to eat with Dinner Call, when close of day arrived with Retreat and when to retire with the Taptoo. I worked hard at what I was learning, allowing my skills to develop. As the weeks became months, I settled down to a routine of chores, drilling and drum school lessons and, gradually, mastered the rudiments of my craft. The Drum Major called by every day to watch my progress. All of the others were much more experienced than I, having been in the regiment longer but they, too, had to keep up their practice as Hicks wouldn't allow for any slacking.

Along with learning the different techniques of drumming, Hicks lectured us on the importance of the drummer's role on the battlefield. 'Soldiers are learning new ways to wage war,' I remember him saying, 'and the battlefield has become a more complicated and confusing place. Tactics have changed and soldiers fight in much greater formations over a wider area making drummers and buglers ever more essential for communication in battle; that's what your job is about. When an officer gives an order, you're the one who passes it on to the men so that they know what to do. Your drum holds them together and keeps their morale high. Without you, they will break formation and become a rabble. So when you're drilling in the field, you must know what you are about because, when the time comes, everything will depend on your calm bearing and skill. And on that!' He laid his finger on my drum.

I never gave matters like that any thought but, that day, when we were back in the mess, McNeilis and The Fox Maguire, being the longest-serving drummers, told me how they had felt the first time they went into battle. They remembered the heart-stopping panic at the start of the action but when they fell back on their training, they were able to manage. They also recalled their dread of playing the wrong beat when passing on the Brigadier General's orders. That was the greatest fear that I had too but they reassured me that all would be well when my time came. I wasn't so sure, though. McNeilis then went on to tell of the many occasions when he was with Wellington's Peninsular Army that the Portuguese, both military and civilians alike, took him for an officer due to the fancy drummer's uniform he wore. 'It often worked to my advantage with the ladies too,' he added, wistfully recalling those stolen moments. 'You'll find that out for yourself in time too, Burns, if you're lucky.'

11

As the newest drummer in the battalion, I was permanently assigned to the 3rd Company, and paired with Reggie. It didn't take long for me to become accustomed to his presence playing alongside me. However, I also began to spend what little spare time I had alone in the school, tapping the practice drumhead, getting my hands and wrists accustomed to the movements. As my lessons developed, I became quite proficient at the rest of the Regulatory Calls as well as learning the tunes of many tavern songs and ballads on the fife to keep the men entertained when we went on long, monotonous marches.

Kennedy progressed me on to the Point of War, the beats that regulate troop movements and formations when manoeuvring and wheeling in the presence of, and engaging with, the enemy. These I found confusing at first, but I soon became reasonably adept at them in the school. Drumming in the square was easy enough with a small file of redcoats at the start, as I didn't have to worry about moving at the same time. It was a different matter when we were drilling on the common for the whole company with the officers shouting commands at us to beat the various signals. My coordination between hands and feet often let me down, especially when wheeling about. Marching on the outside of the column meant that I had almost to run when wheeling to the left and I'd lose my timing as my legs speeded up while my hands tried to maintain a consistent beat. Many an attempt at changing direction failed due to my poor drumming and the column would fall into disorder. When this happened, Hicks would fly into a temper and we'd have to do it all over again until we learned to carry out the manoeuvre properly. But the men would just laugh at me, telling me that I'd either need a bigger drum or a third stick. I soon got used to being roared at or thumped in the back by the nearest NCO for my lack of skill or poor timing. This made me redouble my efforts to improve back in the drum school and Kennedy never failed to encourage me saying, 'It'll come, lad, never fear. It'll come.'

And it was Ned Kennedy who spotted that while drilling with the whole company, I would let Reggie lead by a split second, as I was still fearful of making a mistake. So, when Curley next wanted a drummer for a punishment detail, Kennedy suggested that it was time I should do it on my own. He assigned me for a stint with a couple of redcoats from our company who had committed minor misdemeanours of some kind. After that, Curley saw to it that I had to drum with every punishment detail, which meant that I, too, in effect, was being punished. By his original helpful suggestion, Kennedy had unwittingly put me in Curley's vindictive way again. The others commiserated with me when I grumbled about it back in our mess but even I have to admit that the additional practice actually benefitted my playing.

It didn't come easily to me at the start, as I remember it, but after my first lesson in the drum school, when I saw the standard that Kennedy demanded, I applied myself assiduously. Being interested in the drum is one thing. It's entirely different when you are expected to remember everything about the instrument after hearing it just once, and I struggled with that. 'Talent alone is never enough,' Corporal Kennedy often remarked to me before slapping me on the back, saying, 'Shoulders, arms and wrists, lad. Make them work together.'

When I had mastered the Regulatory Calls and the Point of War, I progressed to learning the Ceremonies, the drumming for special occasions like the Sunday Parade or when the regimental colours were displayed in the presence of Colonel Geoffrey Bartlett Ferguson, the Commanding Officer of the 27th. Performing on those days was especially enjoyable with massed drummers playing together and all three companies resplendent in dress uniform under the admiring gaze of the officers' wives. But all that took time to achieve.

Drum Major Hicks, too, was an inspiring character, reminding us frequently about the necessity of pride and spirit – pride in our drums and spirit in our playing. How I took those words to heart. There was one particular visit by Hicks to the drum school that I never forgot. As soon as he entered, we knew that, unusually for him, he was in a foul mood. He lined up all the battalion drummers and shouted out the different cadences and rhythms for us to play one by one, interspersed with various drill formation orders, just to see if we could switch swiftly from one tune to the next. In the end, he roared at us to cease, declaring that he wasn't satisfied with our performances and proceeded to remind us that drummers needed only three things on the battlefield: accuracy of beat, evenness of tempo and speed of delivery. 'Fast thinking,' he bawled, 'that's what will keep your comrades alive.' Then he glared at me. 'Burns,' he roared, 'drums brought down the walls of Jericho. Your drumming wouldn't bring down a house of cards.' The others waited for Hicks to leave before they had a terrific laugh at my expense.

Sometimes, due to the growing expectation of war in Europe, we drilled with the militias that were garrisoned nearby but as they were only part-timers, we tended to look disdainfully upon them as a totally inferior species to us and we took a perverse delight in showing them up. When the 27th was invited to put on a display for the local aristocracy at Florence Court, a short distance outside Enniskillen, we gave a sterling performance, impressing all the fine ladies with our precision marching and changing formations. I was a real peacock that day, having become quite the master of the instrument by then, strutting around with my new drum and resplendent drummer's uniform. Some of the ladies screamed when the combined companies formed up in three long lines and volley-fired into the air. In the sudden silence that followed, McNeilis remarked that we'd be doing well if our muskets had the same effect on the French.

The battalion marched back to the depot that evening with all our colours flying and drums playing, right through the centre of Enniskillen. I thought I spotted my mother in the crowd of onlookers in Church Street but I couldn't swear to it. If it was her, I hoped she had seen that I was doing well.

Looking back now, it seems that those early days have blended into one, with a routine consisting of drilling, chores, drum school, punishment marching, all mingled with prolonged spells as duty drummer rapping out the changes in the day's activities.

12

I was three months and seventeen days in the army before I killed a man. It wasn't supposed to happen, of course, but the way that Curley and Baxter orchestrated things between them, it was inevitable.

George Benedict Baxter was a captain turned sour in his rank, the worst kind of officer that any regiment could have. One old veteran, serving out his time in our company, remembered him joining the 27th about twenty years before. Usually, ambitious young officers moved from regiment to regiment as they bought their way up the career ladder. It seemed that Baxter had moved more than most but his progress had stalled at the rank of captain and he was stuck in a promotional backwater. Getting ahead in the army then had nothing to do with competence and ability. Instead, it was all to do with connections and money, and a dash of luck thrown in. When the first two elements let him down, he transferred out of the regiment in the hope of a battlefield commission elsewhere but even that approach had also failed him. He hadn't been heard of for many years until, one morning, at parade, he appeared beside Major de Villiers who informed us that Captain Baxter had rejoined the regiment and would take command of our company and that Captain Grant had been transferred to the 2nd. Therein lay our misfortune.

Baxter immediately began to take out his frustration and bitterness on the men. To compound matters, he discovered in Curley as his sergeant a kindred spirit. A good NCO is a godsend to any company, acting as a buffer between the men and military authority. They bring the voice of tough, common-sense experience to leaven the consequences of an officer's upper-class prejudices. But Curley never did that, preferring instead to turn the already harsh life of the common redcoat into an intolerable lot and, with Baxter as company commander encouraging him, that is exactly what he persisted in doing.

Lieutenant Wendell Astwith was the junior officer in the company. He did his best to lessen the petty spitefulness that Curley brought to the conduct of his duties, until Baxter upbraided him in front of the men for being soft, ordering him to place ten men on punishment detail each day for a week and to oversee it himself. Astwith did as Baxter ordered but the men never held it against him, knowing that it was all the captain's doing. Curley added me to the list as duty drummer for the punishment detail for the seven days. Baxter must have spotted my name because, when he was with us a few days, he sauntered over to inspect us as we drilled. He looked at the sweating men marching with heavy knapsacks and me panting alongside, and then said, 'So, you're Burns?'

'Yes, Sir,' I replied, giving a smart salute. He looked closely at me for a few moments before walking off, ignoring Astwith's salute.

The punishment drills continued, with more men being added by the day until, on one occasion, nearly one-third of the company of about eighty men were listed. We quickly became accustomed to Baxter and his ugly ways. He was both indolent and arrogant by nature, possessing none of the qualities that endear a leader to his men. But, from the way he issued his orders, with Curley frequently having to whisper corrections to him, it was obvious that the captain lacked even the most basic understanding of military affairs in spite of his years in the army. Curley was happy to provide this service, ingratiating himself even further with Baxter on the occasions when Colonel Ferguson was present.

We were only a few months in the depot when Francie Doherty, the man who had taken my part against Curley on my first day, went missing. Being neighbours at home, we had struck up a friendship and he frequently joined us in our mess when our duties had finished for the day. He seemed to have settled in well, and even things with his wife, Tess, had been patched up. I never noticed anything amiss with him, certainly nothing that would cause him to be absent from duty.

At parade one morning, when the sergeant major called Francie's name, I was surprised that there was no response of 'Here!' from his place in the line. McGreel shouted his name again but still no answer came.

'By any chance, has Private Doherty reported to the sick bay?' McGreel asked.

'No, Sergeant Major,' shouted Maine, the hospital orderly.

'Did anyone in his mess see him rise this morning?' McGreel's gaze scanned the ranks. There was silence except for a bit of feigned coughing. The sergeant major's voice grew louder, as if expecting the missing man to appear at any moment. Normally, on my days as duty drummer, I'd exchange a nod in greeting when I'd see Francie in the corridor or as we formed into our ranks at Reveille but I realised that I had missed him that morning.

'Corporal Shanley, go check his berth. Double quick!'

Shanley set off at a run and the roll call continued with everybody else either present or in the sick quarters. There was an air of expectation in the square as we all looked for the NCO to come back with a sleepy and repentant redcoat. But the corporal reappeared alone.

'Well?' McGreel asked, lowering his muster board. 'Any sign of the Private?'

'No, Sergeant Major. His bed is made but he's not to be found.'

'I will report him as Absent Without Leave to the duty officer. You will make it your business to find him, Corporal.'

'After breakfast, Sir?' Shanley asked hopefully.

'Immediately!' barked McGreel, 'and take his messmates with you. Maybe going without eating until they find him will help them to remember something.'

Missing the first meal of the day did not suit Francie's fellow roommates but, if they knew or suspected anything, they did not give up any information of his whereabouts.

A complete search of the depot followed but there was no sign of the missing man. Baxter quickly took word of his absence to Major de Villiers who, in turn, reported to Colonel Ferguson. The Colonel was outraged at the news and ordered that Francie be found at any cost. By mid-morning, when the men would usually have some time off to themselves, detachments of redcoats fanned out along the streets and alleyways of Enniskillen, entering every alehouse and drinking den, certain that they'd discover the absconder. But they all returned to the depot without success. I even checked with a few traders I knew in the town but Francie hadn't been seen by any of them.

Search parties were then dispatched a bit further afield in case Francie had decided to sleep off the effects of a whiskey-sodden session in some storehouse or stable on the outskirts of the town but, again, to no avail. By this stage, the Colonel was apoplectic with rage. While most of the 6th Dragoons, the cavalry regiment of the Inniskillings, were then based in England, a small unit remained behind for recruitment purposes. The Colonel requested their assistance. Major Alfred Lunney, their Commanding Officer, readily agreed, treating the search for Francie as he would a fox hunt, a bit of sport before a pleasant dinner in Florence Court to which he had been invited that evening. The Dragoons set out at a canter soon after, determined to apprehend their quarry. From the fixed expressions of the troopers' faces, for Francie's sake, I hoped they would not find him. But they did.

The day was nearly spent when a shrill blast of the bugle announced the imminent return of the Dragoons. The horses clattered into the square, snorting and tossing their heads, their cropped tails swishing from side to side as steam rose from their sweaty flanks. Francie's bowed head was barely visible between two of the horses. His hands had been secured to their saddle-straps. The troopers dismounted and untied him. Francie slumped to the ground, utterly spent. The Dragoons had travelled at a half-canter, making him run the whole way from where they had found him back to the depot. Had Francie not kept up the pace, he was at risk of falling under the horses' hooves and being dragged along the rough and uneven surface of the road. Word of his apprehension spread rapidly into every mess. Soon a crowd of off-duty infantrymen gathered to watch as he was hauled off to the depot gaol. We wondered what had befallen him to make him desert his post all of a sudden. It wasn't long before we heard what happened from the gaol guards themselves.

It turned out that Francie had received word from his wife that their two small children, both girls, one yet an infant, had been laid low with the smallpox. They each had contracted the sickness within days of each other. Close proximity within a small cabin made this a foregone conclusion. The doctor's visit had been brief, his inspection of the girls even more so, and his prognosis held out no hope for their survival. He had agreed to get word of this impending tragedy to Francie who, with breaking heart, asked Curley for leave to see his beloved children for the last time and be of some comfort to his young wife. Curley had refused, claiming that Francie was using his children's misfortune as an excuse to get out of the depot and could not be trusted to return to the regiment. Francie had then asked to see Astwith, expecting he would get a sympathetic response from him but Curley sent him instead to Baxter. Francie pleaded his case but Baxter laughed at him and told him that if his babies died, he could take pleasure with his wife in making more. Torn apart by this heartless refusal, Francie had waited until all his messmates were sound asleep before slipping out of his berth and sneaking quietly down the stairs of his block. Evading the sentries, he had managed to abscond from the depot unseen. By the first light of dawn, he was back in his tiny house, cradling the dead bodies of his two little daughters, tears streaming down his face, while his wife, stricken with grief, sat at a hearth whose fire had long burnt out. That's where he was found by the Dragoons. Distressed beyond all reason, he was dragged away before he could see to his children's burial.

Baxter and Curley had departed that same afternoon on another recruitment drive into south Donegal and were gone for a number of days and so weren't there the following morning when Francie went missing. Otherwise, Baxter would have guessed immediately where he had gone and saved everybody a lot of trouble searching.

A General Regimental Court Martial was quickly arranged. This case was not a matter that required much investigation, Baxter was heard to remark on his return, given that the facts were not in dispute. The soldier was a deserter, pure and simple. All that was needed, he stated, was a hasty conclusion and a fitting punishment to ensure that no man would desert from the 3rd Company ever again.

As for Colonel Ferguson, he was a God-fearing, church-going type, known to the regiment as much for the inflexibility of his moral convictions as for the rigid application of army discipline to soldier and officer alike. Regardless of the reason, as he would see it, a soldier had gone missing from his post and, therefore, a punishment was warranted. We still hoped that Ferguson would take into account the extreme circumstances that had prompted Francie to abscond and that he would find it in his heart on that occasion to be lenient.

13

A few days later, Francie's court martial was held in the Officers' Mess. The large, formal dining room had been hastily converted into a military court, with the Colonel as presiding judge and Major de Villiers as his assistant. Captain Roger Dunne from the 1st Company, a fair-minded man but a stickler for discipline, was prosecutor. Lieutenant William Welter, from the 2nd Company, a junior officer in the battalion, was instructed to defend him. A small number of rank and file soldiers, including Francie's messmates, were allowed to be present to witness the court martial proceedings.

Unsurprisingly, Baxter detailed me as duty drummer. I was unhappy with that as I didn't want to witness the trial but I had no choice. So, that morning, I had to beat a slow tempo for Francie from the gaol block to the Officers' Mess. I threw a few sideways glances at him on the way. Although he was in his dress uniform, he did not carry himself with any soldierly bearing. Instead, he looked utterly exhausted as he shuffled along in the middle of four escorting redcoats with Shanley bringing up the rear. His eyes had the vacant look of one who has little awareness of his surroundings. He even seemed oblivious to the chains that shackled his hands and feet, their rattling an accompaniment to my solemn beats.

McGreel met us at the door and led us into the temporary courtroom. Francie's shackles were removed and he was pushed into a chair beside Welter who was busy scanning a copy of the Army Regulations on the table in front of him. He leaned over and said something to Francie who responded with a shake of the head. He whispered again and this time Francie murmured something back. Welter listened intently, his face betraying both nerves and anxiety at the same time. With his boyish demeanour, he looked completely out of his depth. By contrast, Dunne was leaning back in his chair, giving off an air of confidence, impatient for the proceedings to begin. He had acted in this role on many occasions before, we heard, and by all accounts had never lost a case. It was obvious that he expected to win this one also. A few of the seated redcoats began to cough by way of letting Francie know that they were there until McGreel threatened to empty the room unless he got silence. The tension increased as we waited for Ferguson and de Villiers to arrive, which they eventually did. At a signal from Hicks, I commenced a loud, sustained roll on my drum until the judges sat down, and I finished with a final flourish. An intense stillness filled the room before the major opened proceedings.

'Private Francis Doherty,' de Villiers began, his voice booming around the room, 'you are accused of desertion from the regiment on the 17th of July of this year, and of resisting arrest by His Majesty's Dragoons for the same most serious offence. How do you plead to these charges, guilty or not guilty?'

Welter had to nudge Francie to respond. 'Not guilty,' Francie whispered, his voice just about audible.

'The court did not hear your response, Private.'

'Not guilty,' repeated Francie, his voice a little louder.

'Let the court note that the accused has pleaded not guilty. Captain Dunne,' de Villiers continued, 'are you ready to begin the proceedings for the prosecution?'

Dunne stood, puffed out his chest and loudly declared: 'Yes, Major, I am.'

'Lieutenant Welter, are you ready to begin?'

'No Sir, I am not,' replied the young officer, hesitantly. He gathered himself before continuing. 'I need more time to consult with the prisoner as to his motives for his alleged act, for I am led to believe that there are circumstances that will provide adequate reasons for what he did, and that is why he is pleading innocent of the charges. I also wish to speak to the doctor who treated Private Doherty's children. I humbly beg the court's approval for an adjournment to allow me to do my duty towards the accused.'

With that, the Colonel intervened. His tone was measured but there was a warning edge to it.

'You also have a duty to the regiment, Sir, and do not forget that. Request denied! Let the court martial begin.'

Baxter smiled at this. Welter remained standing, shocked at the Colonel's refusal, until the Major ordered him to resume his seat immediately. Welter had enough sense to know that he risked the Colonel's ire if he persisted with any further objections. More than that, his future progress in the army was at stake as Ferguson had it in his power to block the career path of a young officer. Welter sat down and shuffled the papers on the table in front of him to cover his discomfiture.

Dunne began by laying out the case for the prosecution before the court. On the day before deserting, Private Doherty had a short meeting in the depot with the local physician. After that, he had been in his own mess or with the drummers in their mess all evening before being witnessed getting into his berth that night. Neither Corporal Ward, the duty NCO, nor the sentry, had observed anything amiss during their watch. The Private subsequently failed to turn out for Sunday morning roll call in the square. His messmates should have seen that he was missing and reported that fact to Corporal Ward. They had failed to do so. Therefore, regardless of the outcome of the court martial, they would have to answer for this to their company commander, Captain Baxter.

'Objection!' Welter interjected, rising quickly. 'The prisoner has yet to be found guilty; no grounds exist for anybody to be reported to Captain Baxter.'

Baxter was on his feet in a flash. 'No Junior Lieutenant will tell me how to conduct affairs in my own company,' he snarled.

'Resume your seat, Captain Baxter,' the Colonel barked. 'And you, Lieutenant Welter, are overruled. The Private did desert, without question. We are only here to record that fact fully, and to decide upon a suitable punishment. Lieutenant, you will not interrupt the prosecution again.'

Welter resumed his seat, aghast at the Colonel's outburst.

Dunne then continued, putting it on the record that Francie had absconded for alleged family reasons after being refused permission to return home by both Sergeant Curley and by Captain Baxter, as they were fully entitled to do. He then quoted from Baxter's written statement that: "If every private was allowed to trot off home whenever they heard of a trifling illness afflicting a child or a wife, soon there'd be nobody left in the depot, as every soldier's trull, or one of her brood, would be stricken with on-going illness." This observation prompted a general ripple of amusement among the officers, but I could see that Baxter's words had stung Francie. Welter had to push him back into his seat.

'Besides,' continued Dunne, 'let the court know that Private Doherty has been in front of Captain Baxter on a number of occasions already for a series of recurring misdemeanours and was therefore deserving of no special consideration on this occasion.'

'That's a lie,' shouted Francie. 'I was never stood in front of the captain.'

Baxter again leapt up, his face livid. 'Are you calling your superior officer a liar, Private?' he shouted, the last word being spat out as an insult. At this, a loud murmuring arose from the body of the room. The Colonel pounded the table with his gavel.

'Lieutenant Welter, the Private will contain himself or it will be the worse for him.' He then addressed Baxter. 'Captain, you will resume your seat. Your veracity is not in question.' Baxter sat, a wide smirk on his face. When order had been restored, Captain Dunne resumed where he had left off.

'This is precisely the reason that the army restricts the number of women who can live within the depot, and also why it provides quarters in which soldiers can reside, to free them from such incidental cares that could distract them from their duty. There is no doubt that Captain Baxter's refusal of leave was the correct decision, and one that was therefore binding on Private Doherty. So, when he absconded during the night, it was not a case of being absent without leave. It was a case of desertion, as Private Doherty had no intention of returning to his barracks or of surrendering himself to the authorities. He was discovered "out of uniform" in the half-loft of his cottage, holding his deceased children. Furthermore, when challenged by the Dragoons, he violently resisted arrest. If I may quote again from Captain Baxter's notes written three days following the desertion, he states that "he would not be surprised to hear that Private Doherty, knowing he was about to be discovered, contrived to be found holding his children's corpses in his arms in order to evoke sympathy for himself in the trial he knew was to follow."'

At this outlandish allegation, Welter again jumped to his feet but a sharp reminder from the Colonel made him sit without saying a word. It was too much for the accused, though, who finally exploded. As Welter sat, Francie launched himself towards Baxter, fists flailing. But no blow landed as McGreel managed to place his substantial bulk in the way, saving the captain from possible injury. There was a brief struggle but Francie was swiftly subdued. When order was restored, the Colonel ordered Francie to be shackled again and a new charge was added to the sheet, that of attempting to cause serious injury to a senior officer.

There was a swell of unrest among the observing redcoats at this. Hardened to the harsh realities of the life of the rank and file soldier, this cruel provocation of an accused man was a blatant injustice to them. The disquiet among them increased as they witnessed their comrade in chains again. But, once more, the Colonel intervened, threatening to empty the court if silence could not be maintained. He then called for the prosecuting officer to conclude. Knowing that Francie's outburst had sealed his fate, Dunne quickly ended by stating that the honour of the regiment was at stake and that the punishment meted out by the court must match the seriousness of the combined offences. Welter was not called upon to offer a defence as the facts were deemed to have spoken for themselves. The young lieutenant sat there, totally out of his depth, his case demolished by events beyond his control.

The Colonel deliberated quietly with de Villiers for a few minutes, until a final nod showed a decision had been made. He then addressed the court, saying that there was now no doubt as to the correctness of bringing proceedings against Private Doherty based on the charges laid out by Captain Dunne. Added to this was the aggravated attempt in front of the whole court to injure one of His Majesty's officers. Therefore, the court would now stand in judgment. He then addressed Francie in the following words.

'Private Doherty, it is the decision of this court martial, convened under the authority of the Judge Advocate, and following all proper rules and procedures, and having heard and seen for ourselves evidence of your guilt in the matters of which you stand accused, that you are guilty as charged on each count. You are hereby sentenced to three hundred lashes for desertion. In addition, for attempting to cause injury to an officer of the regiment, namely, your company commander, Captain George Baxter, during the proceedings of this court and in full view of your fellows, you are hereby sentenced to an additional one-hundred lashes. The battalion will parade in the morning to witness the punishment. Perhaps the sight of the lash being laid on with a heavy hand will deter any other man who would attempt either to desert his post or to strike an officer. The punishment will be administered at dawn tomorrow by the duty drummers under the supervision of Drum Major Hicks. The court martial of Private Francis Doherty is now concluded.'

With a sinking feeling, I realised what Baxter had been planning all along; for some reason, he wanted me to flog Francie. First thing that morning, he had changed the roster for the week, assigning me for drum duty on my own instead of with The Fox Maguire. When I saw Baxter smile over at Curley, I knew the two of them were conspiring together. Ned Kennedy had told me from the start that the drum was the pleasant part of the job, the lash was the awful part. The 27th wasn't a regiment much given to the practice of flogging, as efforts were being made to eliminate extreme punishment measures in the army, but flogging still existed and Baxter had ensured the task would fall to me. Meanwhile, Francie sat unmoving, as if unaware of the dreadful fate that awaited him.

Without a backward glance, Ferguson and de Villiers

left the room, everyone present rising as they did so. They had presided over a court martial where justice had singularly failed to put in an appearance. As for leniency or mercy, neither of these qualities existed in the army as they would be seen as signs of weakness. All the same, I was shocked to realise that the whole affair was concluded within half an hour of its commencement.

With a flick of his cane, Hicks signalled me to beat time as the prisoner was led back to the gaol. Francie never said a word on the way; he just walked as if in a trance, his mind, no doubt, with Tess and his lost little girls. As for me, my mind was numb, my sticks striking the calfskin as if they had a detached life of their own.

That was one of the few entirely sleepless nights that I passed in the depot, as I'm sure Francie did too. I dreaded what I had to do and, for the first time, wished I hadn't taken up the drum. At the first light of dawn, the entire battalion in full dress uniform had formed up in hollow square, all facing inwards to the centre, where a pyramid had been made from three sergeants' pikes crossed at the top and tied together, with the bottoms splayed in a wide, triangular frame. Although it all looked a bit rickety, it was very secure. A grim-faced Hicks was standing nearby, a red silk bag hanging from his belt. Then Francie was summoned.

For the first time, on that short walk from the gaol to the middle of the square, I played The Rogue's March, the tune reserved for occasions such as this. I trembled inside for my friend but I also dreaded what was to come next; there was no escaping it. Francie shuffled along, head bowed, shackles clinking loud on the cobbles, making no effort at marching to my beat, unlike Corporal Shanley and the escorting redcoats who kept perfect time. The ranks parted to let us enter, then closed again. We waited in the chill air, unmoving.

The square opened again and Ferguson and de Villiers stomped in with the rest of the battalion officers. Behind them came assistant surgeon Mostyn with his medical holdall, and Maine, the hospital orderly, who was carrying a chair and a pail of water. They took up a position where they could observe proceedings clearly. The Colonel waited for a moment, surveying the ranks in a dramatic fashion before addressing the men.

'Soldiers of the 27th,' he began, 'you are about to witness the punishment of Private Francis Doherty, 3rd Company, Inniskillings, a man who has brought shame upon himself and upon the regiment by being found guilty of the act of desertion, and of attempting an assault on his senior officer. If this were to have happened in a time of war, Private Doherty would hang from a gibbet. Instead, he is lucky to escape with a mere four hundred lashes. The honour of the regiment demands the full loyalty and obedience of every man among you. When you elevate your own will above your duty to the regiment, know that you will be punished severely. The regiment must always come first.' Raising his voice, the Colonel then addressed me directly.

'Drummer, do your duty.'

14

'Strip, Sir!'

With these chilling words, Drum Major Hicks ordered Francie to loosen his shirt. His arms were then tied together to the top of the triangle and his feet to the base. McGreel approached him and placed a red cloth cap on his head and a thick collar round his neck as a protection. Mostyn then conducted a quick examination and declared that he was fit for the punishment.

'Proceed,' instructed the Colonel, 'with force and vigour.'

'Remove your tunic, Drummer Burns,' Hicks ordered, 'don't want blood all over it, do we?' Then, so no one else could hear, he whispered, 'Just do your duty, lad.'

As if I were the condemned man, I slowly placed my drum on the ground, laid the sticks across the rim and began to unbutton my tunic. I took my time hoping that by some miraculous intervention from the Colonel, I would not be called upon to bring such wanton pain to a fellow human being, especially Francie.

'Hurry, lad,' Hicks urged, quietly. 'The battalion's watching. You're doing him no favour dragging out the moment.'

I undid the last few buttons of my tunic and folded it upon my drum. Hicks then handed me the red silk bag from his belt. I noticed that the cloth was covered in dark stains. Blood, I thought; it shows up dark on red. For some reason, that had never struck me before.

'Stop dwelling on what you have to do, Drummer,' Hicks said, sharply. 'Just commence. Twenty-five at a time.'

Curley was grinning over at me. I knew he was enjoying this moment, with all of the redcoats standing in the middle of the cobbled square, relishing the power he had over them. If either he or Baxter had shown any compassion for Francie at all, the matter would never have got this far but both were devoid of even a shred of pity. I reached into the bag, felt the hard, wooden handle, and withdrew the cat o'nine tails or, as every redcoat knew it, the cat. It was the first time I had ever seen one. With a chill, I saw that the handle was actually a drumstick with long strings attached, at first twined round the wood to fashion a grip and then allowed to fall loose, like long tails. Each tail was made of hard, hemp whipcord, with knots at the end to cause maximum pain, and hardened with dried blood. I turned towards Francie. He was spread-eagled on the pikes, his body now bare to the waist and his shirt hanging down over his belt. He gave a slight shiver even though the day was turning out to be a fairly warm one. I held out the lash, trailing the tails almost to the ground and still I hesitated. A drum gave a sombre roll, then stopped. It was Reggie.

'Commence on my count, Private Drummer,' shouted Curley. 'One!'

My first stroke was a tentative, half-hearted attempt. The tails licked across Francie's back, making him flinch. A couple of red stripes appeared on his skin. I saw his muscles tense as he steeled himself for my next stroke. Suddenly, Curley's cane fetched me a severe rap on the back of my hand making me drop the cat.

'Lay it on properly, Drummer,' he shouted. 'That one doesn't count. You barely tickled him.'

Again, I hesitated, feeling the sting in my hand and the pounding of my heart.

'Pick up the cat, Burns,' Curley roared, pointing with his cane. 'Start again.'

I turned to Francie, the marks on his skin more obvious now. Somehow, he contrived to turn his head around. 'Do what you have to, Drummer. It's all right by me,' he whispered hoarsely. I was close enough to him to smell the whiskey off his breath. Perhaps one of the guards had been kind enough to get it for him to deaden the pain. 'Sorry, Francie,' I whispered.

'Proceed,' shouted Curley.

And, I'm ashamed to say that I did. If I hadn't, my half-strokes would have been discounted and the entire punishment would start all over again, just as Curley had threatened. I was obliged to make every lash count, each one accompanied by a single beat of Reggie's drum, Curley calling out the count. After the first twenty-five lashes had been administered, a short break was called. I knew from Kennedy that drummers usually rotated after each round so that a fresh arm was always available. Not this time. Curley and Baxter intended for me to do it on my own.

By the time I had administered one hundred and seventy five strokes, my arms ached and I was greatly fatigued. I stopped to draw breath. Francie's back was a red mass of criss-crossed cuts and tears, the tender skin lacerated by the cat. There was no need for the sharp barbs that I heard were attached to some cats. I had done plenty of damage without those cruel additions. Poor Francie's legs had given out under him and he sagged helplessly, held up only by the ropes that secured his wrists to the frame. Curley was enjoying watching my anguish so much that I refrained from looking at him. It was Hicks who saw how tired my arms were and ordered a break.

'Hold, Drummer, while Mr Mostyn sees to the state of the prisoner.' The Drum Major's voice was flat and emotionless but I have always thought that he was disgusted by the flogging and would have liked to end it then.

'Water!' shouted Mostyn.

I don't know if this was what the assistant surgeon intended but Maine picked up the bucket and poured the entire contents over the injured man. Francie stiffened in shock as the cold water flowed down his tortured back, spilling onto the cobbles and diluting the dark red pools of blood at his feet. His head rolled in agony and he stifled his inner screams. Mostyn whispered into his ear as he examined the wounds, making him wince as he felt the depth of the cuts from which the blood now flowed freely. His grey trousers were stained and discoloured with great red blobs. As I gazed upon the stricken man, it didn't occur to me then that I looked like a butcher's apprentice with my blood-splattered clothes and my wild eyes and the dripping cat in my aching hands.

'What say you, Mr Mostyn?' asked the Colonel impatiently. 'May the punishment continue?'

The assistant surgeon took his time before replying. Then, in spite of Francie's abject condition, he nodded. 'Yes, Sir, it may continue.'

So, my brief rest over, I laid it on again, Curley continuing the count with each stark drumbeat, my strokes taking longer as my tiredness grew. The soldier's code demanded that a flogging be endured in silence and Francie was determined to observe it. He wouldn't have it said that he was a Nightingale, the redcoat's derogatory name for someone who cried out under the lash. Apart from a few agonised groans through gritted teeth, he made no sound, refusing to give any satisfaction to Curley. So, with each lash, with each laceration that cut deep into that man's broken body, I swore that, some day, I'd even the score with Curley. For Francie's sake.

I tried to hold back but Curley, ever watchful, noticed and dealt me a further blow on the knuckles that drew blood but, by then, I didn't care. Francie's back was all but flayed to pieces at that stage with the violence of my actions and continuing seemed pointless. I stopped.

'Again!' Curley screamed. 'Take that one again.'

The savage instinct that had been stoked up within me erupted in a sudden rage; something inside me snapped. I poised to swing round, to lay the bloody cat across that bastard's smirking face and cut him for a change when, suddenly, Hicks had my arm in a vice grip. 'Hold!' he shouted, then hissed in my ear. 'Blast you, Burns. Do you want the cat too? Keep your wits about you, man.' I breathed in deeply a few times, slowly exhaled, then relaxed. Hicks let me go. He had read my violent intent but, luckily, nobody else seemed to have noticed.

'Sir,' said Mostyn, into the sudden silence as the drum ceased. 'The Drum Major's intervention is timely. May I examine the prisoner's condition?'

Clearly annoyed at the interruption, the Colonel had no alternative but to assent to the request. As Mostyn stepped forward, a redcoat vomited somewhere within the ranks. Then others did likewise around the square. I retched also, my mouth filling with bile. It was all I could do to swallow it back. I swayed with fatigue but Hicks steadied me. The sight of Francie's raw, shredded back was too awful to behold as he sagged against the frame, his legs having collapsed under him. There was an uneasy shuffling among the ranks as a buzz of angry muttering arose but the NCOs were swift to intervene. 'Keep still, you men,' they shouted, and patrolled the lines angrily.

Mostyn's examination didn't take long. He peered closely at Francie, poking along his partially exposed backbone. I was near enough to hear the wheezing of his lungs as they fought to take in enough air to sustain life. I couldn't understand how a man's body was able to take such punishment and still be breathing. I stepped close to Francie, wanting to say how sorry I was, but Mostyn shoved me roughly away. He turned to the Colonel.

'Sir, I beg leave to report that the prisoner is unfit for any further punishment. If it continues, he will die for he has lost a lot of blood already. I must recommend a cessation on medical grounds, unless you mean to kill him outright.'

This displeased the Colonel for he seemed fixed on making an example of Francie in front of the whole battalion. He wanted the punishment to be completed in one session but he had to relent.

'Then I release the prisoner into your hands for treatment, Mr Mostyn, after which he will be returned to the gaol. Let the record show that he has received two hundred and twenty-seven lashes so far and that he must receive the outstanding one hundred and seventy-three as soon as he has made sufficient recovery. The sentence will be carried out in full. Major de Villiers, dismiss the men.' The Colonel, with a final contemptuous look at Francie, strode off.

At the Major's order, the men broke ranks and slowly dispersed, with many a rueful glance back at Francie. Being witness to a flogging was a horrific experience and the usual good-humoured banter that accompanied being dismissed after parade was nowhere in evidence. Some of the men had already experienced the cat and Francie's punishment had awakened painful memories for them. Maine produced a surgeon's knife and cut Francie down. A couple of redcoats placed him face down on a stretcher and carried him off to the depot hospital. I went to follow but Mostyn cut me short.

'You've done enough damage for now, Burns, 'he said, fixing me with a stare. 'You're lucky the Drum Major stepped in that time or you'd be next for a flogging.'

'Yes, Sir,' I said, fully aware of the folly I had almost committed. 'I don't know what came over me.'

'Don't thank me, Drummer,' said Mostyn curtly, 'when you treat a man's back after the cat, as I have done, you never want to see a man flogged again, no matter what the reason. And I certainly don't want to see you in my hospital after four hundred lashes because you can't control your anger, you young fool.' He hurried off after the stretcher party. Francie left a trail of blood across the square.

15

Hearing Francie's cries of pain as Mostyn tended to his torn body was torture to me. I sat on the ground outside the hospital, my feelings all in a tangle of despair. At times he screamed aloud, as if the agony was too much to bear. Each sound he made went through me like a hot knife. Eventually I could take it no more so I walked slowly back across the square towards our block, my drum at my side and my tunic slung across my shoulder. When I entered the mess, it was empty. The others had taken themselves off somewhere out of the way, most likely to the canteen for beer. I threw myself on my berth and lay there in a confused state of mind. But Curley hadn't done with me because he suddenly appeared in the doorway, took one look at me and exploded.

'Drummer,' he bellowed, 'you're a disgrace to the regiment. Look at the state of your uniform. Report to me in the NCOs' mess in five minutes with your drum. And stay as you are!' He was gone before I even had the wits to move.

I jumped from my berth and took stock of my appearance. My face and hands were covered with blood, my shirt was spattered and smeared with gore, as were my breeches and shoes. Why he wanted me to remain like that was a mystery. However, without dwelling on it, I raced over to the NCOs' mess where Curley was waiting for me. He dragged me aggressively by the shoulder into the square, where a file of sheepish-looking infantrymen were lined up with muskets and full knapsacks. Curley stalked in front of them.

'This lot weren't man enough to watch a flogging without being sick,' he shouted, 'so let's see if we can toughen them to the sight of a little blood. Burns, you will drill with them until they can look upon you without wanting to vomit. Quick Time!'

Then that bastard had us march back and forth for hours across the exact spot where the pike pyramid had been, me still in my bloodied state, them staring at me, making us step time and time again in my friend's gore, such was the level of sheer vindictiveness that drove the man. And so it was not until much later, totally exhausted, that I presented myself at the hospital door. I knocked gently. Maine admitted me and brought me over to Francie's bed, telling me that the injured man had refused any treatment or assistance from the surgeon since arriving. He lay face down, his flayed back exposed to the cool air. His fingers gripped the wooden edges of the bed frame to control the spasms of pain that wracked his body. His breathing came in quick, loud gasps. I knelt down beside the berth so that he would be able to see me but his eyes were closed.

'Francie,' I whispered, 'Francie! It's me.'

His eyes finally opened slightly. They were bloodshot. His hair was matted with sweat, stuck to his forehead. He gritted his teeth as pain, once again, seized his whole body. I felt my own eyes fill up with tears at the sight of this good man lying on that berth with his back a tangled mess of torn skin, blood and pus.

'Francie,' I said, my face close to his. 'I'm sorry. I really am.'

His mouth moved. 'Water!' he croaked. I gently ladled some cold liquid to his lips and dribbled most of it onto the floor.

'Just wet his mouth,' came Mostyn's voice behind me, passing by. 'That's all he needs for now.' I spooned another drop of water into him and he swallowed it awkwardly. 'Francie,' I began again, but he stopped me.

'No need for sorry, James,' Francie croaked. 'Curley had it in for me from the first day. You're not the only one he's made life hard for. But he certainly has it in for you.' Francie coughed, fresh spasms of pain torturing him. Eventually he relaxed a little and he continued. 'Baxter as well. He knows we're friends. Asked me about you.' He wheezed as he spoke, the effort at words almost too much for him. 'Don't know why. Told me not to tell you. Hoped you'd refuse today so that he could get you punished too. That's why you couldn't say no. You had to do it.' He grabbed my shirt and pulled me to him. I was surprised at the strength that was left in that broken body. 'James, don't let Baxter win, whatever his game is. Curley's only small fry. He's just Baxter's pup. He doesn't matter.' Francie's eyes closed again and his grip relaxed. The effort of talking had used up the last of his energy. Mostyn returned.

'He must rest now, Burns. You can see him tomorrow

after drum school. You have to leave now.'

Without any more conversation, he ushered me out the door. I was utterly despondent as I made my way back to the mess. The others had returned by the time I got there but Curley must have been watching for me because, as soon as I entered, he appeared again in the doorway, a smirk on his scarred face. We jumped up quickly and stood to attention.

'Well, Burns,' he said, 'I hope you enjoyed your little exercise today. You may not be aware of it but you have reason to be grateful to me as there's an additional payment to a drummer who carries out a flogging. It's not quite thirty pieces of silver but it's enough to buy beer for your mates. Too bad that Doherty isn't in a fit state to enjoy it with you. Now, clean yourself up. You look like the shit you are.' And he sauntered off.

Curley's reference to the thirty pieces of silver stung me to the quick. For the rest of the evening, nothing the others said could console me. Even Reggie's usual sense of humour had deserted him. I refused all offers of beer that night despite the fact that Gallagher made several return trips to the canteen. They drank in near silence as the day's episode had been a harrowing one but their sympathy simply washed over me. I assumed that the mood in every mess that evening was sombre. The sight of any man's battered body is hard to take, but why, I kept asking myself, did it have to be Francie? What did he do to deserve that?

I had a broken sleep that night and tossed restlessly for a while, enduring the grunts and snores of my companions, before nodding off. Then, I heard the swish of the cat tearing into Francie's soft flesh again, and I jerked awake, only to lie there in a sweat, panting. Eventually I must have fallen into a deeper slumber – until a sudden bang shattered the stillness of the night.

A gunshot!

I snapped awake instantly. It was still dark. Loud voices and the sound of heavy boots on cobblestones followed as the sentries ran to investigate. I sat up on my mattress, the sheets wet with my perspiration. Corporal Ward's voice was loud in the corridor, shouting: 'Everyone stay as you are. Do not leave your mess. Only the NCOs will turn out.'

Then came the sound of more running feet from the square below. Orders were bawled, muddled and unclear, as the shutters on the windows were closed over, muffling the words. McNeilis lit a candle and the room filled with a gloomy light. We gathered around the table, sitting in an uncomfortable silence, the room chilly as the fire had nearly died out. Only a few stubborn embers glowed in the grate, almost buried in the ashes. Gallagher and Crooks began to dress so, for want of something to do, I did likewise. McNeilis started to clean a musket, pushing the ramrod up and down the long barrel. He saw us staring at him quizzically. 'In case we're under attack,' he explained, as if we were imbeciles.

'It was one shot,' said The Fox, from his bunk. 'We're not under attack by Napoleon.'

'Well, nobody will find me ill-prepared. That's how I survived this long,' and he finished loading the firelock.

We didn't have long to wait. Ward entered. He pointed at me.

'You, Burns, come with me,' was all he said.

With the first inkling of dawn appearing in the sky, he led me over to the hospital. We went in.

'Over here, James,' came Mostyn's voice. I remember him using my Christian name and thought it strange at the time. I immediately took it that something was amiss. He was standing near Francie's berth, the one he had occupied the previous evening when I had left him. The berth was now empty, the bloodied sheets crumpled where he had lain.

'In there,' he said, pointing to the door leading to the hospital storeroom. A faint trail of blood led from Francie's berth to the door and into the room beyond. With growing dread, I went over and stepped through. Wax candles had been lit, shedding flickering light around the room. There Francie lay, with the top of his head blown off. He was on his side with his back to me, his body quite straight, still holding a musket in a tight, two-handed grip that death had not loosened. One leg was twisted up, his big toe curled inside the trigger guard.

'Oh, no, Francie,' I whispered, putting my hands to my head. 'What have you done?' I had fallen to my knees beside him but Mostyn hauled me back saying that I mustn't touch his body, that it had to lie that way until the morning when the regimental surgeon would see to him. Mostyn pulled me to my feet, explaining that there was nothing more that anyone could do for him except pray. Others entered the room. So stricken was I with grief that, to this day, I couldn't say who they were.

Mostyn drew me aside and put his hand on my shoulder, an act of kindness which I still appreciate after all this time, for Francie's act of final desperation was a terrible shock to me.

'He spoke to me last night, James,' the assistant surgeon murmured, his voice low and kindly. 'He said that he couldn't face another one hundred and seventy-three licks of the cat but it had been worth the flogging to see his little children before they died. You mustn't blame yourself. You only did your duty. He would have laid the cat on you had the situation been reversed.'

The salt tears were bitter on my lips. I wiped them away with my sleeve. I didn't know what to say at first. Then the words came into my head and I had to give them voice. It was the one and only time I contradicted an officer.

'You're wrong, Sir,' I replied, my voice shaking. 'It was my fault. No one held the cat except me. Francie might have pulled the trigger but it was I who surely killed him. His blood is upon my hands. And I got paid for it, like a Judas.' I turned and left the room, sickened at the sight of my friend's dead body, and broken with guilt.

Francie Doherty was buried in an unmarked pauper's grave later that day after the surgeon had verified the cause of death as 'by his own hand'. He had been declared unfit to be laid to rest in the regimental plot as he had been found guilty of desertion. He was also denied a church burial in consecrated grounds as he was a suicide. I asked permission to accompany his messmates to the pauper's plot to attend the burial and, to my surprise, Baxter allowed it. He probably thought it would add to my pain to see Francie go into the ground. Nobody else turned up except his messmates and they elected for me to say the words over his grave, the priest being conveniently occupied elsewhere.

Later, back in the depot, I saw Curley and Baxter outside the NCOs' mess. As I passed them, Curley remarked that the 27th was much better off without laggards such as Doherty, and Baxter said that there were still a few more from the Bog Land to be got rid of. They meant for me to hear, of course. It was their way of goading me further. I saluted them smartly, keeping my growing anger to myself.

16

Francie's body had barely been laid in the grave when the routine of formation drilling, musketry practice, barracks' chores, kit inspections and drum instruction resumed. But a simmering unrest lingered on in our company about the manner in which our comrade had been so horrifically treated by Captain Baxter. This became a topic of conversation between myself and Jacob Mulhearn, an old veteran with whom I regularly chatted. I enjoyed hearing his stories about past campaigns in the colonies. It was the closest I could get to finding out more about the kind of things that would have happened to my father. Unfortunately, as with the other veterans, he said he had never been in the same battalion as my father and so could offer no knowledge of him other than that he believed him to be 'as solid a man as had ever served in the regiment, and would never believe otherwise'.

A few days after the burial, Mulhearn joined us in the canteen after drill and the talk soon turned to Francie's death. We spoke in a subdued way in order as not to be overheard. The old veteran said that, more often than not, NCOs became brutes because many officers looked down on the soldiers as common scum and ignored how they were treated. He said that Baxter was the main one at fault as he encouraged Curley in his spite towards the men, and Francie was left with no option other than the one he took. Then he leaned in to me and whispered that if ever I found myself in action with Baxter, I should give him a blue plum, meaning a musket ball, in the back as that was what he deserved.

'The whole battalion knows by now what Baxter has done, may the devil take him,' Mulhearn breathed, and then spat a glob of brown tobacco juice into the hearth. 'In the smoke and turmoil of battle, a man could pull the trigger and who could tell friend from foe at that moment? A mistake can easily be made.' At this, he winked, and smiled conspiratorially. 'Many an incompetent officer, wasteful of his men's lives, was dealt with in this way. Yes, soldiers have to look out for each other. Your friend must be avenged, Burns, and you're the one to do it.'

He patted me on the shoulder as he spat again. I listened to the old soldier's words and planted them in my heart, wondering if it was in me to commit cold-blooded murder. We said no more about it and I left soon afterwards to go on duty. But the topic of Francie's death didn't go away. No matter what we started to talk about, it had a way of coming back into our conversation.

Most of the other gossip was brought into our mess-room by The Fox Maguire. Usually, it was some inflammatory bit of news involving a Skin and a local woman, a dispute over a debt, or a matter involving a piece of land before the court. He always managed to embellish his stories with a humorous angle especially if he could poke fun at some unfortunate redcoat in our company. However, we were in dread of such gossip reaching the ears of our Commanding Officer because of the high standards of behaviour he expected from everyone who wore the uniform. None of the battalion blamed Colonel Ferguson for passing judgment on Francie no more than they blamed me for the cat because, as the facts of the matter stood, he had acted against army regulations, regardless of his motivation. But every soldier agreed that, had Francie been given the opportunity of presenting his case to the Colonel himself, compassionate leave of absence more than likely would have been granted. In the light of what had been placed before him by Baxter though, and given the opinion the officer class had of the common soldier, there was only going to be one judgment at the court martial.

We often wished that the Colonel would pay closer attention to Baxter's antics, though, as he seemed to take excessive pleasure in inflicting daily brutality and, in this, had Curley as a willing lackey. But back then, officers cared little about the stern conditions that applied to the rank and file, and allowed the NCOs free rein in enforcing the harshest of discipline. Baxter and Curley picked on everybody indiscriminately but I continued to be their preferred target and so could often be found performing the most menial punishment duty that they could devise. I still puzzled over what Francie had said about Baxter's interest in me but could not fathom a reason for it. Their ill treatment of me had become so blatant that it was a matter of conjecture, not only around our mess table or in our company, but within the other companies as well. We all knew that Curley was possessed of a nasty streak but

Baxter was on a different level. On account of this, he himself became the subject of mess whispers as to the cause of his spitefulness and bitterness. Having served with more regiments than was usual, we could only guess at possible reasons for his frequent transfers. We began to wonder if financial worries were the root cause of his tendency towards cruelty. It was not unknown for wealthy gentlemen-officers to fall on hard times, and to subsequently take it out on those under them.

However, all this was mere conjecture until The Fox burst into the mess before dinner one evening in great excitement. He had overheard a brief discussion among the junior officers about Baxter soliciting a loan from one of them. Then, Lieutenant John Reihill, new to the depot and assigned to the 1st Company, happened to mention that some gold coins had gone missing from his room the day after he had arrived, upon which another officer claimed also to have lost a sum of money some time ago and that perhaps they should all look to the better security of their valuables until the thief was apprehended. They had then moved away before The Fox could hear any more.

Warnings about theft would be expected in a soldiers' barracks since every battalion in the army contained a fair share of scoundrels of the highest order; thieves, criminals, pickpockets, bullies and thugs, men without a shred of dignity or decency who would cut your throat for a coin. But anyone foolish enough to be caught stealing got a beating to within an inch of his life. For a repeat offence, he would be lucky if he got as far as a court martial before being found with his throat slit or his skull bashed in. On the other hand, theft among officers was almost unheard of as they were gentlemen first and foremost. Hence, the glee with which The Fox passed on to us the gossip he had overheard among the lieutenants.

It was an hour before dawn the next morning, a Sunday, and I was doing some urgent, minor adjustments to the cords on my drum before leaving the barracks for morning parade. A short while before, Reggie, as duty drummer, had given us an extra-loud roll at the bottom of the stairs to rouse us before rushing on to the next barracks' stairwell. When Ward banged on the door, most of us were already out of bed and were busy with our morning ablutions. Sammy Crooks was the exception. He had continued to snore until The Fox Maguire hit him with his straw pillow.

We quickly finished shaving at the buckets left ready from the previous night, then togged out in our fatigues. It was second nature to me by now to make my bed in the required way, to tidy my personal effects, and to make sure that I was properly turned out for inspection, as the officers were meticulous in checking every detail of our attire and equipment. Gallagher, Crooks and The Fox Maguire were already away with their drums, and I could hear them charging down the stairs. Meanwhile, Reggie's insistent drumming and the sound of hob-nailed boots striking the cobbles in the square urged Nosey McNeilis and me to hurry. I had just picked up my drum when I noticed him rummaging in his old campaign knapsack, the one he'd brought back from Flanders. He was feeling right down to the bottom, playing his hand around with quick, jerky movements.

'Hurry, man,' I said, 'we'll be late.'

But McNeilis, in frustration, had thrown the old knapsack down on his berth. He then lifted his mattress and peered underneath before letting it drop back down again, his bedcover now crumpled. The duty officer would have him on report for this when he came around to inspect if he left it like that. It was just asking for trouble. He began to feel the pockets of the spare uniform in his locker, then snorted in exasperation.

'It's gone!'

'What's gone?'

'My pocket watch.'

'But you had it last week in that bit of green cloth. I saw you with it.'

'Well, I don't have it now. And the cloth is gone too.' He squinted at me suspiciously. 'Did you hide it, Burns? Is this your idea of a joke?'

'Don't be stupid! Of course not,' I replied hotly. 'Fix your bed, Nosey. It's Baxter's turn to do the rounds this morning. He'll have you.'

'I care less about Baxter,' McNeilis replied. 'Someone has stolen my pocket watch. I'll kill whoever did it with my bare hands.' He balled his fists and hit them together hard. 'Bastard!' he roared suddenly, and he swung his arms in wide, violent arcs causing me to step back.

All of the messmates knew the story of Nosey's Le Roy pocket watch and of how he came to be in ownership of it. Every redcoat, no matter how low or exalted a character he might be, had a little token or trinket that he treasured. Maybe it was just a worthless brass ring or a shard of mirrored glass for shaving but it was something

115

to remind him of a loved one, or of his home place, or of a close encounter with danger. It didn't matter. These things were not to be touched.

As for McNeilis, his pocket watch meant more to him than anything else. It had once belonged to a French major of Chasseurs à Cheval who had led his squadron in a charge against a company of the 27th. McNeilis and The Fox were company drummers at the time, marching just to the rear of the second line, beating advance. The Chasseurs' major was unhorsed when the company volley-fired at forty yards and was knocked unconscious in the fall. The 27th then charged with the bayonet, stepping over the fallen bodies of men and horses and gave chase to the retreating Hussars. A few men dallied to dip a hand into the pockets of the dead and the dying in quick search of loot. As McNeilis stepped over the major, he spotted the gold chain attached to his uniform and 'liberated,' according to his own description, the Le Roy pocket watch at the end of it, as well as a bag of Louis d'Or coins. Since rum was McNeilis' first love, he drank the coins away. But, for some unclear reason, he became attached to the Le Roy, vowing never to part with it. He had treasured it ever since. Meanwhile, outside in the square, Reggie's drum was still urgently beating when Ward burst back into the room.

'Why are you two still here?' he blazed.

The corporal grabbed me by the collar and started to push me towards the door, shouting: 'Go! You'll be late for Reveille.'

'My watch has been stolen,' shouted the veteran drummer. 'We've a thief in our mess.'

The corporal paused, still holding me by the collar. I wriggled free as I felt Ward's grip loosen.

'Get on parade now, the two of you,' the corporal decided. 'Captain Baxter's already on inspection. Forget the watch until later. Move!' He ushered us out ahead of him. McNeilis went reluctantly.

After parade, we then had to drill with the company. McNeilis was at my shoulder, as we had arrived last, muttering dark threats the whole time. Within minutes, word about the missing watch had passed through the ranks and, before long, with the exception of the officers, everybody in the three companies knew. I could feel Nosey's anger going into his drumming. Even McGreel's berating him for his timing wasn't enough to keep his mind off his loss and I knew that in the end he would come unstuck. Although he was the longest serving drummer in the 27th, he started to beat the wrong cadence more than once before correcting himself. This brought us to the attention of Hicks who came striding over, working his jaw in anger. In my own mind, I was cursing the damned watch for I had, by now, mastered all of the various calls and was confident in my growing skill. Having put in so much extra time at practice, I did not want Hicks to revise his good opinion of me by thinking I was the one at fault. But the close presence of an angry Drum Major brought a greater concentration to McNeilis and we passed the rest of the session without any further mistake. At one stage, when all the drums were massed together, Reggie appeared beside me and asked me quickly where Ward was as he wasn't with the ranks. I barely had time to tell him that he had been in our mess when Nosey discovered his watch was missing. Reggie's expression changed at this but we had no more time for conversation as all the drummers paired off again and I paid no further heed to his question.

It was a tiring drill that morning so we were all relieved when it was over and Major de Villiers, who had arrived to observe the three companies manoeuvre together, finally dismissed us to our various morning chores. I checked the duty sheet and saw that I was rostered as orderly in the officers' mess in addition to my punishment duties. I was about to set off for the officers' block when Hicks called McNeilis and me over. He let us have it in no uncertain terms, telling us that if we drummed like that on the battlefield the battalion could be slaughtered and that, by God, he'd make an example of us if we ever played like that again. As we walked away, it was my turn to let fly at my co-drummer for getting me into trouble. He had calmed down by this stage but he didn't offer to apologise, claiming that it was he who had been wronged in the first place and therefore had justification for being distracted. I was in a right bad temper walking beside him.

As we went up the stairs in our block, we heard a loud commotion coming from way down the corridor. I fixed my forage cap tighter on my head and ran to see what was going on.

17

We burst into our mess and saw Ward standing beside Reggie's berth, a black boot in one hand and a piece of green, cotton cloth in the other. Reggie was shouting and struggling with Ward, trying to grab the boot from him.

'My watch,' roared McNeilis. 'You found it.' He lunged at Reggie. 'You took it, Cox, you bastard.'

Reggie threw up his arms to defend himself as McNeilis took a swing at him. I grabbed at Nosey to prevent the blow from landing but the old drummer was strong and carried me, still hanging on, with him. The three of us landed in a tangle on the floor. We wrestled together for a few moments with me taking a couple of kicks until McNeilis was suddenly lifted from the floor and flung to one side. Curley bellowed with rage as he forcefully pulled both Reggie and me upright simultaneously. He punched Reggie on the side of the head and then, in the same fluid movement, swung his closed fist back at me. My face stung as I staggered backwards, just as when he had hit me on the day I enlisted. The wall saved me from falling and I recovered my balance quickly. I was outraged at being hit for I had done nothing to deserve it. No longer a raw recruit, I squared up to the sergeant in a sudden burst of temper until Ward's big frame suddenly blocked me.

'Back down, Burns,' he warned. 'Don't let this get out of hand. This is Cox's doing, not yours.'

McNeilis shouted from the floor: 'Where's my watch? It was wrapped in that cloth.'

Without taking his eyes off me, Ward shook his head. 'There was no sign of the watch, Nosey, he must have done something with it.'

Reggie got to his feet rubbing his head. 'I didn't steal anything,' he said.

'Well, this piece of cloth was stuffed into the top of your boot and everyone knows that Corporal McNeilis kept his watch wrapped up in it so it must have been you. What did you do with it?'

'Nothing, because I didn't take it.'

'Corporal Ward,' said Curley, 'did you search all of the berths?'

'Yes, Sergeant, and this was in Drummer Cox's boot,' he replied, showing the cloth.

'I didn't take the watch,' Reggie shouted again, defiantly.

McNeilis made another lunge at him but this time Curley caught him in a half-strangle hold and restrained him. The old drummer tried to release himself but there was no hope of escaping that iron grip.

'Stand easy, man,' the sergeant said. 'Stop struggling or I'll lay you flat on the ground. It's only your stripes that are stopping me from hitting you so desist. We'll take this to the duty officer and let him sort it out. You come too, Burns, seeing you're part of it.' He gave me a menacing look. It was on the tip of my tongue to say that it had nothing to do with me but what was the point. If Curley wanted to involve me, he'd do it, but I really didn't want to be brought in front of an officer at that moment. Reggie gave me a worried look but I responded with a 'Yes, Sir' to Curley and followed them to the door.

A few minutes later, we were lined up in front of Captain Grant who had relieved Baxter by then. Ward first explained how he had stayed behind from early parade in order to carry out a full search of the barracks. While we were drilling, he had systematically gone through all the messes until he had come to ours, where he discovered the piece of green cotton stuffed into one of Reggie's spare boots. There was no sign of the watch among the rest of Reggie's belongings in spite of the most thorough search. Curley explained that he had been attracted to the scene by the rumpus and, on entering the mess, had seen three of us fighting on the floor and had put a stop to it. When Grant asked Reggie for his side of it, he denied knowing anything at all about the missing fob. Nor could he explain how Corporal Ward had found the cloth stuffed into his boot. And, no, he was not a thief.

'What about Cox's gambling debts, Sir?' asked Curley, standing beside him. 'The drummer owes money, Sir,' he added.

Reggie gave a slight gasp at this. Of course I already knew of Reggie's liking for cards and of his frequent habit of straying into the back room of Mother Hogan's alehouse late in the evening to join with a circle of other off-duty redcoats who indulged in a bit of wagering away from the depot. But, as his friend, I'd have known if he was in debt. However, given the Colonel's opinion of gambling as the work of the devil, no Skin would want any officer to know in case it got back to him. Curley must have been waiting for his chance to use this against Reggie. Grant immediately took the bait.

'I've heard rumours to that effect, Cox,' the captain said, 'but didn't enquire further as you are not in my company. Have you a liking for cards, by any chance?'

'Yes, Sir.'

'And do you owe anyone?'

'No, Sir.'

'He's lying, Sir,' said Curley. 'That's why he stole the watch.'

'No, Sir.' objected Reggie, but I knew he was shaken by Curley's accusation.

'Did you sell it?' enquired Grant.

'He couldn't have yet, Captain,' interrupted McNeilis, 'for it was there yesterday evening and we haven't been out of the depot since. He must have hidden it.'

'So where did you hide it, Cox?' Grant asked.

'Nowhere, Sir. I don't have it.'

Peeved at this lack of progress, Grant turned to me.

'What have you to add to this, Drummer Burns?'

'Nothing, Sir.'

'Does this matter involve you?'

'No, Sir.'

'Then why are you here?'

'If you please, Sir, I don't know, Sir.'

'Well then, Cox, your friend is of no assistance to you so we'll have to hold you in a cell while we conduct a wider search for McNeilis' watch. But your denials in the face of your obvious guilt do you no favour. Corporal Ward, be so kind as to conduct Drummer Cox to the gaol until we see to this matter further.'

There was no opportunity for me to communicate with Reggie while he was being escorted out. He was really agitated, so much so that I didn't even manage to make eye contact with him. They were hardly gone when I, too, was dismissed. Curley quickly followed me out, not wanting to miss the opportunity of gloating over Reggie's predicament.

'Cox is for it now, Burns,' he sneered. 'He stole that watch to pay a gambling debt. When the Colonel hears of this, he won't like it, and you'll get to flog another of your friends. Let's see if Cox enjoys it the same way Doherty did. He might even shoot himself too. Then you'd have him on your conscience as well. Sleeping easy these nights since you killed Doherty, are you?' I clenched my teeth and said nothing. I started to move away when he suddenly roared at me.

'Don't walk away from your superior officer when he's talking to you, soldier!'

I stopped, turned, and came to attention, keeping my eyes well averted from his. 'Sorry, Sir,' I said, managing to hold my voice steady. Curley waited, but seeing that I wasn't going to react to his provocation, he curtly dismissed me.

On account of all this delay, I was late starting my chores in the officers' quarters. Shanley thumped me when he saw me, and asked: 'Where the hell have you been, Drummer? Taking a nap? Attend to your duties.'

My first task was to assist with laying the table for

their lunch which would be, as always, a lengthy affair, as they frequently dallied over their ports and pipes. Setting the table was a laborious chore as every piece of cutlery had to be cleaned before use and then precisely placed. It was the same with the regimental silverware and glass. I much preferred outdoor tasks.

Some time later, when the officers came in, I noticed that Baxter had arranged to sit next to the Colonel so, while serving, I hovered near them as much as I could without making them suspicious of me. Although I strained to hear the nature of their conversation, I could only pick up brief snatches as I topped up their wine glasses. Baxter must have known everything about Reggie by then as I heard him say that he was expecting trouble in the drummers' mess over a gambling debt. He then added that Captain Grant had known all about it but hadn't bothered to report it so he was doing it, knowing the Colonel's attitude to gambling in the regiment. Ferguson bristled with anger at Baxter's insinuation. Disloyalty to one's commanding officer was unforgivable in an officer, no matter how senior his rank. Ferguson's narrow perspective wouldn't allow any officer to have discretion in a matter concerning the moral welfare of a soldier. All such situations were to be reported to him. By not doing so, Grant's career in the 27th was effectively over.

I moved on without showing any sign that I had heard anything. I shouldn't have been surprised that Baxter would blatantly lie about a brother officer but I was. The ease with which he delivered his twisted words made me realise just how unscrupulous a scoundrel Baxter really was.

Later, while serving dessert, I saw him reach into the fruit bowl and suddenly, the words of the old veteran, Jacob Mulhearn, about worthless officers getting a blue plum in the back, came into my mind. In a flash of inspiration, I determined that there was another way to exact revenge for Francie's death without waiting for such an opportunity on the battlefield. I was in the right place at the right time... and I had the means.

18

When I had finished my chores in the officers' quarters, I left the building and went in search of Captain Grant who hadn't been at lunch because he was still the duty officer. I found him deep in conversation with Ward on the steps outside our barracks, obviously discussing the matter of the missing watch. I went over to them, saluted and waited.

'Yes, Burns. What do you want?' asked Grant.

'Permission to speak, Sir?'

'Go ahead, Drummer,' he nodded.

'I would like a word with you in private, Captain. No disrespect meant, Corporal Ward.'

'I suppose you want to put in a good word for Cox,' Grant said. 'You and he are as thick as two thieves.' He didn't realise what he had said but Ward grinned widely at the indiscretion.

'No, Sir,' I said, staring straight ahead. 'I don't want to put in a good word for Reggie.'

'Oh,' he said, surprised. 'But you wish to speak to me?'

'Yes, Sir.'

'In private?'

'Yes, Sir.'

'So, I'll be off now, Captain,' said Ward, taking the hint. With a smart salute, he strode away.

'Well?' said Grant. 'Speak up, lad.' I took a deep breath and began to talk.

At first, Grant just looked skeptically at me but then, the more I said, the more interested he became. His jaw dropped once but when he closed his mouth again, a determined look fixed itself on his face. He still had that look when I finished speaking. He asked me if I would be prepared to swear to what I had told him. I said I would and, even further than that, I would be willing to repeat it in front of the Colonel himself if necessary. He then told me to go to our mess and to stay there until he sent for me. I thanked him for listening to me and saluted with parade-ground smartness. He hurried off, his sword banging against his leg, a man on a mission. There was no turning back for me at that stage. I had committed myself to a risky course of action which could ruin me.

About an hour later, Lieutenant Welter arrived in our mess and told me that Colonel Ferguson wanted to see me immediately in full dress uniform. I changed quickly as Welter waited at the door impatiently, urging me to hurry. When I was ready, he gave my appearance a quick inspection, straightened the plume on my shako, and declared me fit for presentation. As we crossed the square, he remarked: 'I don't know what you said to Captain Grant but whatever it was, it's caused one hell of a stink.'

We arrived at the officers' block and hurried down a corridor, our footsteps loud on the flagstone floor. Midway along the corridor, Welter told me to wait outside a pair of imposing, double doors. He knocked and entered. A few moments later, the doors opened and he beckoned me in.

The Colonel sat at a long table with Major de Villiers beside him. Baxter reclined on a chair to the side and, by his expression, was barely containing his anger. The venomous look he bestowed upon me pleased me no end and it was an effort not to show it. A quick glance round showed that, to my surprise, the rest of the regiment's officers were present, including Hicks and McGreel. Captain Grant was seated a little apart from the others and gave me a slight nod. Sitting near him were Curley and Ward. Everybody appeared stoney-faced but there was an air of anticipation in the room. The Colonel motioned us forward so we marched to the table and saluted together. My heart beat with trepidation.

'Drummer Burns, Sir, as you requested,' said Welter.

There was silence for a few seconds as Colonel Ferguson glowered at me. Inside, I was quaking at the folly of what I had precipitated and wished I had held my peace earlier. Major de Villiers spoke first.

'Drummer Burns, there's no need for you to be nervous. We just want to ask you a few questions about what you told Captain Grant a while ago. You are required to be truthful in all matters as this concerns the honour of the regiment. Is that clearly understood?'

'Yes, Sir.'

'This is not a formal court martial, Drummer, but Captain Baxter stands accused as a result of certain discoveries that were made following information you supplied to Captain Grant. Captain Baxter denies the accusations and states that you have brought false and malicious witness against him. The Colonel therefore wishes to hear what you have to say about the matter. Do you understand the seriousness of what we are about here?'

'Yes, Sir,' I replied, a slight quiver in my voice. I hadn't expected to be in front of all the officers. I picked a spot on the wall above the Colonel's head and fixed my gaze upon it.

'Fair enough, Drummer Burns. Tell us, then, what you told Captain Grant and how you came to be in possession of such knowledge.'

'Well, Sir,' I began, 'when I finished my chores in the officers' mess, I then went to empty the chamber pots in the...'

'You what?' spluttered the Colonel.

'The chamber pots, Sir. To empty them.' I was flustered at this early interruption and the words I had carefully prepared in my head disappeared.

'And why were you, a regimental drummer, performing such a base and menial task?' asked the Colonel.

'Because Sergeant Curley ordered me to, Sir.'

The Colonel switched his glare to Curley. I wished I could have seen the sergeant's face at that moment but I just kept staring ahead. 'Sergeant Curley, you ordered a regimental drummer to empty officers' piss pots? Is that correct?'

There was a moment's pause before Curley coughed. I heard him stand.

'Em, yes, Sir.'

'In God's name, why?'

'It was a punishment detail, Sir. Drummer Burns has been remarkably indolent in his duties as a soldier. I frequently have reason to reprimand him for tardiness and slackness. He has to learn that the 27th has high standards and that he must meet them, Sir.'

'I see! Have you discussed this with Captain Baxter?'

'Yes, Sir.'

'And what was his response?'

'He said I was to make life difficult for Drummer Burns, Sir.'

'How did he express that wish, Sergeant? What were his exact words?'

Without batting an eyelid, Curley replied. 'He said I was to fuck the little shit at every opportunity, Sir.'

The words were delivered deadpan, with no emotion at all in his voice but they caused great amusement among the officers. In their eyes, the common soldier was the lowest type of scoundrel engaged in every kind of felony, a man who would cut your throat for a glass of whiskey and who needed to be controlled with iron discipline and the lash, so Baxter's words would have been quite understandable to them, if not justifiable. However, the Colonel looked a little taken aback and the officers' laughter quickly faded away. There was a short pause while Ferguson digested this. I didn't move for fear I would be a distraction to him. He turned back to me.

'Drummer, for how long have you been emptying officers' chamber pots?'

'About two or three months, Sir,' I replied. 'I can't be sure exactly.'

The Colonel leaned over to Major de Villiers, raised his hand to his mouth, and conferred briefly with him. The Major nodded. Even today, I still wonder what they said to each other at that moment because it must have been about me. The Colonel turned to the row of officers to his right.

'Drum Major Hicks!' he said.

'Sir,' Hicks snapped to attention.

'Have you reason to be critical of Drummer Burns's progress and performance? Do you consider him to be given to tardiness and slackness in his duties?'

'No, Sir,' the Drum Major replied, 'the lad is a natural on the drum, quick and eager to learn.'

'I see,' said the Colonel, knitting his fingers on his chest. 'Thank you, Drum Major. You may continue, Drummer Burns.'

This digression had given me time to gather my thoughts again so I continued as I had earlier planned.

'Well, Sir, Captain Baxter's chamber pot is a Napoleon Bonaparte one. It has a bust of Napoleon upright at the base. The figure is hollow which means that if you turn the chamber pot upside down you can insert things inside it. I noticed that when I was emptying the pot, Sir. I was curious when I saw a piece of cloth protruding and, thinking it was but a misplaced rag, I removed it. A watch fell out. Also eleven gold coins and some precious stones that I took to be jewels, Sir, never having seen anything like that before. I thought I should inform Captain Grant about the watch, he being the duty officer, because I recognised it as belonging to Nosey, I mean, Corporal McNeilis, Sir.' A few officers laughed again but their amusement was instantly drowned out when Baxter jumped to his feet.

'You blasted liar, Burns,' he roared, sending his chair flying, 'you put the watch there, you little bastard. I'll get you for this. You're a fucking coward just like your father before you.'

The blood pounded in my head as he said that. There was an immediate stir among the officers, too, as both Dunne and Reihill jumped up to restrain Baxter but the Colonel's infuriated bark cut across the room. 'Captain Baxter, you are an officer of the Crown. You would do well to remember that. Your reputation may be in question but it is still possible for you to retain some element of the dignity that goes with wearing the uniform of the 27th Inniskillings. Your reference to a soldier of this regiment who died on the field of battle, a man who is thus unable to defend himself, is unbecoming.' I stared at Baxter, wondering what he had meant about my father. But Colonel Ferguson cut across my confused thoughts. 'Lieutenant Welter, be so good as to fetch Corporal McNeilis.'

As Welter hurried off on his new mission, Baxter reluctantly sat down again, a twisted smirk on his face. The man clearly meant to pay me back for what I was doing but I felt, rightly or wrongly, that there were officers in that room who knew more about my father than they were letting on. My heart thumped uncontrollably in my chest but I resolved to see my plan through. The rest could wait.

19

'May I examine the said Napoleon Bonaparte chamber pot?' asked the Colonel. 'Captain Dunne, if you please, and make sure it is in a presentable, decorous state.'

While they were waiting for the captain's return, Welter re-entered with McNeilis but Ferguson had them stand to one side. When Dunne reappeared, the Colonel took the proffered item delicately in his hands. The other officers could barely contain themselves at the sight of their colonel looking at the small figurine of Napoleon inside a chamber pot, then turning it upside down to feel inside the hollow figure for himself. A look of utter distaste crossed Ferguson's face as he handed the pisspot back to a sheepish Baxter. He then wiped his hands on a handkerchief that he took from his sleeve. Baxter returned to his chair, mortified at having to plant the china clay pot at his feet, leaving it there for all to see. Welter was nearly doubled over with mirth by then, his knuckles stuffed in his mouth. Maybe he was remembering how humiliated he had felt at the court martial and was enjoying that moment of sweet revenge immensely. Ferguson coughed loudly, and a sense of order returned to the proceedings.

'Major de Villiers, did you find the items where

Private Burns indicated?' the Colonel asked, when all was silent again.

'Yes, Sir,' replied de Villiers, 'within the hollow figure, exactly as the drummer claimed.'

Baxter tried to brazen it out. He stoutly maintained his innocence of the theft of the watch but, when asked repeatedly by the Colonel, refused to offer any explanation for the presence of the precious stones and the gold coins other than to say that they were lawfully his.

When Lieutenant Reihill asked permission to enquire if the money comprised of two- and five-guinea coins, the Colonel nodded in confirmation. Reihill then gave a detailed description of the imprints on his missing coins, the theft of which he had already reported to Captain Baxter, who said he would look into it. On examination by the Colonel, the coins conformed to the description given by the Lieutenant. When questioned again, all Baxter said was: 'I had no idea the coins were there. That's the truth.'

With that, the Colonel called McNeilis forward. On being shown the watch, he immediately identified it as his. Clearly delighted with its return, he was asked by the Colonel if, by any chance, he had given it to Captain Baxter. Nosey bristled at the question.

'Absolutely not, Sir,' he replied, turning to Baxter and shaking an angry fist in his direction.

'I didn't steal your damned watch,' Baxter shouted at him.

'You had plenty of opportunity, Captain,' McNeilis retorted. 'You were the inspecting officer yesterday morning while we were on parade. There was no one else there but you.'

'I told you I've no idea how it got there,' Baxter repeated obstinately, raging at the indignity to which he was being subjected by a base NCO, as he saw it. 'How dare you accuse me, you damned Patlander.'

'What about the coins, then, Captain?' asked the Colonel. 'Do you now admit to theft from your brother officer? Or are you suggesting that someone else put them there as well? You have made no secret of your impecunious, personal circumstances so your own indiscreet revelations prompt questions regarding your possession of purloined coins and jewels.'

Baxter's brows darkened at this but he said nothing in reply. He looked away from the Colonel as if he had suddenly become indifferent to the whole process. From that moment on, the outcome of the informal hearing was inevitable. Since there was no adequate explanation regarding his possession of the gold coins and precious stones, his protestations of ignorance regarding the watch went unheeded.

The Colonel conferred with de Villiers for a few minutes, then arrived at his decisions. Baxter was to be confined to his quarters until the completion of enquiries into the ownership of the jewels, after which a court martial would be convened should it be deemed necessary. Concerning the coins and the watch, the case against him was already conclusive. In the absence of any evidence to the contrary, he was deemed to have stolen them. McGreel then escorted the captain back to his quarters and a guard was placed outside. The look he gave me in passing was one of pure hatred but I knew from that moment he could do nothing to me. Even if he got off lightly at a court martial, and I didn't see how that could happen, he would be ostracised by the other officers as long as he remained with the 27th. When word of all this got to the men, the captain would be the laughing stock of the regiment. His inevitable conviction and transfer were only a matter of time, and my intervention had been the vital element in his downfall.

The Colonel then addressed me. 'Drummer Burns, you have behaved honourably in this regard. Your exposure of a common thief in our midst is to your credit. Who knows what further shame and disgrace he could have brought upon himself and on the regiment if you had not spoken up. As it is, Captain Baxter must now reflect upon his conduct and take this opportunity to reform himself. He should be grateful to you, as we are too. Drummer Cox is to be released immediately with no blemish on his character since he has been found innocent of the charge brought against him.' The Colonel paused for a moment before continuing. 'In hindsight, it is now a matter of regret to me that I did not take a more personal interest in Captain Baxter's handling of Private Doherty's situation. Perhaps a more compassionate response would have been the correct one. However, I can tell you that your chamber pot emptying days are over. Sergeant Curley, from now on, when you take issue with this particular drummer, you will bypass Captain Baxter and confer directly with Major de Villiers before you prescribe any punishment whatsoever. That is a direct order.'

'Yes, Sir,' said Curley, and I could feel the man's malice towards me grow.

'If you wish to keep your stripes, Sergeant,' continued the Colonel, 'you will attend to what I have just said and amend your approach to Drummer Burns. Discipline must be enforced in the regiment but it is not a tool for your own, or Captain Baxter's, particular proclivities. You personally will see to it that Drummer Cox is released immediately.'

Curley bristled at this admonishment but he remained expressionless. 'Yes, Sir,' he said, through gritted teeth. He saluted, turned on his heel, and left the room.

'Corporal Burns, you are dismissed.'

I stood frozen to the spot, stunned by the Colonel's words. Corporal? A mistake, it had to be. Hicks appeared in front of me, his big, muscular frame blocking out everything.

'Corporal Burns, you heard the Colonel. You are dismissed.' His mouth crinkled at the edges, with the beginnings of a smile, perhaps.

'Yes, Sir,' I said. Still in a state of shock, I only got as far as the door when my military bearing failed me. Turning around, I saw that Ferguson was deep in conversation with Grant and de Villiers.

'Thank you, Colonel,' I said, across the room, saluting.

'Out!' roared Hicks. I left hurriedly.

A clearly relieved Welter saw me to the exit. 'You certainly did manage to shake things up in there,' was all he said. I felt he wanted to say something to me about Francie but, as he was an officer and I wasn't, he couldn't openly express what was in his mind. He was only a couple of years older than me so I decided to say it for him, as the opportunity might not present itself again.

'Lieutenant Welter, maybe we both let Francie down, and his death is lying heavily on our consciences. But he knew that nothing could save him once he decided to abscond. Now, maybe with this turn of events, I'd say he's smiling again.'

'Thank you, Corporal,' he said, 'I appreciate your saying that.' And, for the first time since entering the depot, an officer actually saluted me. It would be more than a year before an officer saluted me again, under entirely different circumstances. I refrained from smiling until I was well clear of Welter. Then I punched the air with happiness. Imagine! Me, a corporal! I couldn't wait for my mother to hear. I ran back to our barracks and charged up the stairs.

Shortly afterwards, Reggie joined me in our mess, a free man once again, much to the delight of the other drummers. Nosey McNeilis, especially, was full of apologies for believing that Reggie had stolen his watch in the first place. We all cheered as he kissed his precious Le Roy pocket watch and lovingly folded the green cloth around it once more before replacing it in his old Flanders knapsack. As he did so, Reggie raised a quizzical eyebrow at me. He still had no idea what had transpired. I smiled back at him.

We shared a great quantity of beer that evening in celebration, especially as Major de Villiers came over to the mess with my corporal's stripes. McNeilis insisted on sewing them on for me. They all teased me with mock salutes for the rest of the evening, calling me 'Corporal Piss Pot' and the like but I enjoyed their good-natured banter. It wasn't until after dark that Reggie finally managed to break away from the others and corner me. We slunk into the dark washroom. He kept his voice very low.

'What did you do, James? They could have had me for the watch. I only took it for a joke. To hide it overnight. I never meant to keep it. And I don't owe anybody for cards.'

'I know that, Reggie,' I whispered back. 'You don't have to tell me. Look, I was awake too, when you took the watch. I saw you stuff the cloth in one boot and the watch in the other. Of all the stupid hiding places! I waited until you were asleep again and removed the watch thinking to turn the joke on you. But then I heard the sentry approach and, not knowing whether he would enter or not, I got back into bed quickly. After that, Crooks got up to piss and he was so long gone that I fell asleep. It was too late to replace it when we got up for early parade even though I dallied, hoping I'd be last out but Nosey missed the blooming thing before I could put it back so I shoved it under my forage cap. There was no opportunity at parade to tell you what I had done so I kept it there all day. I was convinced that I would be found out but they never thought to search us. As for Baxter, I found the gold coins and jewels when emptying his piss pot a few days ago. I did nothing about it because I thought they were really his. Then The Fox told us that Reihill had money stolen so when all this happened, I figured that as Baxter was a thief already, he might as well be found out for the watch too. I planted it there after lunch when the officers were having their port. Nobody spotted me. Baxter had it coming anyway for what he did to Francie and for what he said about my father. He's a right bastard.'

A visibly relieved Reggie shook his head in disbelief at what I told him. He laughed a bit at first, then turned serious.

'James, I never thought that McNeilis would kick up such a stink about that watch. If Ward had found it in my boot, it would have been the lash for me. Everyone would have believed I had stolen it to pay off a card debt. I'd never have survived the cat, no more than Francie could. You saved me, James. I owe you, and some day I'll repay you, that I promise.'

I shook my friend's hand. 'It was nothing,' I said.

'To you, maybe, but it's everything to me, Corporal,' he said, giving me a good-natured salute.

It was almost two weeks later that the matter of the jewels was resolved. A letter arrived for the Colonel confirming that they belonged to a Major Packenham of the 88th Regiment, the Connaught Rangers. They had disappeared from his personal baggage while on his way home from France the previous year on board the *Cyclops*. Baxter had been on the same homeward bound ship as the major and must have found an opportunity to steal them. He then made a nuisance of himself appealing for a transfer back to the 27th, his first regiment, until, finally, his ill-natured persistence, and the matter of a small bribe, paid off.

On being informed of all this, Baxter, as before, denied any accusation of theft but still obstinately refused any explanation as to how the jewels came to be in his possession other than to say they had been planted there. The resultant court martial was a swift affair. He was found guilty of scandalous and infamous conduct unbecoming an officer and a gentleman, in that he had stolen from his brother officers and from one Corporal Ignatius McNeilis. He was sentenced to be stripped of his rank and cashiered from the regiment. He was further barred from ever serving in any other regiment of the King's Army. The written verdict of criminality was to be read in every mess in the regiment as was a statement of Reggie's complete innocence in the matter of the watch. The gold coins were returned to Lieutenant Reihill and the jewels forwarded to Major Packenham.

After that, Curley became wary of how he spoke to me. But I knew that he was harbouring a festering grudge and would serve me ill if he could, so I was equally wary around him. As for Baxter, Reggie and I were accorded the pleasure of drumming the disgraced ex-captain through a gauntlet of booing and hissing Skins out of the depot and out of our lives.

My happiness would have been complete had I been able to find out more about my father. Baxter had accused him of being a coward, yet I fervently believed that was not the case. But how could I discover the truth when those who could enlighten me were not prepared to do so?

20

By the spring of 1814, the war with America rumbled on while, in the depot, the 27th was still building up numbers to replace men lost on active service and through sickness. At the beginning of May of that year, two significant things happened. First, just after Baxter's departure, we had the arrival of our new company commander, Captain Stuart Logue, a fiery Scotsman who had seen action with Wellington in India and the Peninsula. Secondly, startling news arrived that Napoleon had abdicated and had been exiled to the Island of Elba in the Mediterranean. At least, with the Emperor out of the way, McNeilis immediately observed, if we were sent to fight the Americans, we had an experienced man in charge of the company.

There was mixed reaction in the depot to Napoleon's departure. Some were delighted that after so many years of war, things could finally settle down and a period of peace and stability would bring greater prosperity. Others felt that they were being denied an opportunity to progress their careers in the army as the rate of attrition in time of peace would be much reduced. As for me, I began to entertain hopes that I might be with the next batch of replacements destined for Canada. The idea of finishing my service there, and of then putting my name down for an allotment of land to start a farm, was attractive to me. It wouldn't take me long, as I imagined it, to earn sufficient to pay for my mother's passage to join me so that I could take care of her properly. That was the plan I began to nurture but I still had five years of service ahead of me before I could realise my dream.

The rank and file soldier, regardless of which army he is in, has very simple needs: to eat his fill, to get drunk often, to have opportunities to loot, and to sport with free-spirited maidens. These needs might be met separately at times, but they seldom all coincided. The army, though, presents a different set of relentless, simultaneous demands in the form of drilling, marching, manoeuvring and musketry, with every facet of each dictated by the drum. The sole purpose of all this effort was to prepare the soldier to engage with the enemy wherever and whenever he presented himself, and to emerge the winner. Napoleon went a lot further, holding out the vision of glory to his men, as well as the promise of victory in battle, which he nearly always achieved. Apart from losing at the pyramids in Egypt early in his career and again, much later, in the campaign in Spain and Portugal, he was the total master of warfare, enjoying a remarkable series of victories over the armies of Europe. But the destruction of his *Grande Armée* in Russia, in 1812, marked a turning point for the Corsican, when the aura of French invincibility was seriously dented and his military reputation tarnished. When we subsequently heard that Napoleon was bound for Elba, the veterans among the companies wagered that he wouldn't last there for too long. 'The thin red line will be needed again, you'll see,' old Jacob Mulhearn remarked. 'Keep your muskets clean, boys. Bonaparte won't be finished until he's dead.' All the veterans remained steadfast in that opinion.

The three companies together began to drill, march and practise musketry as a larger unit, under the supervision of de Villiers, until everything we did was precision-perfect. Drumming in conjunction with the others became second nature to me. In this way, the months passed by and I became as proficient as Ned Kennedy and Drum Major Hicks could have hoped for. However, during that same period, Napoleon's restless spirit bestirred itself. Possessed of boundless energy, unbridled ambition and unshakeable self-belief, a small island could hardly provide him with the kind of attention he craved. No, Bonaparte could only be content on the world stage. It took but ten months for the veterans to be proved right.

At the end of March, 1815, when the news spread like wildfire throughout the country that Napoleon had escaped his tiny island realm and was already on his way to Paris, there was little surprise in the depot. Even though the Emperor sent out messages far and wide claiming that his people had requested his return and that he wished from then on to live in peace, nobody believed him. Being Napoleon, it was impossible for him not to extend the vista of *la Gloire!* once again, and his battle-hardened veterans flocked to rejoin including the Old Guard. Everyone knew it would only be a matter of time before the French were on the march again.

Anticipation grew in the depot with each passing day. Every dispatch rider, on entering or leaving, was quizzed by curious Skins for any hint of news that would indicate what the future held. As far as we could glean, something was stirring as there was an increase in orders to the local merchants for flour, salted pork and other provisions. Then, one morning, de Villiers commanded that every redcoat's equipment and kit should be inspected and that, where it was wanting or worn out, it should be replenished from the Quartermaster's stores. Word soon came that companies of the regiment being trained in other garrisons were to join us. At this, our excitement mounted. We would soon be at full strength for the first time since my enlistment.

In ideal circumstances, a battalion consisted of about one thousand men, organised in ten companies, each with about one hundred effectives, as men present and fit for action were called. When officers, NCOs and drummers were added, the total could be up to eleven hundred. More usually, a battalion consisted of around seven hundred and fifty effectives, and that was about the number our combined companies had in total on muster.

A week later, dispatches arrived from Army Headquarters in Dublin ordering the battalion to make its way to Cork forthwith and to proceed from there to the Low Countries to join the army being assembled by the Duke of Wellington. On the same day, the newspapers reported that the Imperial Guard had been given back its old eagle standards. That meant only one thing – war! In a flash, my dream of Canada evaporated and a more serious proposition faced us, dealing again with Napoleon's army.

The depot went wild with excitement and became a hive of activity. Our preparations to leave didn't take long as we had expected it for some time. We were told what to bring with us and, since there would be no accompanying baggage train, everything would have to be lugged on our backs. Our knapsacks could scarcely hold all that we were expected to carry. By the time we stuffed in a spare shirt, white waistcoat jacket, breeches, gaiters, undergarments, shaving kit and mirror, and a myriad of other small items that are needed to keep our equipment and weapons in good order, they were bursting at the seams. Along with our knapsacks, however, we also carried a linen bag on the hip that contained a wooden bowl, a pewter mug, a day's ration of bread and salted beef, hard tack biscuits and a lump of cheese, together with a knife, fork, spoon and a full canteen of water. The redcoat may be a trained soldier but, on the march, he is nothing but a lowly beast of burden.

For many soldiers, packing the knapsack was an easy task in comparison to the painful leave-taking of loved ones. Soldiers with families living outside the depot were given permission to spend a short while with them to say their farewells. As Reggie had nobody connected to him in Enniskillen, he came with me to see my mother. To my eternal disappointment, there was no sign of her at our cabin even though the fire had been lit earlier in the day and the embers were still glowing. I shouted for her in the fields and in the nearby wood but there was no response. Standing there, wishing for even one sight of her, I recalled her words to me when I told her I had a mind to enlist, about her not having it in her heart anymore to watch me go. I think she was being true to her word that day and maybe had decided to avoid me as news must have reached her of our imminent departure. I wanted so badly to show her my corporal's stripes, to tell her that I was doing well, and that, no matter where the regiment sent me, I would come back one day to take care of her and bring her to Canada. But I never got to say those things. I have never made my peace with that.

On the day of our departure, thus laden, we assembled in column formation and, with drums and fifes playing, and regimental colours flying unfurled in the breeze, we marched forth from the depot in Enniskillen on our way to face the Emperor of France himself, Napoleon Bonaparte. Distraught women and children, many in tears, ran alongside the column, calling out to fathers, brothers, husbands and lovers. Yes, there was an air of excitement among the troops but there was also heart-wrenching despair, for the unspoken thought in every mind was that many of the men would not come home. However, we were all resolute and put on our best display as we marched.

The Colonel didn't accompany us due to a recurring bout of illness but I thought he appeared quite downcast at our departure from the depot, leaving only a skeleton garrison behind. As Major de Villiers was awaiting a transfer to the 32nd Foot, Captain Dunne, as the next senior officer, was elevated to overall command of the battalion. Lieutenant Reihill was put in temporary charge of the 1st Company, Grant had the 2nd, and Logue remained in ours, the 3rd. Coming with us, of course, were all the other battalion officers and NCOs, most of whom we knew well.

A few women, overcome with grief at the separation,

clung on to their men and were half-dragged along with the column. This distressing scene continued as far as the bridge until the sergeants intervened and forcibly detached them, telling them they were only making a show of the regiment. Curley actually threw one young girl to the ground and threatened her with his hand if she came after us again. The small number of women who were allowed to accompany us faced an arduous and hazardous trek. Also heavily laden, they would find it difficult to keep up with the pace of the march and were not expected to rejoin their menfolk until after dark each evening, that is, if they managed to reach our campsite at all. They brought up the rear of the column.

A large crowd had gathered at the bridge to see us off and to wave a final farewell. Maybe it was wishful thinking on my part but I believe that I spotted my mother peering round the back of a hawker's cart. I couldn't wave to her as I was drumming. To this day, I couldn't swear it was her but, if it was, I hoped she was a little bit proud of me, wearing my dress uniform with my corporal's stripes on the shoulder, drumming the battalion in marching order with our colours flying.

All too soon, we crossed the bridge and left Enniskillen and its familiar noisy streets and peaceful lakeshore paths behind. What I didn't leave behind were my regrets about not getting to say a last goodbye to my mother. Those, I brought with me.

21

The trek from Enniskillen to Cork was the longest we had undertaken so far with each day bringing us further south across the midlands. We created quite a spectacle as we marched, our drums keeping the whole column on the move and the soldiers of the different companies trying to out-sing each other in order to pass the time. The drummers worked in pairs, laying down the pace of the march, normally Ordinary Time, seventy-five beats to the minute, mile by mile, sometimes on roads that were just about passable. A vanguard cleared the way for us because, with the column moving at pace, it was an unstoppable force. Maintaining a marching tempo was second nature to me by then and I felt we could have gone on forever. I had learned hundreds of tunes by heart and we kept up a lively beat as the men sang every marching song they knew. Then they'd start all over again.

Passing through towns and hamlets, most of the locals were entertained by our displays, especially the youngsters who tended to follow us imitating our march. But, in a few cases, our red coats must have stirred memories of the rebellion in 1798 as insults were occasionally aimed in our direction. These we mostly ignored, although, in one small town, stones were thrown at the column and we were sorely provoked. When Logue detached the last three ranks of our company and made ready to fire a volley, the culprits quickly scattered. We laughed as our muskets weren't even loaded but they weren't to know that.

At night, fatigued after the day's marching, we either sheltered within the walls of a welcoming garrison or, for the most part, bivouacked in a field. When we slept in the open, we made rough tents for ourselves along the hedgerows by lopping branches off trees as uprights and joining our waterproof sheets in fours to provide cover from the heavy dew. As for cooking, we used the large iron pots and kettles that we had brought along, ate in our groups and cleaned up before turning in. I have always felt comfortable with the rough-and-ready nature of hunkering down in the open to eat, where the conversation among the drummers would flow without regard for manners or convention. By contrast, the officers were billeted in local houses or inns that had been procured for them along the way by a mounted advance party under Lieutenant Welter. We didn't really think to envy the officers their crisp, clean sheets. We were just glad to be away from the constraints of depot life and the constant drilling and the shouting of the NCOs. Of course, the Regulatory Calls still marked the routine activities of the day, regardless of where we were, from our rising to sleeping. The army day didn't change much, even on the march.

Although we were an infantry battalion, we had a number of horses trotting along in the body of the column.

These were the spare mounts belonging to the officers in case of loss or lameness. Being on horseback, the officers had much more comfort than we had, only stopping to change animals at intervals so that each was exercised in turn. Unlike us, officers only walked when they wanted to stretch their legs.

Thankfully, Curley mostly kept clear of me, apart from sending me a few spiteful looks. Since Baxter's departure, he had also restrained himself in his dealings with the men, probably because of Ferguson's words to him. But, once we were free of the depot, he reverted to type and devised a new form of punishment to inflict on us – carrying stones. For a trivial breach of discipline, an unfortunate redcoat had to add a certain weight of stones to his knapsack. The more serious the perceived offence, the heavier the loading. I recall that on one day's march, more than half of our company was carrying an additional burden. During the day, Curley was perverse enough to carry out spot checks to see that his victims weren't shirking their punishment and, in the evening, to supervise the emptying of bags to make sure the stones had been carried the whole way. Shoulder straps bit deeper into soft flesh, making the carrying of the knapsack excruciatingly painful. I have never heard an NCO being as consistently cursed as Curley was. It was probably the Colonel's admonishment that protected me, that and my corporal's stripes, so he targeted Reggie instead. Curley never discovered that I shared Reggie's load as we were very careful not to be found out. To our disgust, Logue didn't seem bothered by this unusual treatment of the men so Curley persisted with his stone-carrying punishments for the whole length of the journey. To the rank-and-file soldier, though, it became another reason to complain, not that we were ever short.

Although we joked about going to war against the French, few of us had any real idea of what it was like to stand on a battlefield. Even the old campaigners had stopped their yarn-telling around the campfires. Their silence and the distant look in their eyes told us that deep memories had been stirred up. Back in the depot, they would wind us up with exaggerated descriptions of their deadly engagements with the enemy. Now, with conflict looming again, and us marching to meet it, they deflected the conversations towards harmless topics as if to protect us inexperienced recruits from the real horror of war. McNeilis was an exception. He laid it out for us.

'We're going to be in the thick of it, lads,' he'd say, any time there was a lull in the conversation, 'us and our drums. But the good thing is we'll be with our own. There's nothing worse than going into battle with unknown troops when you're not bound to them by any ties. You can't fight beside those you don't know.' We just laughed at him when he said things like that. I'd go quiet then, wondering if I had it within me to be brave when my turn came, and what I would do if the man beside me was smashed by a cannonball and I had to carry away the bits. Would it make any difference whether I knew him or not? I lay awake for a while each night that we were on the road, brooding on these matters, knowing that the time was coming when I would find out the answer to all these things.

Finally, a week after leaving Enniskillen, we arrived in

Cork itself. The 27th created quite a stir as we marched through the busy streets. Drum Major Hicks had taken up his place at the head of the column and was putting on a great show for the populace, bellowing his instructions to the Skins following close behind him as he directed the column around each corner in perfect formation, our drumming marking time. He would throw his long staff in the air and march on, catching it as it fell, without missing a step. 'Make way for the King's troops,' he'd bellow, when our steady advance didn't quite clear the road in time. But nobody stayed in our path long enough to risk being hit by the Drum Major as his heavy staff had a long reach. Some onlookers shouted their resentment as we passed but since, for the most part, it was good-humoured, we paid little heed to it. We were greatly fatigued by that stage and were glad to be near our journey's end.

I imagined Cork to be a bigger place than it was, but I remember Ward commenting on it as being 'exceptionally neat and well-presented' as we marched through the streets. We joked with him about that afterwards, asking him where he learned words like that and why couldn't he make himself look a bit more like Cork? I was sorry we weren't staying there for it had great alehouses, so McNeilis told us. He had been there before and knew the best places. But we didn't stop to sample them, much to our regret. On we went towards Middleton, where we were to remain until it was time for us to embark on our sea crossing.

A squadron of Dragoons came out to meet us and escorted us to our temporary home. We bantered affably with the troopers as they trotted alongside the column and before long we entered Middleton Barracks. At last we dropped our knapsacks and bedrolls and looked forward to taking our boots off after the fatigue of the long march south. It had taken its toll on our feet. Despite all the aches and blisters, not one man had fallen out of the line on the way and we were proud of that.

22

For the next few days, we had a chance to carry out running repairs to our equipment and our uniforms. The officers spent a lot of time at meetings while the NCOs drilled the whole battalion in formation with the local militias. They lacked the polish that we had but it gave us a taste of what it would be like to manoeuvre with other large formations. As if to underscore the seriousness of what was in store, much more attention was paid to our musketry skills until we were able to prime, load, present and fire at a rate of four times a minute. This applied to drummers as well for we were expected to shoot like any line soldier. It also got us used to the deafening sound that so many guns made when all fired together. Then we'd concentrate on bayonet practice until each man was as adept at handling his Brown Bess for stabbing as well as for shooting. Finally, we practised swinging the musket around to use as a club, with Curley constantly reminding us that the heavy, walnut butt was the ideal tool to make sure that a man stayed down. We joked about what we'd do to the enemy when we met him but, privately, we were becoming more anxious as the day was fast-approaching when our lives would depend on how skilled we were with our weapons. Then we'd lay the muskets aside and pick up our side drums again for that's what we'd be facing the enemy with. We laughed at the short swords we carried. What use would they be against a loaded gun or a bayonet?

Barely a week had passed when news came that our transport ships had arrived at East Ferry and we were ordered to move out. Logue and Curley inspected our company before we left the barracks. They were in a fierce temper as they worked their way through each man's uniform, weapons and knapsack, criticising this and finding fault with that but, since we were boarding ship, they weren't able to put anyone on punishment detail. This mood was widespread as we saw redcoats from other companies at the receiving end of their officers' tongues and fists. But we survived all that and, fully prepared, we once again packed our kit. Finally, nearly three weeks after leaving Enniskillen, we marched out in column and proceeded the last few miles to the dockside and the waiting transports. We arrived at East Ferry full of expectation and beheld our vessel.

The *Rascal* wasn't much to look at. It was an old merchantman from the East Indies fleet with its glory days, when it brought silks and spices to the home ports, long in the past. The ship was typical of the kind then used for transporting troops and provisions. But if the *Rascal* was past its prime, its master, Captain Richard Hawthorne, recently retired from the Royal Navy, had a solid reputation.

The first three of the battalion's companies went on board, all of us crammed in together on the middle deck, which had been separated into large compartments. We stowed our knapsacks between the rows of rough mattresses laid on the bare wood. The other companies of the 27th who had joined us on leaving Enniskillen boarded different ships. The middle deck was a gloomy space indeed except where the disused gun ports could be opened slightly to let in light and air. These would be closed when the East Indiaman sailed. The cannon had been removed of course but I could easily make out the marks on the floor where the gun-carriage wheels had scored deep gouges in the wood. The *Rascal* was also taking crates of provisions and casks of water on board for the coming campaign. All of these went into the lower holds where a couple of flickering lanterns dispelled the gloom.

The drummers rushed to claim the best spot near a gun port. With so many men berthed close together, it would not take long for the air to go stale so we were pleased with our patch. We dropped our knapsacks, stacked our drums and hurried back on deck. We were allowed to stay there to watch the ship in its final stage of preparation on condition that we did not get in the way of the harried crew. There was little of the orderliness and discipline that one would expect to see on a ship of the Royal Navy but, of course, these hired transports did not demand the same standards as a fighting Ship of the Line. It was hard to see how the *Rascal* could ever have been mistress of the oceans.

Most of the battalion had never been to sea but McNeilis and The Fox were among the small number of veterans who had been to the colonies. They told us of the tedium of weeks on end living in cramped conditions with sparse rations and impure drinking water. Even when you arrived at your destination, they said, there was the risk of catching a fatal, tropical disease or a debilitating fever not to mention being attacked by hostile natives. 'Comfort on a ship depends on two things,' Nosey said in that pompous, knowing way of his, 'wind and water; wind to blow us to our destination and water, not to sail on, but to drink. Thirst on a ship would drive a man mad.' With that, he jammed his clay pipe back into his mouth.

We watched from the rails as wagons arrived on the quayside. At first, when we saw such a quantity of provisions arrive for our ship, we thought we'd eat and drink our way through the whole passage. Then an old deckhand informed us that these were extra stores for the army and that we'd be lucky to be fed at all unless we had brought our own supply with us. This disheartened us greatly as we were mostly young men with big appetites that our old, iron pot bravely struggled to feed. The thought of there being little enough to fill our bellies while on board did nothing for our general spirits. We tortured ourselves by asking him about the contents of the casks being hoisted over our heads.

'Mostly wheat, flour, oatmeal and grotts,' the old salt said. This last was new to us but he told us that they were small cakes, or nibs, which he believed were much liked by the Russians. 'And they can keep them,' he added, with a snort, 'for they are seldom fresh, being mostly as hard as small round shot and don't taste much better.'

'Sounds like our army biscuit,' quipped The Fox.

We all cheered when told that the last casks swinging

over us contained beer that had just been brewed in the victualling yard. We looked at the sailor in disbelief but he assured us that it was true. He said that each seaman was rationed a gallon of beer a day, as it was safer to drink that than the water. This caused great resentment among the Skins as there was supposed to be a beer ration in the army too, apart from what we could buy in the canteen, but we only got it occasionally. No doubt our stock went to somebody but it certainly wasn't us. We watched where the casks went and prayed for a dark night as we knew that, with the particular set of skills in the company, a quantity of that beer would come our way. It was fortunate that it was not the summer since beer brewed at that time of year tended to go sour quickly and became undrinkable. It was probably like the brown swill I had sampled on my first night in the depot.

There was a delay in hoisting the officers' horses on board as sufficient stalls hadn't been prepared for them. The ship's carpenters got busy and for the next couple of hours the sound of sawing and hammering came from below decks. We relaxed on piles of untidily coiled ropes and spare canvas and passed the time easily, sipping newly brewed Cork beer that had already, by some strange mysterious means, found its way into our canteens. We toasted the other transports in our convoy when they slipped their cables one by one and set sail, leaving us behind. After a while, the *Rascal* was the only ship left in East Ferry and still the carpenters continued to work. We didn't mind. We didn't have to march anywhere. Finally the chief ship's carpenter emerged on deck and announced to Captain Hawthorne that all was finished. The crew busied themselves again and soon the horses were hoisted on board and lowered into the hold. Once settled in the stalls, they were hobbled for added security.

Last of all, twenty cattle were herded on to the ship, slipping and sliding up the gangway. These would provide fresh meat for the army. Cattle could walk without any loss of bulk and could be slaughtered as needed, unlike pigs whose meat had to be salted and casked. Sitting on the deck, watching so much food being stowed, it was no wonder that our thoughts kept turning to our stomachs. The beer served to quench our thirst and put us in good spirits but it did little for our hunger.

In conversation with a gnarled old deckhand, I wasn't surprised to learn that sailors are just as adept at grumbling as soldiers and mostly about the same things: rotten food, stale bread, incompetent officers, shortage of women, daft regulations and not getting enough sleep. It seemed to me then that a sailing ship and an army depot had much in common.

23

The *Rascal* set sail for Portsmouth five hours behind the rest of the convoy. Fourteen ships were ahead of us and yet, when we cleared Roches Point, they were long gone. As dusk fell, we watched the land disappear below the horizon with only the small sails of local fishing boats in our vicinity. Sammy Crooks wistfully voiced what the rest of us were thinking: 'Would we ever see our homeland again?' That silenced us for a while. The stiff breeze filled the sails over our heads, pushing the ship through the choppy water, taking us further away from Ireland.

Looking around, it was noticeable that many of the crew were older men, a common enough feature on ships that had been leased by the Transport Board. This was because the navy stopped all passing ships at will in search of suitable replacements for those lost to disease and sickness on long voyages, a frequent result of poor victuals and sheer hard, dangerous work. With the youngest and fittest creamed off by the press-gangs, merchantmen like the *Rascal* had to make do with a scratch crew of mostly older hands who were willing to stand on a heaving deck for another couple of years. There was no shortage of takers as most had no home other than the ship they served upon. They were experienced and competent sailors but the strength in their bodies was like an ebbing tide and while they might have a will to fight should the need arise, they were well past their prime. Still, the passage was going to be a short one.

The first night at sea was a novelty to us but there was no escaping the cramped sleeping area, the stinking air and the low ceiling where the tallest of us had to walk bent over like an old labourer beaten down by a lifetime of toil. But we managed to get some rest all the same, lulled by the movement of the ship and by the creaking sounds of its timbers. A few redcoats nearby decided to try out the hammocks that had been slung for us. Reggie opted to sleep in one as well. Most of us made do with the smelly, straw-filled mattresses on the floor. There was liberal use of the slop buckets as some of the lads were seasick. With the smell of vomit mixed with the other stenches that filled the compartment, it was all I could do to hold my few meagre mouthfuls down. But despite the unpleasantness of our quarters, we all settled eventually after a fashion and the night passed peacefully enough.

The next morning was bright and clear with a boisterous wind urging the ship along and we enjoyed a light breakfast. We became somewhat accustomed to our living conditions and had adapted to the heaving movement of the ship. The air had become tolerable as the old gun ports were partly opened again allowing a gentle wind to waft in, along with chinks of bright light. All in all, it was not as unpleasant as I had expected it would be. Our orders were to remain below deck so we amused ourselves with conversation and cards as if we were at home in our mess. I noticed that a few had engaged in reading books they had brought along. One soldier who was absorbed in his Bible told us that we were all sinners and that the Wrath of God was going to come down upon us with fire and destruction. He kept saying it until a blasphemous redcoat told him that God had better hurry up if He was going to do it, otherwise Napoleon's wrath would be upon us first. The soldier stayed quiet after that. Word was passed along that the men would be allowed on deck in sections of twenty for exercise so we waited impatiently to be called. It was mid-morning when Curley came down and ordered our group on deck.

It was a relief to be in the open again with the stiff breeze tugging at our clothes and the salt air strange in our nostrils. Reggie and I spoke to one of the crew for a couple of minutes. He told us that we had progressed beyond the Lizard Point in Cornwall and were making good time beating up the channel. When we told him we were drummers, he pointed out the capstan to us towards the bow of the *Rascal*. This was the spool-shaped apparatus used to winch the ship's anchor cable up or down. He told us that the top, by coincidence, was called a drumhead because that is what it resembled. As we made our way along the deck to take a closer look at it, there was a loud call from high in the rigging.

'Sail, ho! On the starboard bow.'

There was an instant reaction from the poop, the raised deck where the First Mate, a man named Knowles, stood near the ship's wheel.

'Keep a close eye on its direction,' ordered Knowles. 'Summon the Captain.' There was an immediate buzz of excitement among the crew around us as the First Mate hurried over to the ratlines. He climbed up a few rungs and extended his telescope. Deckhands paused to scan the horizon until the petty officers bellowed at them to get back to work. Out of curiosity, we hurried over to the starboard rail and looked but could see nothing. Captain Hawthorne appeared on the deck adjusting his cocked hat. Although we were just out of sight of the English coast, we might as well have been in the middle of the ocean as there was no sign of land in any direction. It was a strange experience. We kept well out of the way, not wanting to be sent below. We stared at the horizon until we saw it, a tiny speck of white in the distance, still a long way off.

'Well, Knowles,' shouted Hawthorne into the ratlines. 'Can you make him out yet?'

'Two masts, Cap'n,' replied the First Mate. 'A brig, by the looks of it.'

He clambered down and joined Captain Hawthorne. We sidled closer to overhear.

'Definitely converging with us, Captain, but still too far away to know who it is.'

I was wondering why the sight of another sail should cause such animation. Surely it wouldn't be unusual to meet another vessel in such busy waters as these.

Then Knowles said, 'Might be a privateer, Sir.'

'Bloody French corsair, that's what I think too,' agreed Hawthorne, 'and, God help us, look at what we've got.'

With a frustrated expression, the captain glanced around the untidy deck. I imagined what he was thinking. The *Rascal* might have been a formidable vessel in its day, well capable of defending itself but now, reduced to the lowly role of transport, it lacked the threatening appearance of a man-of-war. Furthermore, without its guns, it could not be expected to put up much of a fight. Should it be attacked, all it had by way of armament was four carronades, the short, stubby 32-pounders that were devastating at close range but useless at a distance. These were placed on the foredeck, two on each side. With no escorting vessel and lacking the protection of the convoy, our lone transport made a tempting prize.

'As good as pirates, they are,' muttered an old tar, sidling over to us. 'Damned privateers!'

'What's a privateer?' I asked.

'A bloody corsair with a licence to plunder,' he replied. 'A brig coming from the French side can mean only one thing. We're in for it, and no mistake. Privateers have good vessels. Reminds me of that time I was on the *Emerald* when we took a Spanish brig off Cadiz in 1805.'

'That's cod's talk, Billy,' one of his companions quipped, 'you were in the heads having a slash when that happened, I heard.'

There was some raucous laughter until a petty officer roared at them. They shuffled away quickly.

With everyone on the deck now preoccupied with the unknown vessel, more redcoats lined the rails, a scattering of our officers among them. They were as curious as we were. Our position on the deck was perfect for viewing as Hawthorne and Knowles had again swung part way up the ratlines, their long scopes trained on the brig. It wasn't too long before the speck of sail became more visible. The mystery ship seemed to be heading in the same general direction as we were but, as the sails gradually became more defined, even we, who knew nothing about boats, could see it was on a course to intercept us. As for Captain Hawthorne, he had seen enough. He dropped back to the deck with Knowles and they conferred together. Both looked worried.

'A privateer for certain,' Hawthorne said. 'He can outrun us no matter what we try. And as soon as he closes with us, he'll see that he outguns us too.'

'True, Sir,' said Knowles. 'He's carrying eighteen guns too, judging by its length. We're no match for him, ship to ship. That Frenchman could stand off and pound us until we are forced to strike our colours or we sink.'

'Yes, Mr Knowles,' Hawthorne said, a wistful tone in his voice. 'We don't have much of a fighting option, do we?'

On overhearing this, an idea that had been festering in my mind then crystallised. There was no way that I could ignore it so I approached our senior officers and saluted. They didn't notice me at first. Then Logue spotted me. 'What the devil do you want, Burns?' he snapped.

'Sir, Captain Hawthorne thinks he has too few guns to fight the Frenchman,' I began.

'And you know better than Captain Hawthorne, Corporal? Is that it?'

His sarcasm didn't encourage me but, as I had started, I couldn't just walk away.

'We have more than enough firepower, Sir, under the right circumstances.' I paused, suddenly regretting my audacity.

'Corporal, you forget your place,' rapped Logue impatiently but Captain Dunne cut across him.

'Just a minute, Logue. Go on, Corporal. I know you have an idea. Spit it out, man.'

Thus emboldened, that's exactly what I did. When I had finished, Dunne stared at me for a moment, then said: 'Wait here, Drummer.' Abruptly, he spun around and joined Hawthorne and Knowles and spoke urgently. Whatever way Dunne had communicated my idea, the ship's master seemed happy with it.

Things happened quickly then. The battalion officers gathered and another brief conversation took place after which the NCOs were summoned and rapid orders were issued to them. Curley stomped over to us with a belligerent attitude.

'Seems like you've given them an idea, Burns, you cocky little upstart. Just remember the Colonel isn't around to protect you here, Logue doesn't give a curse about you, and I still have that extra stripe. So go fetch your drum. You too, Cox, and get yourselves to the Captain's deck. Leave off your tunics. Fatigues only. Don't want you resembling real soldiers, do we?' And he headed off after the other NCOs.

When we went below, the middle deck was in a state of frantic activity as our lads prepared for action. Boxes of cartridges were opened and the men were detailed to take sixty apiece, the amount issued when going into battle. While most were excited at the prospect of action, a few were praying. Reggie and I were soon back on deck in our fatigues, the bright paintwork on our drums now hidden under their ticken covers. Captain Dunne, divested of his officer's tunic, beckoned us over to the poop.

As we joined him, files of Skins appeared from below

deck in their shirts and breeches only, clutching their muskets and cartridge pouches. Bayonets were slung in their belt scabbards. NCOs had them lie on the deck close in under the rails where the approaching brig wouldn't see them. As they settled down, a small group of white-shirted sharpshooters climbed the ratlines to what was called the tops, the platforms on the masts that would give them a steady base for accurate firing.

In the meantime, the ship's officers had taken off their uniforms and changed into casual, seafaring clothing. Captain Hawthorne briefly assembled the ship's deck crew and issued unusual instructions. They were puzzled first but, when he gave a brief explanation, they hurried off to comply. A few moments later, the *Rascal* started to pitch and roll in the water as some of the main sails emptied of wind. The ship presented the appearance of being a sloppy transport vessel commanded by an inept captain in the hands of an inexperienced crew.

One of the junior midshipmen appeared on deck with a folded ensign in his arms. He hurried to the stern of the *Rascal* and hauled in the Navy Jack. Soon a different ensign fluttered from the stern in the stiff breeze. A silence descended upon the ship apart from the creaking of the wood and the flap of the wind. Reggie and I stood on the poop deck near Hawthorne and Dunne, our drums concealed at our feet, our hearts hammering, wishing we were back in Enniskillen.

24

The unidentified brig kept coming closer until it was within range of using its cannon but it stood off for a while, suspicious of us. Suddenly, as if it could read our minds, an ensign burst free at its stern – The Tricolor.

'I knew it,' said Hawthorne, his scope still fixed on the approaching ship. 'It's the *Annalise*, an eighteen gun brig taken two years ago on the way home from Malta, as nimble a ship as ever was built for swift sailing. They must have liked the name as they didn't bother to change it.'

Across the stretch of sea, there was a flash of reflected light from the brig's deck. Its master was doing the same as Hawthorne, weighing up the *Rascal* before getting too close. I wondered if my ruse would work. I glanced along to our stern where the ensign of the Kingdom of Holland, with its horizontal bars of red, white and blue, now flew in the wind. Luckily, Captain Hawthorne still had one in his possession. It certainly came in useful as the *Annalise* held fire while submitting us to intense scrutiny. But was she curious enough about us to fall into our trap? Just at that moment, the ports on the *Annalise* opened and the guns were run out. I imagined the frantic movements of the gun crews on board the privateer as they loaded their pieces. Even one broadside at that range would do us considerable damage; a couple would finish us. The tension around me mounted.

'He's having a good look at us,' Captain Hawthorne remarked, meaning the French ship's master. 'He knows we're a transport and therefore more valuable as a prize than sunk. But if he suspects we're carrying troops, he'll keep his distance and reduce us with his guns.'

The wait became nerve-wracking as the privateer continued to hold off, wary of coming any closer, maintaining a course that was almost parallel with ours. The *Annalise* slackened sail to keep station with our ponderous progress. Whatever qualms Hawthorne had earlier about our capacity to defend the *Rascal*, he now appeared totally unperturbed by the proximity of the privateer. Movement below the main hatch on the deck attracted my attention. Flashes of red uniforms became visible as more Skins gathered there. Captain Dunne slouched over to us, a shabby coat now covering his white shirt.

'Well, Burns,' he said, 'we'll soon see if there's any merit in your plan. On my signal, you two will drum The Attack. This is your first time under fire so keep your wits about you. Your drums will start off the action, unless they fire first, of course,' he added wryly.

'Yes, Sir,' Reggie said.

Dunne then went to the main hatch and leaned down. I couldn't hear what he said but there was a low muttering response to his words. Someone wished him luck as he straightened up. Dunne touched his forehead in acknowledgement. He deliberately sauntered back over to the poop where Hawthorne had been making a conspicuous show of ignoring the privateer while in reality he was keeping a covert eye on it. All of a sudden, the *Rascal*'s captain shouted something indecipherable and descended the few steps to the main deck. His voice was loud enough to carry across to the privateer as he berated a bunch of deckhands for their ineptitude. They hauled on the heavy ropes and the ship's sails filled again. The ship took a heave forward as it caught the full power of the wind. This charade was enough to entice the Frenchman closer.

A sudden shot came from one of the brig's guns and a cannonball skimmed across our bow. Immediately Hawthorne ordered the sails to be reduced again and, in a few moments, the heavy vessel had slowed considerably. The *Annalise* rapidly closed the gap. Speaking through a loud-hailer, the privateer's master asked us in halting English to identify ourselves. On hearing Captain Hawthorne's reply that the *Rascal* was an unarmed transport heading for The Hague with a cargo of cotton goods and gin, we were ordered to give way and allow him to come alongside. The *Annalise* changed tack and swiftly closed, a sleek greyhound to our lumbering beast.

'Lower all sails or I will open fire,' the French master said, his voice carrying across the narrowing gap. 'We are going to board you.'

The sails of the *Rascal* rapidly emptied in compliance, flapping idly in the breeze. Through its open gun ports, we could see the crews hunched around their guns, looking up at our higher, imposing side the closer they got. Towards the stern near the helmsman stood the brig's master surrounded by his officers, all of them focused on us. The privateer's deck swarmed with armed men, weapons glinting in the sun as they prepared to board. A number of them scrambled up the brigs's ratlines carrying muskets and took up positions high in the rigging. Even though there was little enough chance of being hit at that range, especially with the heaving of the ships, I kept moving around, just in case. With their muskets aimed downwards onto our deck, they might not spot our sharpshooters much higher up on our masts, concealed by sails. The Skins were good marksmen, no doubt, but that was on the range. How true would their aim be in this situation?

Grappling hooks snaked up onto our deck, landing with a series of loud clumps. The ropes were pulled taut, binding the two ships together with a jolt. A few Skins lying at the rails were nearly impaled but they wriggled free of the lines without injury. A loud, exultant roar arose from the deck of the *Annalise* when suddenly Dunne shouted.

'Now, drummers, now!'

We dropped to our knees, ripped the covers off our drums, and commenced beating The Attack. A hundred Skins suddenly stood, leaned over the rails and volley-fired down onto the deck of the privateer, taking the would-be boarders totally by surprise. The crack of our muskets was drowned by the thunderous roar of the brig's cannon as they fired at point-blank range into the *Rascal*'s wooden sides. The ship pitched as if someone had punched it hard in the ribs but the ropes held fast and we remained attached to the *Annalise*. There was no way of telling how much damage had been done but the fear of being sunk galvanised the 27th into frantic action. Our sharpshooters opened fire upon the privateer's rear deck where its captain was one of the first seen to fall. At the same time, redcoats poured from the main hatch to join the fight. They sprang over to the rails and added to the weight of fire being directed onto the privateer.

Suddenly, our two starboard carronades belched flame and a cluster of Frenchmen fell when our well-aimed canister-shot tore them apart. The din was so loud we could barely hear the sound of our own drumming as we stomped up and down on the deck. At that stage, Astwith and Welter had organised the redcoats into two companies to volley-fire in relays while Reihill organised the third company into a boarding party. More of the enemy fell screaming as the relentless fire began to tell on their numbers, making any attempt by them to board us impossible.

Another broadside lifted the *Rascal* but it wasn't as severe a jolt as the first one. For some reason, only a few of their cannon had fired the second time but we needed to board quickly. They all had to be silenced. A gap opened at the rails and Reihill was away with his men, dropping on knotted ropes to the deck of the privateer below. They were among the enemy before they knew what was happening, cutting and slashing their way through the crowded deck. Shanley, following close behind, led his platoon down the stairwell to the gun deck underneath where the desperate struggle continued in the confined space.

A few foolhardy Frenchmen tried to climb unnoticed on to the *Rascal* but Knowles frantically cut the lines before any of them reached our rails. They fell into the narrow gap between the heaving vessels and were crushed. One French officer, a giant of a man armed with an axe, tried to rally his countrymen between the brig's masts but one of our sharpshooters took him down with a musket ball in the mouth. Two redcoat bayonets ran forward and finished him off as he lay writhing in agony. Yet more of our lads clambered down to the brig where they joined in the vicious hand-to-hand fighting around the mast.

All this time, the supporting musket-fire from the rails of the *Rascal* continued unabated, the redcoats switching their murderous aim to the rear of the brig in order to avoid hitting their comrades. Under Reihill's command, the Skins on the *Annalise* formed into a makeshift line, volley-fired at close range, then charged with the bayonet, stepping on the bodies strewn in their way. A few privateers fired their pistols into the advancing red wall, then reversed them to use as clubs but neither club nor sword was a match for the bayonet. The Skins fought not only the way they had been trained but also like the tough scrappers they were. The French casualties mounted steadily as they were pushed the whole way back along their own deck until the surviving officer, his face bloodied from a scalp wound, signalled his intent to surrender by holding his sword to one side. Slowly, the two sides disengaged as the fighting came to a gradual stop. The French officer shouted to his men to lay down their arms. Some did so reluctantly but a few prods of the bayonet put a stop to any thought of prolonging the resistance.

As quickly as it had begun, the fight was over. The redcoats on the bloody deck of the *Annalise* gave a loud, victorious hurrah and were immediately joined by the rest of us on the *Rascal*. That was my first action with the French and I had come through unscathed.

25

As I looked down, the deck of the *Annalise* was like a vision of Hell. Men lay at odd angles, the wounded with limbs hacked and faces slashed, the dead with the shocked, frozen expression of those abruptly plucked from life and thrust into the next world in one violent instant.

The surrender of the privateer marked the end of the redcoats' task; that of the drummers was about to continue as we took up our other duties. While our surgeon, Mostyn, busied himself on the deck tending to Skins who had received superficial wounds, we took to ferrying the more seriously wounded down to the *Rascal*'s sick bay where the ship's surgeon, a barrel of a man named Andrew Felton, awaited them. It wasn't long before we had a queue for his attention lying outside. The surgeon pointed to a redcoat with a shattered leg and told us to carry him inside. I didn't recognise the injured soldier at first but when we laid him on the soiled table in that cramped, airless bay, with the swinging lantern overhead, I saw that it was Patrick Magee, a man who had lost his sergeant's stripes for drunkenness and brawling, and one of the best marksmen in the company. Felton cut away the man's trousers, took one look at the leg and made an instant decision.

'It has to come off, soldier,' he said. 'I can't save it.'

A desperate expression crossed Magee's face at this verdict. 'No!' he whispered, 'not my leg.'

'If I don't take it,' stated Felton, 'you'll die.' He turned to the side table where his instruments lay. Handing me a bottle, he said, 'Get this into him. It's rum, for the pain.' I raised Magee's head a little and poured as much of the raw spirit down his throat as he could swallow. He coughed as it burned inside him, then reached out for more. A moment later, Felton stuck a short piece of wood into his mouth.

'Bite on that,' the surgeon instructed. He then called for three more drummers. Gallagher, Crooks and Reggie joined me at the table. We knew what we had to do. Magee's hair was matted to his skull with sweat as he gripped my hand like a vice. On first sight of the crooked knife in Felton's hand, Magee turned away and moaned pitiably, his teeth clamped on the wood.

'Hold him down well, drummers. He'll kick like blazes at the first cut but I must take that leg above the knee in one go.' Felton's words were chilling but he was right. It took all our strength to restrain Magee. His eyes bored into mine and he panted heavily as Felton's knife bit deep into his thigh, cutting deftly through muscle and tissue as far as the bone. The surgeon's hands were bloodied beyond his wrists but he knew his trade well. Magee's screams through clenched jaws were loud enough to be heard on the deck of the *Rascal* but Felton never hesitated. When he had cut in a circle as far as the bone, he switched to the saw. At that point, I had to turn away. I thought Magee was going to wrench my hand off with the fierce grip he had on me. The surgeon sawed away, the blade gnawing through solid bone. Magee fought us all the time, writhing and squirming, his eyes bulging in his skull as he frantically sucked in air. Suddenly, the sawing noise stopped and the surgeon lifted the amputated limb away from the bloody stump. It was a clean cut.

'Done,' he grunted, throwing the remains of Magee's leg in a bucket. But Felton never got to cauterise the wound as Magee seemed to slump inside himself and his grip on my hand relaxed. His eyes glazed over, as if he were staring at something far away in the distance. His last few breaths rattled in his throat and he expired there and then, right in front of us.

We stood in disbelief at the macabre scene, staring at the dead man in shock, never having seen the like before. Felton had the appearance of a crazed butcher as he stood there holding the grizzled saw, his apron soiled and stained, his arms and shirtsleeves bloodied to the elbow and an exhausted look on his face. I shivered, although I was anything but cold. It was truly a nightmare vision around that table, with our wild expressions visible in the light of the swaying lantern.

'He's gone, poor fellow,' Felton announced in a flat voice. 'Take him away, boys.' And he wiped the table in preparation for the next wounded man in line. The strip of wood was so tightly wedged in Magee's jaws that we weren't even able to remove it. Reggie covered Magee's face with a ragged linen cloth to hide his contorted features and to give him some trace of dignity in death. The queue of injured moved aside to let us pass, their eyes wide with terror at the prospect of what the surgeon might do to them. The sound of Magee's screams must have unnerved them but none seemed to be severely hurt so we tried to offer some level of reassurance.

When Felton and Mostyn had eventually finished with our own wounded, they offered to see to the French. The most seriously hurt was the privateer captain. Hawthorne had him hoisted on to the *Rascal* where he regained consciousness on the deck. He tried to say something but we couldn't understand him, his voice being barely above a whisper. He moaned with pain as we carried him down the narrow stairway to the surgeons. As soon as Felton cut away the Frenchman's coat and shirt, we saw a mass of blood and exposed bone where his chest had been shattered in two places by musket balls. Felton's blood-spattered features looked demonic in the dim light as he worked on the Frenchman but the wounds were fatal. The brig's master died on that table with the surgeon's hands inside his chest cavity feeling for the balls that had done the damage. I watched him draw his last breath and then helped to carry his body back on deck where it was placed alongside that of Patrick Magee.

When we returned to the sick bay, Felton said that our services were no longer needed as the rest of the brig's wounded were being kept on the *Annalise*. He thanked us and then we were dismissed. Relieved to be back on deck again, we sucked deeply on the fresh, sea breeze that blew the horrible stench of blood and gore from our nostrils. While we were occupied below with the wounded, the remaining, uninjured privateers had been taken on board the *Rascal* and secured in a hold. First Mate Knowles was appointed commander of the *Annalise*, given a scratch crew and orders to sail immediately for Portsmouth. Felton transferred to the brig to care for the enemy wounded on the short passage, leaving Mostyn with us. We Skins lined the rails, cheering loudly as the brig departed, no longer raw recruits but soldiers who had been blooded. And it felt good.

As it turned out, Magee was our only fatality that day. Considering the viciousness of the fight, we had escaped remarkably lightly. Dunne had the companies assemble on deck as Captain Hawthorne read a short passage from the Bible over Private Patrick Magee and the privateer captain. Then we drummed as they were slipped over the side, a sad end for two brave men.

The frantic activity of repairing the damage to the *Rascal* continued for hours after the *Annalise* left us. Fortunately, the French only managed the two broadsides, neither of which hurt us below the waterline. The two ships had been so close that when the first one had been fired, shards of splintered wood had flown back through the brig's gun ports causing fearsome injuries to some of their own gunners, hence, the second was much reduced. Shanley and his men overpowered them before they could fire a third. Yes, we had been lucky. The relative calmness of the sea played in our favour as well. Had it been rougher, the *Rascal* could have taken on water and our situation would have been considerably worse. The ship's carpenters had worked wonders plugging the holes and by late evening we also were under way again with a strengthening wind taking us in the wake of the *Annalise* that had disappeared from view. As the *Rascal* was short of hands due to the loss of those transferred to the brig, some of our lads helped with the ropes under the close supervision of the petty officers.

We were all elated, both crew and redcoats, cheering and singing well into the night. When Captain Hawthorne, accompanied by our own officers, came down to the middle deck to thank me personally for my 'inspired idea', he handed me a bottle of the best Jamaican rum. Dunne and Grant clapped me on the back and even Logue condescended to congratulate me. But the sight of Curley's resentful glare reminded me that I had given the sergeant yet another reason to hate me. The redcoat army is a brutal place for a lowly private but, since I now had two stripes of my own, I kept telling myself that there was little he could do to harm me. So I opened the bottle and poured the tawny liquid into the waiting cups of my mates. To hell with Curley, I thought as I sipped my rum. I could handle him. We slept the sleep of the exhausted that night.

The next morning, the *Rascal* arrived in Portsmouth with the tide. We cheered as we passed the *Annalise* and followed a pilot boat to our appointed place at the quayside. Knowles and the prize crew waved back at us. This put us in good form as we disembarked. The three companies then formed column. We marched off led by a mounted officer from the nearby Gosport Barracks to join the rest of our battalion which had arrived the day before with the convoy. We sang the whole way there.

At Gosport, great news awaited us. The 1st Battalion

of the Inniskillings was already there. The men had been away since 1793, when they left for the Flanders campaign, my father among them. Since then, they had been stationed for prolonged periods in Malta, Egypt, Sicily and then Spain, where they had fought as part of Wellington's army. They had arrived in Gosport from New Orleans where they had been involved in the recent fighting with the Americans. Unfortunately, they also had endured a mishap on their sea passage, encountering a severe storm after setting sail from Jamaica, which resulted in them becoming separated from the ships carrying all of the regiment's senior staff officers. As they still hadn't arrived, Captain John Hare was their acting Commanding Officer. Being senior to Dunne, Grant and Logue, he assumed command of our companies as well.

We all mingled together that evening, sharing beer and conversation in equal measure, we listening to their exotic tales of the places they'd seen while they were eager to hear the news from home and of our encounter with the privateer. Some of them had been away so long that, with the passing years, they had lost all touch with their friends and relatives. I asked a couple of the older men about my father but they evaded my questions so I learned nothing from them. Instead, they clammed up when I told them who I was. Hicks overheard me pestering them and told me to stop making a nuisance of myself. I couldn't hide my frustration at that but the Drum Major then told me to let sleeping dogs lie, that there'd be another time to talk. I passed a restless night.

The next day, the troops who had travelled on the *Rascal* were merged with those who had returned from

America so that a new battalion formed. After that, Captain Hare addressed us all, reminding us that regardless of our experience, whether we were new to the battlefield or seasoned warriors, we were all Inniskillings, and should remember that we are as strong as the image on our regimental badge, Enniskillen Castle. Nothing would move us, he said. We would be rock-steady no matter where in the line we were placed, and would stand by each other, man to man, no matter what came against us, or would fall together. Prophetic words, indeed, as it turned out.

During our short stay in Gosport the quartermasters ensured that we had all of our equipment and necessaries in our knapsacks and, with frequent inspections by the officers, we were as well prepared as we could be. A week later, rested and refreshed, the 27th Inniskillings left for Portsmouth again at the same time as the 23rd Regiment of Foot, the Royal Welsh Fusiliers, who had been in Gosport Barracks with us. They too were embarking for the Low Countries.

When we arrived back at the quayside, the familiar sight of the *Rascal* riding at anchor in the harbour cheered us. There was no sign of the *Annalise* this time, though. Our company was again one of three allocated to the old East Indiaman. As soon as we set foot on deck, all signs of the recent action with the privateer had been removed and the ship was spotless. The deckhands welcomed the 27th on board like old friends, telling us that our passage this time would be another short sea hop to Ostend, adding that, as the *Rascal* was to sail in the company of other transport ships with an escort of frigates, it would be a foolhardy corsair that would attack us. Captain Hawthorne came over and dallied with the drummers for a few minutes, telling us that it was a pleasure to have old comrades on board again but this time he hoped for an uneventful trip so that I wouldn't have to come up with any more bright ideas. A short while later, the Captain left us and we went below to stow our gear in the same place as on the earlier crossing. As we settled in, it was obvious that the mood had changed among the redcoats. We were much more sombre.

26

The *Rascal* sailed with the tide, taking up its lumbering place in the convoy. Further out in the channel, a frigate cut through the water with all sails catching the wind. What a glorious sight it made while we bragged anew to anyone who would listen about our exploits the previous week. The veterans among us more than matched our single exploit with stories of the many engagements they had experienced.

It was a contented ship that settled down that night. When the lanterns were finally extinguished, soft footfalls on the deck above told us that the night watch had taken over. I slept soundly on my mattress until I was awakened again by the ship's bell ringing, followed immediately by a distant voice calling the time and announcing that we were off Ostend. It was almost pitch dark in the compartment. Sitting up, I pushed the porthole open a trifle. A rush of balmy air wafted through the crack as I saw the twinkling of many lights. More feet rustled on the deck above as sailors ran to slacken sail and the *Rascal* started to wallow. Then came the rattle of the capstan as the anchor was dropped. In the hammock above my mattress, Reggie woke also. I heard him groan. Mixing beer and rum always leads to a sore head.

'Go back to sleep, Reggie,' I whispered. 'All's well. We're off Ostend already. We'll be going ashore when dawn comes.'

I tried to fall back to sleep with the comforting movement of the sea beneath me but for some reason my mind was perturbed and sleep evaded me. Being thirsty, I thought that a drink of water would settle me and so padded over to the barrel. Barely had the cup touched my lips when I thought someone whispered my name. A chink of light flickered through the open door. I heard my name again. Not thinking straight, I crossed the compartment floor, carefully avoiding the sleeping men on the mattresses and the rows of gently swaying hammocks. As I drew near the door, I stopped.

'Who is it?' I whispered. The gap opened slightly wider and I discerned a figure in a red uniform holding a lantern that barely threw off any light. Slowly, he motioned me forward with a crooked finger, and the light disappeared. My curiosity thus sparked, I tiptoed to the door and went through. The figure with the lantern had already crossed that compartment also, avoiding the sleeping men there and again motioned me forward in the gloomy light. I followed. He led me down to the centre hold, crammed with sacks and crates. I knew we were then almost directly amidships for the main mast dropped from the ceiling above, occupying the centre of the hold, and disappeared down through the floor. The flickering lantern lay on the floor beyond the mast, near an open stairwell that gave access to the lower deck.

Drawn to the light, I walked between the crates, past

the mast and went over to the opening. Thinking that the soldier, whoever he was, had gone down to the hold, I bent to pick up the lantern. Suddenly, I was grabbed from behind. A rough hand clamped over my mouth and another pulled me upright. I struggled for a moment until I felt something sharp stick into my back and a voice I instantly recognised hissed in my ear.

'Stand easy now, like a good lad,' Curley whispered, 'and I'll let you go. We must have a little talk, you and I. To get things straight, like. If you shout out, you'll feel the rest of this,' and the point prodded through my shirt to my lower back. I felt the warm trickle of my own blood going down my body, making me shiver.

'I'm going to let go,' Curley hissed, releasing me. 'Turn around now, slowly. One wrong move and you're dead.'

I did as he asked. The sergeant stood before me with a bayonet in his hand and a mad look on his stubbly, scarred face. It was obvious from his crazed demeanour that he was full of rum. His eyes were wild and bulging as he pressed the sharp point hard against my stomach, forcing me back against the mast. Only the strong weave of my tunic saved me from injury.

'It's time we sorted a few things out, now that it's just you and me,' he muttered, his voice so low I could barely hear him. 'It was down to you that Captain Baxter got discharged, you and your damned interfering. I don't know how you managed to plant McNeilis' watch on Captain Baxter but he has sworn to get you for it. He paid me handsomely before he left to fix you, if I got the chance, but you're having a charmed life with your corporal's stripes and the Colonel's protection. And now you've become quite the hero again with Hawthorne. Even Captain Hare has been told what a great little soldier you are. Well, now, Burns, I'm giving you a chance to save your life by owning up to planting McNeilis' watch and the rest of the stuff on Captain Baxter. If you don't, some day soon you'll feel this bayonet going through you. I know my way around the chaos of a battlefield. I'll appear out of the smoke in front of you and do the job I've been paid to do, and you won't see me coming until it's too late.'

While he was muttering all this, he kept me pressed back against the mast so I couldn't move. I was in a sweat at first but, when I saw what he was at, I let him talk in the hope that he'd drop his guard.

'You feel this bayonet, don't you?' he rasped, sticking it through my coat.

'Yes,' I croaked.

'Well, it was Baxter's. He gave it to me and said I was to use it on you. And, dammit, if I don't have the chance now. So, maybe I'll just finish you here instead of on the battlefield.'

Curley leaned his weight back slightly as he said that, and I made my move. Wily old soldier that he was, though, he had eased back on purpose, intending for me to try something. As I moved, he went with me, tipping me over. We fell to the ground in a tangle of arms and legs, him on top of me. He smashed my head on the wooden floor, stunning me momentarily. Then he pushed his snarling face into mine and in the shadowy flicker of the lantern, I saw him raise Baxter's triangular-bladed bayonet high over his head, twenty inches of killing steel, poised to strike downwards into my heart.

'But why wait, Burns?' he hissed, 'I'll do for you now,' and he stabbed downwards.

As Curley moved, a hand suddenly appeared out of the gloom and grabbed his wrist. Another hand bashed into the side of his head, snapping it sideways. He grunted in surprise but held onto the bayonet. The fist hammered into Curley's head again. Seizing my chance, I rolled free of him and lay there for a few seconds in a daze, wondering who had saved me. I looked up. Even though my saviour was standing over Curley with his back to me, I recognised Reggie's shape as he raised his leg to stomp down on my attacker's face. But the sergeant dropped the bayonet and, with his two hands grabbed Reggie's foot and pushed hard, throwing him back against the mast with a hard thud, dazing him. Curley was on him in a flash; his big hands went around the drummer's throat and he began to squeeze. Reggie's eyes bulged as he flailed wildly in Curley's strong arms, fighting for air.

My head cleared and I sprang to my feet, grabbing Baxter's bayonet as I did so. I gripped the socket end with my two hands and, with all my strength, rammed the long blade into the middle of Curley's back as far as I could. I felt it snag momentarily against his backbone, then it went right through. Curley gurgled as his lungs were punctured. He released Reggie and grabbed at the mast for support. One hand then went down to his chest and it came away covered in blood. Reggie sagged to the floor, breathing noisily but he had the good sense to wriggle away from Curley who still had his back to me. I had buried the bayonet in as far as it would go; only the socket was visible protruding from his red tunic. In the ghostly light of the lantern, the sergeant made a pathetic sight as he held on to the mast for support, his head lolling in surprise at this sudden turn of events. He slumped to his knees making horrible, sucking noises as his life ebbed away. I took a step back without taking my eyes off Curley as Reggie regained his feet, rubbing his neck where the marks of the sergeant's hands could be clearly seen.

'Is he finished, James?' croaked Reggie.

'Not yet,' I whispered.

Curley's breathing was then but a rasp as, with great effort, he succeeded in pulling himself up using the mast as a prop, leaving a bloody trail of hand marks on the wood. He slowly turned towards us, his face contorted with pain as the air wheezed into his lungs only to immediately hiss out again through the holes. He looked down at the point of the bayonet sticking a clear six inches out from his chest. Blood dripped from his mouth as his last few breaths gurgled in his throat. He was dying on his feet. Curley looked at me. 'I didn't think you had the balls for it, Drummer Boy,' he gurgled. His face contorted with a mixture of shock and pain as he tottered back unsteadily, one hand gripping the bayonet that skewered him while the other flailed uselessly, seeking support to keep himself upright. I closed right up to him and looked straight into his eyes.

'You're never coming out of the smoke at me, you bastard. This is for Francie.' And I pushed him. Without uttering a sound, Curley fell back through the open stairwell, banging his head on the edge as he went through. I heard the loud snap as his neck broke. He tumbled down along the wooden steps to the deck floor below. There was a heavy thud and then silence.

Breathing heavily, I leaned over the opening and saw the darkened huddle that was Curley lying at the foot of the stairs. He wasn't moving. In the gloom, I could see that his head was at an impossible angle to his body. There was no question about it. Sergeant Nathan Curley of the 27th Regiment of Foot, the Inniskillings, was dead.

'Now he's finished, Reggie,' I whispered.

27

As I stared at the crumpled heap in the near darkness below, the energy suddenly drained from my body and I almost collapsed. I reached out for the sturdiness of the mast. It was tacky to my touch. Curley's blood! I jerked my hand away as if I had been bitten but then sensed a reassuring presence at my side.

'Thanks, Reggie,' I gasped, turning. 'You saved me that time. We'll have to tell Captain Logue about this.'

'What? Don't be mad, James,' Reggie heatedly objected. 'Listen to me, Curley's dead and there's only us here. Nobody else needs to know. He meant to kill you, in case you don't remember.'

'Yes, but when they find his body, there'll be all sorts of questions. They're bound to find me out.'

'No, they won't, unless you tell them. Then what? You, a corporal, have killed a sergeant, your superior officer. No matter what the reason or justification, you'll hang. Nobody will listen to me because they'll say I'm just sticking up for you. And I could hang too, for what I did. Look at the justice Francie got. Why should things be any different for you?'

In spite of what I knew I should do, there was sense in

what Reggie said. His hangover seemed to have disappeared as he was thinking more clearly than I was.

'We have to get out of here,' he hissed. 'We can't afford to be seen. Leave the lantern.'

I stepped over to the hold again for a last look down, maybe just to make sure he wasn't going to come after me, in spite of the evidence of my eyes a few moments before. Curley still lay where he had landed, a dark stain visibly spreading around his crumpled body. There was no question about it. He would never move again.

Silently, we crept back to our compartment without disturbing anyone and were soon in bed once more to my great relief. Reggie must have guessed that I was still having doubts about what I should do as he leaned over in his hammock and whispered down to me.

'James, as long as we keep our mouths shut, nobody will ever find out anything. There's nothing to tie us to Curley's death. So don't go thinking you should do the honourable thing just because you're a corporal. There's no honour on the scaffold. And I don't want to swing beside you.'

Reggie was right, of course. I saw that, and accepted that no good purpose would be served by my owning up to Curley's killing.

'Tomorrow's going to be interesting,' I whispered back. 'What'll they do with the body, I wonder.'

'Dump him over the side, most likely,' Reggie hissed. 'Too bloody good for him.'

He was snoring again within a few minutes, obviously not bothered by any qualms of guilt about what had happened. But then, he hadn't killed Curley, I had.

Sleep evaded me for a long time until I eventually drifted off, exhausted. But that last look down into the hold kept coming back to me. I woke up screaming because Curley had fixed his head back on the right way and was climbing the steps with a nightmarish grin on his bloody face and the bayonet still sticking out of his chest and him saying he was coming to get me. Reggie shook me and I came to my senses. The other drummers were all staring at me in the gloomy light. And finally, I understood the kind of demons that make soldiers wake up at night. I muttered an apology for disturbing them and they lay back down.

'You okay?' Reggie whispered.

'Yes, I'm fine,' I said. 'Just a nightmare. I'll get over it.' My clothes were drenched in sweat and I lay shivering in the cool air.

'Did I say anything?' I hissed to Reggie.

'No,' he replied, understanding what I was asking, 'go back to sleep.'

However, there was little enough time for sleep after that. It seemed like only minutes before Ward roused us and told to beat Reveille on the deck but, before we could fetch our drums, Welter countermanded the order and we were told to stay put instead.

'This is it,' whispered Reggie. 'They've found him. Just act normally.'

We made empty conversation with the others as we tried to stay calm, waiting to see what would happen next. My heart was thumping in my chest with the suspense. Supposing we had been seen and hadn't noticed? I kept looking at the door expecting at any moment to see

Captain Logue arrive with an armed guard to arrest me for murder. We occupied ourselves with checking our equipment and drums. And still we waited.

Then, suddenly, there was a babble of sound in the next compartment. Everyone in ours wondered what was going on until Ward burst in with the news that Curley's body had been found on the lower deck with a broken neck and a bayonet through him and that an investigation was to take place. He said that assistant surgeon Mostyn was examining the body in the sick bay and that the battalion officers were awaiting the outcome. Then he added under his breath, 'I don't know why they're bothering. Curley's no loss to the regiment.' And he left us in a hurry in case he would miss any further developments. The others were all stunned, of course, and we, too, feigned surprise, but it didn't take long for the muttering to turn to Curley's ill-treatment of the company. By their reaction, none of the redcoats regretted his death. McNeilis went so far as to say that Curley had it coming and wished well to whoever had done the deed. He glanced at me as he said that but I stared back at him, betraying nothing in my expression.

Some time later, Captain Logue entered and we sprang to attention. He came directly to the point, asking us if we had seen or heard anything unusual during the night, or if we had seen anyone arguing with Sergeant Curley the previous evening. We all said that we knew nothing, not having seen the sergeant since our last period on deck. Crooks was bold enough to ask if it could have been an accident. Logue sarcastically replied that it would have been impossible for Curley to have hit himself twice on the side of his own head, stab himself in the back, and then break his neck in a fall down a stairwell, all without assistance of some kind. 'No,' Logue stated, 'this was murder, pure and simple. Curley was strong so it would have taken more than one to put him down, and we're going to find the guilty parties.' He went on to say that they were checking every man on board to see who was missing a bayonet or who had been in a fight. Beside me, Reggie twitched, adjusting his right sleeve so that the cuff would hide his hand. Logue scanned the room, asking us if we knew of anyone who had it in for Curley. To distract him from Reggie, I said: 'Permission to speak, Sir?'

None of the others moved as Logue stepped right in front of me.

'You again,' he said. 'What have you to say, Corporal Burns?'

'All of us, Sir.'

'What?' he asked.

'You asked if we knew of anyone who had it in for the sergeant and I said all of us, Sir. All of us in the company who he made carry stones to Cork, that is. And for the insults and thumps and kicks and endless punishment drilling back in the depot. But that doesn't mean it was one of us, Sir.'

Logue stepped right in to me, almost nose to nose. His eyes narrowed.

'Very smart, Burns. Yes, Sergeant Curley told me all about you and how you lied to Colonel Ferguson about Captain Baxter to get your stripes. You think you've become a big man in the regiment because of the action with the privateer but, to me, you're just a drummer.

You're not untouchable, you know, Corporal, so don't toy with me. I can have your stripes.'

I felt Reggie's boot press against mine and I knew he was warning me not to go too far. I didn't need another enemy.

'Yes, Sir.'

'Have you anything else to say?'

'No, Sir.'

'Hold out your hands.'

'Sir?'

'Hold out your hands. Palms down.'

I held them out. Logue bent over to examine my knuckles, my mind racing as he did so. If he thought to check Reggie next and saw the injuries to his knuckles, we'd be undone. I was just about to say something else to keep his attention on me when there was a thudding of boots at the door and Captain Dunne entered. I remained with my hands outstretched as I hadn't been ordered to lower them.

'What's going on here, Captain Logue? What's keeping you? We need the rest of your company on deck now.'

'I was just checking the drummer's hands,' Logue replied, straightening up 'to see if he had bruised knuckles.'

'Oh, for God's sake man, they're drummers. They don't have bayonets. It couldn't have been one of them that did for Curley. Corporal Burns, do the drummers need their hands checked?'

'No, Sir,' I replied, emphatically.

'Logue, check the rank and file for a missing bayonet.

See to it, man. You're holding up the whole disembarkation, wasting time with the drummers.'

We saluted as Dunne left.

'Bayonets,' bawled Logue, turning to the rest of the redcoats in the compartment. He walked up and down between the rows of men as each showed a full scabbard. Then, angrily, he stomped towards the door, pausing only to order us to assemble on deck with all our equipment immediately. He kicked at a mattress in a temper on the way out. Reggie nudged me as we picked up our knapsacks. 'You pushed your luck there, James,' he whispered. 'He didn't like that.'

'You just keep your cuffs down over your hands, at least until we're off this ship,' I hissed. 'And to think,' I added, with a grin, 'this was supposed to be an uneventful trip.' We both laughed. It was good to relieve the tension.

When we got on deck, we saw we were still anchored outside the port as the *Rascal* was too big a ship to cross the sandbar that lay at its mouth. Only vessels of shallow draught could enter safely. Soon, all three companies crowded the deck, lining up as if on early parade. A barge pulled alongside and we drummed a colonel on board. The officers saluted as the 27th presented arms. Hawthorne ushered the colonel and the battalion officers into his quarters. We waited stoically on deck, with the NCOs striding up and down between the ranks, until the officers finally reappeared and the colonel prepared to take his leave. We drummed him off the ship again.

Captain Hare climbed to the poop deck to address us. He told us that the investigation into Sergeant Curley's death would have to be deferred as we had been ordered to disembark immediately and to join Wellington's Army with all haste. The 27th was soon going to be in the thick of it again because that was where we belonged. In the meantime, if any soldier had suspicions or knowledge as to the circumstances of the sergeant's death, that man was to approach his company commander and, if warranted, an appropriate reward would be arranged. I was mightily heartened at this unexpected development.

As Hare finished speaking, a small fleet of barges arrived alongside to take us ashore. But Reggie and I had one last, unexpected, task to perform before leaving the *Rascal*. Logue called us over to him. For a split second, I thought we had somehow been found out but instead he ordered us to accompany him to the stern of the ship with our drums. We had no idea what was going on until we saw Captain Hawthorne, Bible in hand, and the stained, cotton shroud on a plank beside the rail, and we knew why we were there. Hawthorne read a few verses for the soul of the deceased sergeant. Then, irony of ironies, Reggie and I drummed as Captain Logue tipped Curley's weighted-down corpse over the side of the *Rascal* and into the sea. I felt nothing but relief as the corpse disappeared under the surface of the grey, choppy water. Like Baxter, he was gone from our lives. We then hurried to rejoin the other drummers and wait our turn to climb down into a barge to be rowed ashore.

Various, outlandish rumours went back and forth among the groups of redcoats regarding what had really happened with Curley. As for me, I was heartily glad that the order to join up with Wellington's Army had come when it did. The longer the investigation was deferred, the better for me, and I secretly hoped that the whole affair would be passed over eventually. I was almost certain that no suspicion could fall upon me and, therefore, the quicker we were ashore and away from the *Rascal*, the more at ease I would be.

I carried not a shred of guilt for what I had done, believing that it was Curley's unwarranted attack on me that was the cause of his own death. Needless to say, I was extremely grateful when we finally stepped ashore in Ostend and left Curley's corpse to rest where it lay.

28

We saw nothing of Ostend itself other than the road that ran right through it. Even when the town lay behind us, we still marched on until at last we were directed into a field for the night. After the events of the two sea passages on the *Rascal*, I was more than ready to resume a daily routine on land again. I was still shaken by the affair with Curley, half-expecting to be arrested yet, as I lay under my cover, I didn't feel the slightest bit remorseful over what I had done. The man had intended to kill me and without Reggie's intervention he'd have succeeded and it would have been my corpse at the bottom of the sea instead of his. So I pushed Curley's death from my mind and fell asleep.

On the following morning, a staff officer rode up with orders for the 27th to proceed with all haste to Ghent. We formed up in company columns and before we had even drummed the battalion out of the field, the customary grumbling had begun in the ranks at the prospect of another long march bearing full knapsacks. But the redcoats' moaning was cut short when we learned, to our surprise, that we were to proceed by barge. Unbeknown to us, a canal linked Ostend with Ghent by way of Bruges, a picturesque little town with canals for streets, quite unlike any place that I had ever heard of. So, for the next few days, we travelled in style along the waterway towed by draught horses, calling out to all the fine ladies we passed, and spending the evenings at pleasant bivouacs. Some of the barges contained our food supplies so, each night, after a restful day on the canal, we bedded down with full bellies thinking that a soldier's life wasn't so bad after all.

We were assigned a new sergeant in Curley's place, one Josiah Bennett, newly promoted from the ranks. He had been with the regiment in Spain and had recently returned from America. He was reputed to be a different sort entirely to Curley. Indeed, events bore this out for, in his dealings with our company, he turned out to be devoid of ill mood or temper. It didn't take long for us to be impressed with him. All too soon, though, our easy life on the canal came to an end and we arrived in Ghent.

Captain Hare ordered that the whole battalion drill as a large single unit so that we would become accustomed to manoeuvring together. Hicks kept a much closer eye on how the drummers performed but we had become so adept that he could find little fault with any of us. With the growing awareness that the time for confrontation was drawing closer, there was room for nothing else in our lives except our preparations so we practised until our hands ached.

Having bade farewell to their families and loved ones weeks before, the troops were fairly well adjusted to being far away from them. However for the small number of women permitted to accompany the battalion, this marked the beginning of a period of particular worry. I began to imagine my mother all those years before helping my father prepare to leave camp with his company, and then the long-drawn out wait she had for his safe return, until the day she could no longer endure such agony, and came home to give birth me. I observed in these women small signs of growing anxiety as they busied themselves with every kind of activity to pass the time until their men came back. Strange as it may seem, I began to understand why it was better for a soldier to be detached in every way when preparing for battle rather than to have to worry about a loved one who could fall into the clutches of the enemy if things went wrong.

Then word arrived in our camp that we were to be part of Sir John Lambert's 10th Brigade along with the 4th, 40th and 81st Regiments, all experienced troops. In total, when we joined with the others, the Brigade numbered about two thousand bayonets. Every campfire was alive with gossip at the end of each day's drilling and musketry practice. As if proof were needed that we were pulling out soon, we were allowed a short visit into the town of Ghent under the watchful eye of the Provost Marshall and his deputies, who were there to ensure that nothing untoward should take place between the soldiers and the townsfolk. With things coming to a head, we were determined to enjoy our last bit of freedom.

On the day we visited, the streets were full of people going about their business, apparently untroubled about the news of Napoleon's approach. We saw many wealthy individuals who were on the Grand Tour of the great cities, totally unconcerned about the coming battle. It seemed as if the sight of so many soldiers was a happy reassurance to them rather than a grim warning of the inevitable conflict.

Redcoats were everywhere but as we had hardly any money to spend and, with a battle pending, there was little point in attempting to purchase anything other than foodstuffs and wine. As we passed a dingy, nondescript shopfront, McNeilis drew me inside and purchased a quantity of lint and a roll of rough, bandage material. He advised me to do the same, saying: 'You'll never know when you'll need it, Burns, maybe even for yourself.' But I kept my few coins in my pocket, little knowing I would have reason later to regret not doing as he suggested.

When we came out, a group of civilian men on horseback trotted by with new pairs of field-glasses around their necks, shouting that they were now better equipped to observe the coming battle than Wellington himself. They tried to persuade an open landau full of ladies to accompany them to Charleroi, saying they would purchase a champagne picnic for the outing. We were amazed that the upcoming battle could be reduced to a spectator sport for the wealthy. The gentlemen persisted until a bunch of wild, drunken Hussars came upon the scene, pushed the men's horses aside, and propositioned the ladies with outrageous gestures. One of the revellers unwisely objected, at which the ringleader of the Hussars drew his sabre with an unsteady hand, threatened to expose the hothead's manhood, if he could find it given the state he was in, and then remove it in front of the ladies. The rest of the Hussars circled the men's horses, brushing against them menacingly. At this, the instigator's friends quickly apologised to the Hussars on his behalf, exited the circle at the first chance, and led him away for his own safety. This exchange, typical of the excessive behaviour of Hussars, greatly amused us. The scene must have encouraged a few among our party to try their luck with the next group of ladies we passed but, as far as I could see, it was only one drummer from the 40th who had success there. Or so he bragged later.

It was while we were in the town that news of crucial developments arrived because the provosts suddenly began to announce that all soldiers and officers had to return to their battalions immediately. These calls were of such urgency that disquiet began to spread among the civilian population. Then a rumour that Napoleon's heavy cavalry, the Cuirassiers, were almost in Brussels triggered an immediate panic. As we hurried through the crowded streets back to our camp, the talk among the populace of Ghent was of impending defeat and the streets rapidly emptied as people hurried home to gather their belongings. Not long afterwards, the roads leading towards the sea ports began to clog with the carriages and wagons of those seeking a safe haven from the French. But there was to be no such haven for us.

The 27th quickly reassembled and broke camp, stowing everything that could not be carried onto the supply wagons. Knapsacks were more carefully packed than usual as anything protruding would stick into the body during a forced march, causing blistering and bruising. The overcast skies promised rain so we placed leather covers over our shakos, knapsacks and drums before heading off. Marching in the wet was always an unpleasant business; a forced march, fully-laden, in rotten weather was even worse, and that is what we were prepared for.

With everything finally ready, we sat and watched the staff officers gallop hither and tither passing on orders to the various battalions encamped in the wide, open fields all around us. Since it was usual for drummers to remain close to the senior officers, we generally managed to overhear news brought by the staff riders and, in turn, were then able to tattle it on to the ranks. Most of it was of little consequence to the 27th until a Hussar major, one of Wellington's aides-de-camp, galloped up with a note for Sir John Lambert confirming that Napoleon had taken command of the *Armée du Nord* and had already left Paris at his head.

'Which direction has he taken?' asked Lambert.

'Why, north, of course,' the Hussar major replied, saluting. 'To Brussels!' The cavalryman wheeled his horse round and galloped away.

'Then that's where we're going, gentlemen,' Lambert announced, reading the note again. 'Wellington is assembling the army at a place called Waterloo, a little south of Brussels, so we must get there with all speed. The brigade will leave within the hour.'

Lambert gave the order of march to the various commanding officers and they all returned to their battalions. The air filled with the sound of drums beating The Call as the columns formed up, ready to move out. We had little time to think of anything but our duty so there was a smartness in our drumming at the prospect of meeting the French at last.

'This is it, lads,' Sergeant Bennett said to us, solemnly.

'Be sensible. Only carry what you need.' Then he moved on to the next group of soldiers, I assume with the same words of advice because I saw a couple of them take things from their knapsacks and throw them away.

I clearly recall, just before we left, seeing McNeilis in close conversation with one of the women. He handed her something and whispered earnestly into her ear. Then I recognised what he had given her. It was his Le Roy fob watch, his most treasured possession, the one I planted on Baxter. She nodded, wiped a tear from her eye and embraced him, before putting the watch inside her clothes. McNeilis rejoined us. He looked at me for a moment, then said: 'Ellie's minding it for me, Burns, as a favour. It's safer with her than where we're going. If anything happens to me, I told her it's yours. If it wasn't for you, I wouldn't have it at all.'

I didn't know what to say to that because I felt bad about the amount of upset the whole watch affair had caused McNeilis; I never felt bad about Baxter, though.

'I don't want your watch, Nosey,' I replied. 'You'll be back to collect it yourself.' Without another word, McNeilis walked off to get his knapsack and drum.

The soldiers of the 10th Brigade were not the only ones on the march that morning. Indeed, it seemed as if the whole of the Allied Army was on the move. Extended columns of infantry snaked along the road with thousands of cavalry in the adjacent fields, Hussars and Dragoons, interspersed with long lines of horse-drawn artillery and an endless stream of supply wagons. The provosts were active in moving everything along with the drums keeping everyone to a regular pace. A screen of Hussars on our right protected us from any raiding French cavalry. The dust raised by so many marching boots hung in the air, hurting the eyes, getting inside collars, tunics and socks, mixing with sweat, irritating the skin and causing blisters.

Every now and then, a man would stumble as he trod on some heavy items like a discarded boot or unwanted rations. I actually tripped over a lump of raw meat still on the bone; on another occasion I picked up a book but when I saw it was only a volume of Lutheran sermons, I threw it away. Eventually, it became easy to tell where the brigade had passed by the sheer scale of the material that had been cast aside as every man tried to lighten his burden. Most common among the debris were packs of playing cards. Maguire said they brought you bad luck if you carried them with you into battle. Better to be rid of them.

The march continued with little time given for rest as each battalion commander understood the need for speed and pushed the men as hard as they could. I don't remember much grumbling at that stage. Everyone knew the serious nature of our enterprise and so we just kept going. Even when night fell and the darkness made our road uncertain, the provosts lit lanterns and, somehow, managed to keep the brigade on the move.

The rain that had threatened since we arrived in Ghent started to fall as drizzle at first, then slowly became heavier, until a veritable squall arose, and wind and hail assailed us without mercy. The hard march became more difficult as the full storm took hold. The 27th stuck at it, maintaining the forced pace all night, while the rain swept down upon us in torrents, soaking every man to the skin.

Nothing was impervious to the wet. But still the men kept going, urged on by the shrill blasts of the officers' whistles and our incessant quick-step drumming. Whereas the men had set out at first in lively fashion, talking quietly in the ranks, or breaking out into song to pass the time, it didn't take long for the rain to quell their spirits. Great, tumbling clouds seemed to take delight in dumping their contents right on top of us, with every drop adding to our stock of misery.

And so, the columns continued in sodden silence, long into the wet Belgian night, treading with weary feet to the cadence of our drums, with the growing certainty that every step was bringing us closer to the final contest with Napoleon.

29

The surface of the road was churned into a heavy, cloying sludge, cut up by the wheels of wagons and carriages of every kind. We marched doggedly on, nearing the Forest of Soignes. The road ahead was clogged with streams of refugees seeking to escape the approaching conflict. As the 27th was at the head of the column, it fell to us to force a way through the disorderly, panic-stricken throng. Much additional misery was heaped upon these unfortunate creatures as we pushed their carts and barrows with what little belongings they held into the ditches on both sides of the road. Howls of dismay and not a few curses followed us as we forced our way through the jumble of humanity but what else could we do. The road had to be ours as we were determined to join with Wellington as quickly as possible. Nothing was permitted to slow us down. In times of war, there is no room for sentiment or sympathy, and so we continued to clear the way for the rest of the brigade coming hard behind us.

In the course of pushing everything except military traffic off the road, a few scavenging Inniskillings discovered that some of the abandoned wagons contained brandy. Wellington's strict instructions to all ranks forbade any stealing from the civilian population but, because of the darkness of the night and there being few provosts around, the opportunity was too good to be missed. Nobody was likely to be caught. Word quickly spread among the other companies and soon a mad scramble ensued. Brandy not consumed on the spot was poured into canteens or stashed in knapsacks for trade. As our company had already passed by when the stock of brandy was discovered, we couldn't go back and so missed our chance. Later on, though, a couple of bottles were passed along the line to us as we marched. These we stashed away in our linen bags for later consumption. Brandy can assuage fear as well as warm the stomach.

We entered the Forest of Soignes with reluctance. As soldiers are prone to being superstitious by nature, they have an instinctive distrust of being surrounded by trees. At night, a forest becomes a place of trepidation with strange sounds and flitting shadows, holding its mysteries and secrets fast unto itself. That's how we felt as the battalion marched on, enclosed by massive trees rooted to the earth for decades, not knowing what dangers lurked behind them, while we insignificant mortals passed anxiously through their midst. Great boughs spread their canopies of leaves over us and, with every gust of wind, shook themselves free of great drops of water that landed on our already saturated uniforms like a punishment for daring to trespass on their territory. The odd outburst of nervous laughter could be heard as some tried to dispel their anxiety but the presence of the trees looming overhead combined to crush our spirits. A heavy, leaden silence descended upon the column and we seemed to close in upon each other. Even our drumming was muted. We trudged on, filled with a brooding uneasiness until, at last, the trees began to thin out and our humour lifted.

Eventually we came out from under their spell and we left the forest behind. There was a different quality to the darkness then, not the enveloping, inky density of being under the trees but a sense that it had been softened and lightened somewhat. We entered open farmland again and a few of the soldiers found their voices but then the wind pressed our sodden uniforms to our chilled bodies as the rain sheeted down anew, drenching us. The conversations that had restarted soon died again. I had never known such utter misery or despondency on a march as on that awful night.

And still we slogged on, a sorry-looking lot with soggy, stained uniforms, boots covered with clinging mud and leather-covered shakos battered and heavy with dripping rain. Despite our scruffy, woebegone appearance, we were part of an army on the move, and we were heading for a fight. There was a grim determination about us as we forced the pace. Provosts at each bend in the road urged us on while mounted staff officers galloped back and forth on their various errands.

On a few occasions we had to make way for cavalry as squadrons of Dragoons and Hussars passed us out, their bedraggled horses tossing their manes and snorting in the cool, pre-dawn air. When the rumble of artillery limbers came from behind us, the provosts ordered us off the road altogether. We were glad to rest for a while as cannon lumbered by, heavy 9-pounders, lighter 6-pounders and then the howitzers, all pulled by teams of the strongest horses the army possessed. These poor beasts had such a job hauling their heavy loads, slithering in the sludgy mud, that artillerymen frequently had to dismount to lend their assistance to get the guns through. Mounted officers urged the men on in an effort to keep these machines of war moving.

To ease the boredom, we cheered whenever a gunner fell into the sucking slime but a mean-faced artillery sergeant angrily threatened to make us push the guns instead so we desisted. The churned up road became so choked with horse-drawn supply wagons and ammunition caissons that we took to the cornfields alongside, flattening the tall stalks with our boots. Lifting our feet became a nightmare as the cloying muck stuck to our boots making progress almost impossible. Many troopers ended up walking barefoot as their boots surrendered to the mud. There was no chance of retrieving them as successive ranks were coming on relentlessly behind in an unending line. Finally, word spread that we were nearing the village of Waterloo and, at last, we veered back onto the road again. It was still dark so we had no idea of what our surroundings looked like but we could make out long lines of cavalry horses tethered along the approach to the village, the bigger mounts of the Dragoons easily distinguished from the lighter chargers of the Hussars. In the dim light of scattered lanterns, farriers moved among them, checking their hooves for loose iron to avoid losing a shoe. A lame horse in the charge could cause many others to fall with drastic consequences.

And so we entered Waterloo, the village that none of

us had ever heard of before that day. It was an unremarkable, run-down place, as only a peasant village can be, with a cluster of houses dominated by an inn on one side and a church on the other. It was the same as a hundred other places we had marched through except that now, even at this hour, Waterloo was a hive of activity.

In spite of the sopping rain, flaming torches and lanterns lit the main road through the village. We were told that the inn had been taken over as Wellington's headquarters but we didn't know whether the great man himself was there or not. The few houses we passed had officers' names chalked on their doors. They, it seemed, had been assigned billets and were going to sleep in warm beds. The local inhabitants weren't there to object as, by now, most of them were sheltering from the coming battle in their cellars or had taken to the road to escape. Water dripped off our bedraggled shakos as we looked enviously at the inviting warmth and comfort that the few houses offered but no order to halt was given. So we drummed the Inniskillings through Waterloo and out into the dark countryside once again. We were dead on our feet, thinking that our march that night would never end.

A bit further on, chilled to the bone, soaked to the skin and caked with mud, we arrived near a place called Mont St Jean where the Allied Army was assembling. In a state of near exhaustion, we were led into a field with the soil already churned up by thousands of marching feet. My hands had no feeling, ready to fall off with the effort of drumming for so long. At my side, Reggie was as drained of all energy as I was. We were so tired that we were incapable of marching any further. Finally, Sergeant

Bennett shouted '1st Company, Inniskillings, Fall Out!'

It was the most welcome order we had ever heard. Some of the men literally collapsed where they stood, flopping down into the mud. They were asleep in an instant.

30

Beside me, Reggie folded into the thick slime, eyes already closed, clutching his drum while I just relished the relief at being able to stand still after such a harrowing march. Officers squelched up and down in the downpour, glowing lanterns in their hands, urging the men to rest, but we were in the middle of nowhere. Some Skins still had the energy to erect bivouacs, joining their waterproofs together to make loose, tent-like covers but I had had enough of being exposed to the elements. My body was jaded but mentally I was still alert. There was no sign of the other drummers yet so I left Reggie where he was and sought shelter from the beating rain under a bush or a patch of more solid ground to spread my canvas. I came upon the surrounding hedgerow almost immediately and a voice hailed me through the sheeting rain.

'Hey, mate, your uniform? You a drummer?'

Looking around, I couldn't make out anything but I answered in the affirmative all the same.

'Then come on over here, mate, and join us,' the voice said. 'We're lighting a fire.'

Whoever it was, I thought, must have had eyes like a cat to see in this blackness and getting a fire going in this rain would require nothing short of a miracle. I was wrong because, just at that moment, a flame licked out of the darkness. I slithered over towards the struggling fire, the sucking mud trying to hold my boots fast. By the light of the flickering flames, I made out three heads close together under a straining, canvas roof they had rigged up using broken branches as supports. They had found a good spot, taking advantage of a hollow in the scraggy hedge. They made room for me so I crawled under the shelter, dragging my drum with me.

'We're the 95th, The Rifles,' the voice explained. 'My name's Jarvis. This here's Tanner and that's Craven.'

'Burns, 27th,' I replied, shaking hands all round. I eased in a little more under the makeshift shelter to escape the flow of water that coursed over the edge of the canvas, preferring the thickening smoke to the non-stop rain.

'The 27th?' shouted Jarvis beside me. 'You're a bloody Skin! And a Patlander to boot! Throw him out, the bloody Irishman!' teased Craven. They all laughed. 'We're drummers too,' Craven added, 'but we use bugles in The Rifles.' He tapped the brass instrument at his side. 'Not as awkward to carry as a drum, it ain't.'

I took out my canteen and offered it to them. 'Brandy!' I explained. 'The lads found it on the march. It's good.' They each took a swig, grimaced, then laughed, toasting the health of the 95th Rifles. A second swig and they toasted the health of the 27th Foot. They passed back my canteen and I glugged a mouthful. The brandy burned all the way down but it gave instant warmth to my chilled body. Jarvis clapped me on the back and told me I was all right, that they'd make an exception for one Skin. And that was how easy it was, on that miserable night, to make friends. The thought that all around us thousands of men were doing the same thing, seeking comfort in sleep or in easy company, didn't cross our minds. We created a little cocoon, happy that our long march was over.

The buglers informed me of the latest news that was doing the rounds. They had been at the crossroads of Quatre Bras the previous day when Wellington's forces just about held the left flank and prevented the French from breaking through. They had then withdrawn to this place, bloodied but unbeaten. Meanwhile, to the east, Field Marshal Blücher's Prussians had failed to gather in sufficient numbers to defeat Marshal Grouchy's French Corps and had been badly mauled at the village of Ligny. Blücher had retreated, his army becoming further separated from Wellington's, with Grouchy somewhere in pursuit of him. As for the eight thousand Dutch-Belgians who had also been at Quatre Bras with Wellington, the three buglers laughed in derision at the way they had at first wavered, then had broken at the sight of the advancing French. Craven spat.

'Run like rabbits, they did,' he said with contempt. 'Fired one volley and then bolted. You can't rely on them foreign troops.'

'You can't say that about them all,' objected Jarvis. 'The King's German Legion will fight as good as any of us.'

Jarvis and Craven continued to argue contrary views. Tanner just snorted at them, saying it didn't matter a monkey's, we were all cannon fodder anyway.

'True!' Jarvis and Craven agreed. 'Napoleon's

beautiful daughters will blast us all to eternity.'

'I didn't know he had any daughters,' I said, in mock ignorance. My joke about Napoleon's pet name for his cannon caused them to nearly choke with laughter. When they calmed down, a silence fell upon our little group, the kind that leeches all the energy out of you. I didn't like the melancholy atmosphere that seemed to be taking hold, preferring the laughter of rude banter since that had a way of keeping everything else at bay.

'So what happens next?' I asked, feeling somewhat like Tanner's rabbit myself. 'Will the French really come this far?'

'Aye, Boney's on the way, no doubt about it. He has split us from the Prussians and thinks we're on the run. He wants to send us all the way to the sea.' Thinking of the hard road we had travelled, it seemed an awful long way back to the depot.

Again, there was a silence. Looking at their earnest faces in the firelight, I knew that they felt the same as I did, only none of us could admit to it. Fear doesn't pick and choose who it infects. It's just there, like a dark thing in the corner, refusing to go away. They had already rubbed shoulders with injury and death at Quatre Bras, and yet, there they were, ready to give it a go again. They saw me looking and stared back, their faces blackened and streaked with mud, their eyes white and vacant. The fire crackled, taking hold, its slight warmth drawing us in further from the sheeting rain. Steam rose from our wet clothes as they began to dry on our bodies. Our soggy feet were closest to the fire, the heavy mud still adhering to our boots.

A sudden commotion broke out in the darkness around us as word spread that a quartermaster's wagon had somehow got through with a supply of bread, meat and rum. We scurried over. Already, a frantic melee had broken out among the cold and hungry soldiers until mounted officers carrying lanterns arrived out of the night to put order on things. They made us queue, the threat of the flat of their swords enforcing obedience. I bumped into Reggie in the crowd. He looked ghastly, only half awake. He wondered where I had been so I tugged him along beside me. We grabbed what the wagon attendants handed out to us and together returned to the makeshift shelter where the buglers were already biting into hunks of bread. They made room for Reggie but it was a tight squeeze. The bread was hard, the meat was grizzly, being cut from some obscure part of an animal, and the rum was watered down. Still, it was better than nothing. As soon as I put some bread in my mouth, I found I had no appetite but I forced myself to eat.

Conversation soon reverted to what the morrow would bring. The buglers seemed to know what they were talking about. The Duke depended on his Allies to form the bulk of his army. There was no doubt but that the King's German Legion, the KGL, as well as the other Rhineland troops, mostly from Hanover, Nassau and Brunswick, would hold their own against any man's army even though many of them were young and inexperienced. As for the veteran redcoat regiments, including the 27th that had been with him in India, Spain and Portugal, they would hold fast against the best the French would throw at them. They would fight to the last bullet and then charge with the cold steel. But the Dutch-Belgians were different. Everyone knew that they had fought as part of Napoleon's army until a few years previously. Now, the big question was whether they would stay and fight against the Emperor they had followed for a decade? If they turned and ran, as they did at Quatre Bras, the much-vaunted French cavalry would pour through the gaping hole they'd leave in the line, divide Wellington's army in two, and then roll up the flanks, annihilating them. That was a nightmare possibility but it could become a reality. How would Wellington address that, we wondered, as our regiments had never before encountered the armoured Cuirassiers on the battlefield. We eventually drifted off into a damp, uneasy sleep, leaving the question to be answered in the morning.

31

'Geddup, you drunken Skin drummers!'

I slowly opened a bleary eye to see Sammy Crooks's dirt-streaked face in the dim light of the fading fire. He was leaning over me, shaking me with one hand while waving a brown bottle in the other. 'I brought you breakfast,' he said. I pushed his hand away and straightened up.

'Have a swig of this...nectar,' he slurred, satisfied he had thought of the word. He stuck it again into my face. 'You wouldn't get this quality back in Mother Hogan's, sure you wouldn't.'

'Get off with you, Crooks,' I said, waving my hand out from under the shelter. 'It's not Reveille yet.' The rain had eased off but it was still quite dark. My damp clothes stuck to me as I crept out. Reggie followed on his hands and knees. 'What do you want?' I asked.

Crooks belched loudly before answering. His breath stank. 'Captain Hare has called for all the battalion drummers. Took me a while to find you. He's got orders. We must be moving again, damn it. Just when we were settling in. There you go, lads. A present from the Skins.' He threw the bottle back into the shelter. Tanner, Jarvis and Craven dived for it and a manic struggle ensued within. Crooks shuffled off like a man going to his death, his drum almost dragging on the ground. We said our goodbyes to the buglers and wished them well as we left. 'Whatever happens, we'll be where the shooting is,' Jarvis called out.

As Reggie and I made our way through the scattered bivouacs of the battalion, we could make out the dark shadows of the sentries standing down with the approach of daybreak. It had been a miserably wet but uneventful watch for them. McNeilis, The Fox Maguire, Gallagher and Crooks had already gathered around the battalion's officers by the time we arrived. The Regimental Colours hung wet and uninspiring from the poles that Welter and Astwith held, both of them trying hard to belie their youth by looking stern in their officers' uniforms. The NCOs stood nearby, with the big frame of the Drum Major in the middle. Some of the NCOs were swaying gently, probably due to the quantity of brandy they had consumed earlier. Bennett slipped in the mud as he arrived and almost fell, much to the amusement of the others, but a glance from Hare brought the mirth to a sudden end. In normal times, being drunk when turning up for duty was a punishable offence but, with hours to go to what was expected to be a crucial battle with the French, there was little point in pursuing the matter. Anyway, a man sobered up quickly enough on the battlefield when the cannon balls started to fly and if he faced his Maker it wouldn't be the smell of his breath that would keep him out of Heaven. No, those were not normal times. The officers conferred for a while, with Hare issuing instructions. When the circle broke up, he gave us the signal to drum Reveille.

We beat like demons, as much to warm ourselves up as to rouse exhausted men from their short alcohol-induced slumber. The drums of other regiments could be heard floating to us on the breeze. An army was waking up. A fleeting thought crossed my mind that we were calling men to what might be their last day on earth. How they must have cursed us and our damned drums. They crawled out from their muddy, sopping bivouacs, those who had bothered to make them, and stood shivering in the rain as they gathered their scattered wits. Some men just rose up from where they had dropped, their uniforms caked with slime, while the rain still sluiced down. There was frantic activity for the next few minutes as soldiers attended first to their muskets, tearing away the oily rags that covered the firing pieces, uncorking the muzzles, pumping the ramrods up and down to clean out the barrels and then priming the weapons for firing. All around us came the sound of muskets being popped off to make sure that they would fire properly when loaded and then they were covered again. There would be no battle if the guns couldn't fire.

Having seen to their weapons, the redcoats attended to themselves. There was no question of shaving on this particular morning but most men made an effort at scraping excess muck off their uniforms and boots and generally trying to make themselves look like soldiers, a difficult job given the conditions.

A short while later, distant cavalry bugles sounded Stand To, and the men instantly formed up to repel a sudden attack. It wasn't long, though, before a patrol of

Hussars rode up to tell us that we could relax as the French were too far away to be a threat to us. Nobody was disappointed when Hare ordered us to stand down. Whatever was happening, it seemed that it wasn't going to involve us. And if there was no sign of the enemy, there was no sign of breakfast either. The supply wagons were held up again in the sludge somewhere towards the rear and, with the sheer number of men requiring food, getting it to us was a near-impossible task. All we had was what was left in our linen bags, scarcely an appetising prospect. There was still a quantity of brandy about, but raw spirit wouldn't fill our stomachs, nor did it dispel the gnawing fear.

Since I was a corporal, I was detailed to stay close to Hare as he and the other officers did the morning rounds of the men. I told Reggie to stick by my side so we accompanied Hare as he strolled from group to group, chatting amiably with the Skins, answering their questions and urging them to be calm and steadfast, that the day would bring victory over the French, he was sure of it. He repeated the same words over and over, urging the 27th to do their duty and not to give way. Some old hands cheered him and wished him luck as they drank from their canteens, the strong spirit kicking them into life; others had managed to light their long, clay pipes and were puffing balls of smoke into the misty air as they listened to him. Many seasoned redcoats, lacking a pipe, simply chewed on their plugs of tobacco, pausing every now and then to spit as they patiently awaited for what the day would bring.

The last flashes of lightning lit up the sky, revealing

momentarily the mass of men present in the fields, only for them to disappear when it became dark again. Lanterns burned low in their bowls, the pools of light from them getting smaller. By then, the last few desultory fires had died out, having given up the fight against the rain. We were loitering with the other drummers when a mounted rider was heard splattering across the field shouting for the commanding officer of the 27th. It was one of Wellington's staff officers. Hare hailed him, saluted briefly, and took the proffered note. He scanned it quickly by the light of a lantern before handing it back, saying: 'The 27th will do its duty, Sir.' The officer had barely swung his horse away when Hare ordered us to beat The Assembly. Our drums sounded loud across the field as the men, guided by their sergeants, quickly jostled into line, relieved that the waiting seemed to be at an end. Hare then issued further instructions to his officers.

'Tell the men to drop all knapsacks and blankets,' he ordered. 'They won't be needing them now. See to their cartridge pouches too as this might be the last supply of ammunition they'll get before the shooting starts. We're moving forward to the reserve line.'

The company captains scattered, passing on Hare's orders to the NCOs, reminding them especially about topping up on cartridges at the armourers' wagons as we passed. There was a sense of apprehension in the ranks with this stark reminder.

Within minutes, knapsacks and other personal effects had been piled for the battalion wagons to gather and the companies of the 27th formed into columns ready to move. It was hard enough carrying a loaded knapsack on a long march but any soldier would tell you that he preferred to be free of any encumbrance on his back going into action. A few, including me, cast a wistful glance at the pile, wondering whether any of us would come back to claim our few miserable possessions. Orderlies led the dripping horses over and helped the officers to mount. Then, with a loud roll, Reggie and I strutted off in the gloom beside the head of the column, passing where we thought we had shared the buglers' shelter but, if that was the place, there was no sign now that anyone had been there. Their fire had fizzled out and the shelter was gone. I imagined Jarvis, Tanner and Craven moving out with the 95th Rifles and wondered where they were at that precise moment.

We tramped on as the first chink of light appeared in the sky, keeping up a steady tempo for the short distance from our bivouac to our designated place with the other reserve battalions. On this march, we beat Ordinary Time, seventy-five paces of thirty inches each to the minute; every single step, every tap on the drum counting down the seconds, taking us closer and closer to our meeting with Napoleon's *Armée du Nord*.

The swampy tract of land over which we passed was mostly devoid of ditch or hedgerow. The tall cornstalks and wheat that had been standing proudly the previous day had been trampled underfoot, the year's crop destroyed. After a while, we were directed off the road and took up our position with the rest of Lambert's 10th Brigade on the slope behind the ridge that marked our lines. The men flopped down on the waterlogged ground again, grateful that the distance had been so short. It was still not light enough to make out exactly what lay before us but gradually, as the sky grew brighter and the rain clouds began to disperse, we looked forward to drying out. The officers immediately cantered up to the crest of the ridge. McGreel and Hicks set off too, striding after them. Half-way there, the Drum Major paused, turned and called for me to accompany them.

'You too, Reggie,' I said eagerly, and we raced off, our drums bouncing against our legs, to join the officers at the top of the ridge.

In the dim light of early dawn as we beheld the rolling, green landscape that gently sloped away from us down to the misty valley below, we had absolutely no inkling of the momentousness of the event that was about to take place there that very day. It was the morning of Sunday, June 18th, 1815. All across Europe, people were preparing to go to church. We were getting ready for battle.

ʒ2

With a broad sweep of the eye, we observed the two long, curving ridges that effectively created an oval-shaped arena, shrouded in the early-morning mist. We stood near a crossroads facing south, with the road behind leading back to Waterloo and Brussels, while in front of us, it ran down the valley and up to the opposite crest, leading towards Charleroi. Another road bisected that, running along the top of our ridge to the left and right, dropping in places below the level of the ground on either side, becoming in effect a sunken road.

Three large clusters of farm buildings occupied the valley, each of them forming a considerable obstacle to an attacking army but equally forming a stout bastion of resistance for a defending one. I didn't know the names of these farms when I first beheld them but they have been carved into my memory ever since. To the left, lay the imposing presence of the farm known as Papelotte. In the centre, two hundred metres below the crest lay the white-washed, walled farmyard of La Haye Sainte, with an orchard to its rear and a sand-pit opposite. On the extreme right of the valley lay the walled enclosure of the Château d'Hougoumont. Much nearer to us, beside the crossroads, was a grassy knoll on which stood a solitary elm tree.

Our viewing was disturbed by a battery of 9-pounder cannon that struggled by, escorted by a troop of Light Dragoons. They moved out onto the slope to our left, the horses slithering on the soggy ground as they strained to pull the huge guns. The artillerymen dismounted and pushed at the spokes of the wheels. Away on the horizon, a troop of Hussars galloped near a small wood, acting as the eyes and ears of the army, the distant thundering of their horses' hooves carrying across to us. When they had disappeared into the trees, the officers left the ridge and returned to where the battalion was relaxing on the wet reverse slope. We stayed near the colours, awaiting further orders. We were still cold and miserably wet.

With the arrival of full daylight, a low, watery sun forced its way through the breaking clouds and we earnestly hoped that the rain was over at last. Our attention was diverted from looking skywards as a large group of horsemen cantered towards us from the direction of the sunken road. They reined in their mounts and quietly observed the arrival of more artillery. From their uniforms, plumed helmets and glistening mounts, it was obvious that they were the senior officers of the Allied Army. I immediately recognised Sir John Lambert, our Brigade Commanding Officer, having seen him a couple of times while we marched but I couldn't identify any of the others.

One man in particular, though, stood out. Carrying himself with an air of ease and command, he sat on a magnificent brown charger, dressed in a blue civilian coat, buckskin breeches, high riding boots and with a cocked hat on his head. As I stared at him, he spurred his horse in our direction and I became aware of a quiet stir behind me. With a quick glance round, I saw that the 27th were standing up and forming in line, with Captain Hare and the rest of the officers sitting stiffly astride their horses in front of them. The rest of the drummers wordlessly joined me, a frisson of excitement crackling among us.

'The Duke,' Sammy Crooks whispered beside me, 'it's Wellington himself, come to see us off.'

I don't know what came over me at that moment as I didn't stop to think but I suddenly snapped upright, ramrod straight, fixed my drum in front of me and commenced a terrific roll that the others immediately followed. In a second, with every 27th drummer beating in perfect unison, the whole battalion presented arms without any instruction being given, and we saluted the Duke with a tremendous, rousing cadence that ended with a dramatic flourish. With perfect timing, each drummer paused with drumsticks crossed and held aloft, before ending the roll. It worked so perfectly it seemed we had been rehearsing for months for that moment.

In the sudden silence after the last beat had died away, the Duke raised his hat to us before he spurred his horse on. No one said a word as he went by, followed by all of his staff officers, knowing that he disapproved of cheering in the ranks. Nor did he say anything to us. He simply held his hat aloft as was his way. I'd swear when he passed that he looked me straight in the eye and gave me a nod as if he knew I was the one who had instigated the drumming specially for him. It was easily the most stirring drum roll I had ever played. It was all over in seconds.

As soon as the Duke and his staff had gone, Hicks strode over, planted himself in front of me and, hands on hips, loudly berated me in the most crude manner saying that if I ever made a spectacle of the regiment again in front of the Duke of Wellington by a breach of drum protocol, he would see me unceremoniously kicked out of the 27th.

'Consider yourself severely reprimanded, Corporal Burns,' he ended. Hicks then winked at me and went back to Captain Hare and the other officers. I sat down on the flattened corn beside the others, aghast at the nerve I had shown in precipitating what had just happened. Gallagher slapped me energetically on the back, saying, 'Thought you'd make sergeant for that, didn't you, Burns?' The lads were greatly amused. Soon, though, everybody had relaxed again and the battalion settled down.

Even though it was mid June, the rain had left a chill in the air that had yet to be dispelled. As the sun rose higher, it began to burn off the rising mist, bringing a cheer to our spirits. It was the first we had seen of it for days. We prayed it would shine long enough for our clothes to dry out properly and give some badly-needed warmth to our bodies. Looking around then, it seemed that the whole of the Allied Army was assembled on that slope. All around us, men busied themselves with last minute preparations for battle, cleaning their muskets again, replacing the flints in their locks and pointing their bayonets. When finished, they slumped back down, still weary after the long, non-stop march from Ghent and the lack of any proper sleep the previous night. We were happy to be at our ease in the lee of the crest, our drums resting on the drying ground beside us.

As we reclined, with the rattle and hum of our assembling army coming from all around us, another more distant sound began to intrude. Slowly, and ever so gradually getting louder, the strains of martial music carried across the shallow valley floor from the far ridge. A hush came over the Allied Army, and into that silence came the growing sound of massed drumming, bugles and singing. The French were arriving. Every man strained to make out what was happening on the ridge opposite. From our position with the reserves on the reverse slope, we were unable to see the enemy but the thin line of redcoats now standing along the top of our crest had suddenly gone very still.

As we listened, we began to make out a few of the actual melodies that the French bands were playing as their music floated over to us. It seemed as if their bands were competing with each other, their tunes gradually merging into a frantic medley. It was impossible not to be impressed even by the sounds alone. Captain Hare mounted his horse again and spurred forward to the crest, Grant and Logue following suit. Hicks started out for the ridge on foot, calling for McNeilis and me to go with him.

The scene before us had changed utterly. Hearing Napoleon's *Armée du Nord* arriving on the crest opposite was daunting enough; actually beholding it was so awe-inspiring that I was filled with sheer excitement. The southern slope was alive with dense columns of blue-uniformed infantry, extending in perfect rows down into the valley as if rehearsing their attack. As they marched, more and yet more troops spilled over the crest, eagle standards held high, regimental flags flying with mounted officers at the side of each battalion. Artillery pieces lumbered into sight, rolling ponderously into position just below the crest in a long line. Their crews were like ants milling around as they unlimbered the guns, slowly man-handling them on the marshy ground until their gaping, iron mouths faced across the valley directly towards us. I lost count of how many cannon they had.

McNeilis, having watched in silence for a while finally found his voice. 'That's his Grand Battery,' he observed, pointing at the lengthening row of massive guns. 'Napoleon understands artillery. If he's concentrating most of his cannon in the middle of his line, that's where his main attack is going to be, straight over towards where we are now.' He spat. 'That's after they've softened us up a bit,' he added.

'But are they not too far away?' I asked, in my ignorance.

'Don't be fooled, Burns. We're well within range of those pieces. They'll hit us hard. Their artillery officers already have their telescopes on us spotting the juiciest targets. It's as well we're back in reserve. Whoever stands here is going to be hammered when the show begins.' I said nothing after that, just watched in admiration of the unfolding spectacle.

Still the French came on, their bands playing as if it were for a Sunday afternoon performance. By then, the entire, distant, downward-sloping landscape was a moving mass of thick blue columns of infantry. Lines of horse artillery lurched forward in between them with the soft light playing on their polished barrels. On the flank came rows of Hussars screening the fringes of the infantry. Thousands more cavalry followed, the blue uniforms of the Dragoons a contrast to the green of the Chasseurs à Cheval and the cherry-red of the famed Red Lancers. Each of the Lancers was armed with a fearsome, nine-foot long, spear with its red-and-white, swallow-tailed pennon unfurled. Away to one side galloped the elite of the French cavalry, the feared Cuirassiers, whose powerful, shock-charges had ensured many a victory for Napoleon in the past. Last into sight came the Imperial Guard, complete with its own cavalry and artillery, masters of the battlefield, whose mere presence was enough to unnerve the most stalwart of opponents. The sight of the French army arraying itself with admirable discipline in preparation for the assault was truly an unforgettable spectacle. And still, from across the valley, came the floating sounds of the regimental bands and drummers, their joyous melodies carrying clearly over to our ridge.

I lost track of time looking all around at the sheer size of the force deploying itself against us, wondering how we were going to face it. Nosey McNeilis was watching them too, his veteran's eye making more sense of what they were doing than I ever could. He indicated to me how four columns seemed to be taking up assault positions to the left and right of the French centre with the cannon of the Grand Battery covering them but I was too dazzled by the display of martial superiority to absorb what he was saying.

'Well done, the Duke,' observed McNeilis eventually. 'He's chosen well for defence.'

'What do you mean?' I asked.

'No matter which flank Napoleon attacks, he'll have to stream his men around either Papelotte Farm on one side and Hougoumont on the other. It's the same if he tries a frontal attack. He can't come straight at us because La Haye Sainte below us is already occupied with the King's German Legion. You can see their green uniforms. The French will have to funnel around it. They'll be cut down. Look, some of the 95th Rifles are down there in that sandpit too.'

As he said that, the sound of bugles floated up to us from the farm and we saw a lot of movement around the walls. Obviously, the King's German Legion and The Rifles were preparing to defend it stoutly. A happy image of Jarvis and the others from the previous night came to me. I doubted whether they were still so content. When the guns opened up, they'd most likely be in the thick of it, just as they expected.

When, at last assembled, that huge mass of men started to cheer as one, their voices combined into a single chant of '*Vive l'Empereur.*' The atmosphere became altogether more menacing, and I finally understood the purpose of this whole sinister demonstration. It was staged to intimidate and dishearten even the bravest of men, a tactic that had worked so many times before on different battlefields the length and breadth of Europe. I still recall the deep shiver that went down my spine at that moment caused by pure, naked fear.

33

The lips of old warriors are sealed. What they have seen and done is kept locked away since the recollection of painful events leads only to deep anguish and heart-felt regret. I know, since I too have repressed for most of my adult life memories of certain dark deeds such as the killing of Sergeant Nathan Curley. In fact, I have banished them from my mind so successfully for over sixty years that sometimes it seems as if they never happened. But there comes a time in everyone's life when the accounts book must be balanced and I suppose I have reluctantly arrived at that stage now.

And so it is with a degree of difficulty that I have come to record not just killing Curley on the *Rascal* but also the other events that happened on that extraordinary Sunday in June. It is not because my memory is fading. On the contrary, these events are as fresh in my mind as on the day they occurred. Rather it is because I find the other associated memories so distressing that they will disturb the fragile peace that I have managed to construct for myself. The pain caused by bitter loss bites deep into the human soul but I must face it now with the same determination with which I tried to avoid it for so long. Of the thousands of men who died on that momentous day, many whose faces I looked into at the moment of death, two in particular have remained in my memory. One I already knew; the other I have never spoken of, until now. If fact, I hadn't even met him as I gazed across at the French lines on that fateful morning.

As any soldier will tell you, it's always the waiting that is hardest to endure. Our orders were to remain in reserve with the rest of Lambert's 10th Brigade until called forward into the line. As I sat there looking at my comrades, the men for whom I had drummed all the way from the shores of Lough Erne to this rural part of Belgium, I wondered how many of them were thinking the same as me – would I be alive or dead by nightfall?

Had they been able to see the size and might of the French army across the valley, as McNeilis and I had, maybe even the veterans among the 27th would have agreed that the odds on being killed were inordinately high. Of course, they trusted Wellington's leadership and ability but they had serious doubts about William, Prince of Orange-Nassau, and would not be shaken in their poor estimation of him. It was the talk of the army that the Prince was completely inept when it came to leading men. Even though he had been with Wellington's staff in the Peninsula for nearly three years, Slender Billy, as he was called, was reputed to have learned nothing. Yet, because the Prince's father was King William I of the newly founded country, the Netherlands, the Duke had no alternative but to put him in charge of 1st Corps. However, he took the precaution of providing experienced and resolute officers for the Prince's staff and placed him on the right flank of the allied line. This took him away from the centre, where the walled farm of La Haye Sainte was expected to take the brunt of any frontal assault. The Duke's intention, as far as we could made out then, was to minimise the damage that the young Prince could inflict on his own men and, by implication, on the rest of the Allied line.

A muted drone of human sound came from across the valley, the extraordinary murmuring of thousands of men talking while they moved slickly into prearranged formations. There was movement on our ridge too as other redcoat battalions arrived and stretched out in a long thin line with other Dutch-Belgian and German battalions on the downward slope in front of them. We later understood the wisdom of Wellington's tactical deployment. He had dispersed the allied units among the redcoat battalions in order to 'put steel in their backs,' as I remember McNeilis commenting. Wellington also placed his batteries on the downslope, scattering them along the line with a clear field of fire across the valley but he had far fewer guns to aim at the French.

'I don't mind taking a musket ball,' muttered Reggie, as we lay on the damp clover, 'but God preserve me from coming up against a Lancer when the time comes. I don't want to be skewered.'

'God preserve us from both as I don't want either of them,' I replied.

Lieutenant Astwith detached himself from the other lieutenants and came over to me. He pulled me aside for a moment, a worried expression on his youthful face.

'Corporal Burns, I've a favour to ask of you,' he said

quietly.

'Sir?' I asked.

'I've a premonition about today, Burns. If I'm severely wounded, I don't want to linger. You're a stretcher-bearer. If you find me in a bad way, I want you to cut my throat. Finish me off quickly. Promise me that.'

I stared at him in shock. Although he was an officer, he wasn't much older than I, and was probably just as scared. We were all in dread of serious injury but, youth being youth, we pushed the thought away – we were too young to die, weren't we? And yet, here was Astwith, indulging the possibility of being fatally wounded and making plans for that eventuality.

'Promise me, James,' he said again.

What else could I do other than say yes. He then shook my hand as if we had just struck a deal, thanked me profusely and walked off to rejoin Reihill and Welter. I prayed his dark premonition wouldn't come true for either of us. I didn't want any more blood on my hands.

The sun rose higher in the morning sky as mounted staff officers continued to race up and down among the battalions passing on orders. Soldiers continued to file past in orderly lines, taking up positions much further along the ridge trailing out in a long double line in full view of the enemy. We remained out of sight of the French, lying on the flattened corn on the sheltered side of the crest facing back along the road to Mont St Jean. Since first light, it was clogged with wagons containing ammunition and provisions of every kind. We watched as a couple of large tents were erected further back. 'Temporary hospitals, I'll wager,' said Gallagher. 'They'll be full soon.'

Muddied after their long treks, cavalry were also assembling on open farmland to our rear, flattening the early crops as men and horses were ordered to lie on the wet ground. Further back, more squadrons of Dragoons and Hussars had dismounted and tethered their horses to rope-lines that had been quickly erected. Being well back out of harm's way, these troopers stood in clusters with nothing else to do except light their pipes and wait. Some didn't even bother to dismount. Farriers moved among the skittish animals, rubbing their necks, talking quietly to them, helping to keep them calm.

As we lay there, muskets stacked near to hand, I remember seeing steam rising from the soldiers' drying uniforms adding to the slight mist that still lingered in the air. The junior officers and NCOs continued to move among the men, stopping frequently to offer quiet words of encouragement. Sergeant Bennett hovered near us for a few moments. 'It won't be long now,' he said, 'you'll be all right when it begins. You'll see.' He continued along the line of prone redcoats, bringing a veteran's calm to anxious men who had never stood in the line before.

'Why the delay?' I asked McNeilis, as I made slight adjustments to the cords of my drum. 'Why hasn't Bonaparte opened fire yet?'

'Can't fight in the mud,' replied McNeilis. 'If he fires his cannon, they'll dig into the soft ground and he won't get them out to fire again. Same goes for his cavalry, they can't charge on marshy terrain. They'll just cut up the surface and make it impossible to ride on and then, for the infantry, it would be like trying to charge across a ploughed field. No, he's waiting for it to dry out a bit.'

The Skins took advantage of the wait to continue enjoying a lingering smoke on their long, clay pipes. I have never been one for that but, since that June morning, whenever a whiff of tobacco drifts across my nostrils, it takes me back to that very spot and that agonising period of waiting.

To our amazement, a wagon trundled up with a supply of rum and a generous ration was passed around to each man but, as there was no sign of a food wagon, we had to make do with whatever scraps we had managed to save in our bags. Reggie shared his last piece of stale loaf with me while I gave him a few bites of a small lump of hard cheese I had scrounged from a passing artilleryman. The rum made me retch but I managed to keep the half-chewed mash of bread and cheese down. Then I closed my eyes and lay back.

To pass the time, I began to separate out the drifting sounds, identifying them one by one – the murmur of men talking quietly among themselves; the whinnying and snorting of stamping horses; the chink of harness, the rasp of swords and bayonets being sharpened, and even my own anxious breathing. Yet still, the tortuous waiting endured. I have often wondered at Napoleon's prolonged delaying for he must have known that the later the hour for commencing the battle, the greater the disadvantage to him. He might not have finished with us by the time Blücher arrived with his Prussians, as we all prayed he would.

Suddenly, louder than all other sounds, there came the distant boom of a cannon. My reverie ended abruptly. I opened my eyes and looked round at my startled, fellow-drummers as a cannon ball whistled by somewhere over our heads. Then a second thundering crack came as another ball whizzed by somewhere further down the line. And then a third cannon roar was heard, echoing across the crest.

'It's started!' McNeilis said, jumping up. 'Three shots! The French are attacking.'

34

With that three gun signal, the fifty-four guns of the Grand Battery disappeared in a cloud of smoke as every one of them fired, the thunderous roar making the ground around us shake despite the three-kilometre distance that separated us from them. The air filled with strange whistling sounds as the French gunners quickly got into their stride, increasing their rate of fire, pounding our side of the valley. Even though we were not in the line of fire, we crouched down into the wet earth seeking shelter from the barrage. I wondered why there was no immediate reply from our guns until I heard an officer bellowing at our artillerymen during a short lull not to fire until ordered to do so or they'd answer to Wellington. Bennett slid down beside us.

'The French are only warming up, lads,' he said. 'Be grateful we're out of view rather than exposed like those poor devils up there.'

As soon as he said that, a cannon ball hissed over the top, bounced on the muddy ground and rolled on slowly down the slope. A redcoat from the nearby 40th regiment stood up and stretched out a leg intending to stop it. The ball just took his whole foot clean off and kept rolling.

Screaming in sudden agony, the soldier collapsed on to the crushed corn, the bloody stump of his leg pointing into the air, bone and sinew exposed. His companions rushed to help him and clustered around but there was little they could do other than offer him comfort.

'Get him out of here,' roared one of their officers. A stretcher-party of 40th drummers carried him back to the hospital tent as the wounded redcoat clutched the severed foot still in the boot that his mates had thoughtfully placed on his chest – as if the surgeons would somehow be able to magically reattach it. The sight of his bloody stump of a leg and his agonised screams shook us more than the sight of the whole French army.

'You've been warned, lads,' shouted Bennett, as we settled down again. 'See what can happen. Leave these things run themselves out.'

More cannon balls flew over the crest as the French gunners perfected their aim. They were slowly adjusting the range and elevation of their bigger artillery so that their projectiles would skim over the top and fall among the men who they knew were lying out of sight. The balls bounced, rolled for a bit and then finally stuck in the soft ground. There were plenty of targets on the reverse slope with the bulk of Wellington's infantry gathered there and, further back, more brigades of cavalry and ammunition wagons for the artillery.

Slowly, the French began to have more success. Along with solid roundshot of different weights, they began to load shells, fuse-lit, hollow balls filled with explosives and broken shards of iron. When fired, the lit fuse continued to burn until it reached the charge inside. It then exploded sending jagged, metal pieces flying in all directions. Anyone within a short range would be horribly mutilated or killed outright. Luckily most fizzled out in the wet mud when they hit the soft earth. A few reckless redcoats extinguished some at great risk to themselves. I recall that Ward pounced on a hissing shell that landed among us and pulled the fuse right out of the hole. He then danced around in the muck, holding the still-burning fuse in his hand while making a fizzling noise, until he suddenly shouted 'Boom!' and flung himself to the ground. Even the officers joined in the laughter at this, until the next shell exploded among us killing a man and seriously wounding four others. Their screams of anguish unnerved us further as they were the first 27th casualties to be carted away. That incident put an end to the laughter and a sombre mood attached itself to us. We were quiet after that, quiet in a way that only nauseating fear can bring. It was a strange experience lying there, out of sight of the French artillery yet not out of danger's way. We spared a thought for the men holding the line on the crest who were standing fully exposed to the guns. Better them than us.

The rate of French fire noticeably increased and the sound of distant shouts and screams came to us. The earth beneath us shook once again with the tremendous pounding of the guns, hurting our ears with each resounding roar. Another ball struck not far from us, just missing a group of Skins, spraying our already filthy uniforms with globs of muck. As Gallagher wiped his face, he grinned broadly.

'It's heating up over there, lads,' he said. 'They'll

attack soon. They're concentrating their fire on the centre, that's where the attack will come. The longer we stay out of it, the better.' But we weren't out of it; nowhere on that battlefield was safe, with roundshot and shell skimming the ridge top regularly as the French improved their aim. Every now and then, Hare rode to the top of the ridge with officers from the other regiments, observed what was happening, and then returned.

Suddenly, a cannonball pulverised two unfortunate soldiers directly ahead of us on the crest, smashing their bodies into a bloody pulp and wounding a few others. We were ordered forward to help remove the wounded. It was a messy business stepping over the smashed bodies, too much for Sammy Crooks who vomited until there was nothing left inside him. He said it was worse than anything he had seen in Spain. The young soldiers watched the rising number of casualties with growing alarm as balls continued to land in their vicinity. Hare saw that the Nassauer troops were young and inexperienced under fire so he joined their officers riding up and down their line, talking to them, encouraging them to stand firm.

For a while, we trundled back and forward to the hospital tent with other casualties. Apart from drummers doing stretcher duty, it was normal practice for infantry also to carry an injured comrade off the field but they were expected to return to their place in the line. It was reported afterwards that many of the Dutch-Belgian battalions, having dropped off a wounded colleague, kept going and didn't stop until they reached Brussels. There, we later heard, they added to the growing panic among the populace by spreading stories about the invincibility of the French and the inevitability of Wellington's defeat. Blasted cowards! After a while, Captain Grant told us to stop removing the injured. The casualty rate was mounting so much that our small number couldn't cope so we went back to our drums. From then on, anyone who got hit lay where they fell or hobbled from the line by themselves if they were able.

The trickle of injured men soon became a flood, all streaming back over the crest, their heads and bodies bloodied, arms in makeshift slings and dazed looks on their faces, all of them despondent and demoralised. A few paused to tell us about the mercilessness and brutality of the French artillery. One soldier, a Hanoverian Jäger, his head wrapped in a soiled, white handkerchief, smiled broadly as he passed us using his musket as a crutch.

'You'll all be dead by the time I get to Brussels,' he shouted at us.

There was no talk among us by that stage. That Jäger was telling the truth.

35

The Inniskillings around me maintained a stoic silence, absorbing all the punishment that Napoleon's daughters could dish out, as we waited for our chance to pay them back. Then one of our ammunition wagons took a direct hit and exploded with a deafening roar, ripping a team of horses and two drivers apart. The ground under us shook with the force of the explosion.

More shells came, falling further back down the slope as the French sought to build on their success. Another wagon loaded with barrels of gunpowder blew up. Men and horses disintegrated in the blast, splattering blood and gore in all directions. The tethered, cavalry horses, frightened by the explosions, broke free of their ropes and tried to bolt but were quickly corralled by the farriers. Other wagons were urgently pulled further back but that made things more awkward for our own guns as fresh cannonballs, shells and kegs of gunpowder then had to be carried by hand over a longer distance. Our artillery needed a steady supply of munitions as they had started to return fire. However we had no idea what was really going on and, short of going up to see, there was no way of finding out.

As if on cue, a staff officer rode over to Captain Hare with news of the battle. He told him that an assault had begun on Hougoumont on our right flank where the Coldstream Guards were placed with good support from some Dutch-Germans in the small wood beside it; that the exposed centre battalions were also taking a pasting from the French artillery and that the main attack was still expected there. If it turned out to be so, Hare was to hold the 27th in readiness to move forward and counterattack. There was an immediate stir among the men as this news spread like wildfire. But still we had to wait.

It was hard lying there listening to the booming of cannon, the rattle of musketry and the distant screams of men locked in close combat while we reclined in relative safety, our muddied uniforms starting to dry out in the strengthening sun. All we had to worry us was the random fall of shot that landed in our part of the reserve line, and the casualties they caused. We could only imagine the death and devastation at Hougoumont as Napoleon committed more infantry to the attack. So our frustration and anger grew as we lay there allowing the French to hammer us at will. We itched to get back at our tormentors.

Then, miraculously, the bombardment eased off and we knew something was happening because mounted staff officers began to gallop to the various brigade commanders to the rear of the line. In that short respite, we could distinctly make out the *Rum-tum-tum* of the French drums.

'That's coming from in front of us,' said McNeilis. 'The guns have stopped to let their infantry pass. They're attacking the centre.'

We listened as the sound of the bands gradually grew louder and the guns of the Grand Battery opposite fell silent, and we were able to make out the strains of marching music, an incongruous sound on such a bloody day. The veteran Skins checked their muskets again, even though they had done this over and over already. An air of nervous anticipation spread among us but the NCOs were quick to intervene.

'Stay down, boys, stay down,' the shouts came. But it was impossible not to be agitated under the circumstances. Then a huge cheer came to us from across the valley, thousands of lusty voices shouting in unison, over and over again.

'*Vive l'Empereur!*'

From the enthusiasm they were displaying, I believe the Emperor himself was there but our lines remained unperturbed through all of this. Their drums began to play again, non-stop this time. The French were obviously coming for a fight and we wanted to give them one. But it wasn't the 27th Foot that had been ordered to advance to repel the enemy attack. Instead it was our own Inniskillings cavalry, the 6th Dragoons, with their big horses and straight, heavy swords, who had been given that honour along with the rest of the Union Brigade. Lined up some distance behind us, they mounted up and moved towards us at a walk, hundreds of men on snorting beasts, impatient to get at the enemy. We stood to give them a mighty cheer as they passed through our files and formed into squadrons, increasing speed to a canter, building momentum up the slope towards the crest. We were still cheering when they disappeared from sight over the top. Their canter became a gallop as they charged downhill, knee to knee, crashing into the mass of advancing French infantry. The sound of their horses' hooves was soon lost in the mayhem of the ensuing battle.

After that, we had no idea how things unfolded and so, when the excitement died down, we were again ordered to be patient and hold our position. I occupied myself with examining my drum, scraping off the small bits of clay that had dried on the paintwork and tightening the cords. It wouldn't pass inspection back in the depot, but then, we weren't in the depot. I wiped the calfskin top with my cuff and tapped it a few times. It sounded normal. Through the smoke, a couple of wounded Scots Greys, who had also charged with the Union Brigade, staggered back on foot and told us that they had managed to stop the attack but had then been subjected themselves to a counterattack by the Cuirassiers. Worst of all, the French were coming on again with fresh columns of infantry. The troopers continued their despondent walk to the rear. The French artillery again began to land their roundshot on the slopes where we lay so we knew they were firing over the heads of their own infantry on their way up towards our lines.

'When the guns stop again you'll know they're almost upon us,' explained Gallagher. 'They won't want to hit their own men.'

The Fox Maguire clapped his hands over his ears to drown out the sound and Crooks closed his eyes as if in prayer. A shell landed among a cluster of redcoats from the 4th, blasting them to pieces, the shock waves reaching where we lay. Bits of broken muskets and separated limbs flew high into the air. This had become an all-too-common sight. I glanced at McNeilis. To give the old veteran his due, he was calmly lying on the ground with his arm around his drum as if it were a long, lost lover. He nodded encouragingly at me as the firing grew in intensity again. I kept my head down, wondering how the battalions on the exposed ridge could possibly survive the onslaught. Surely our turn couldn't be far away.

Suddenly, Captain Logue was leaning over me, pulling me by the jacket. At first, I couldn't make out what he was saying. Then, in a brief lull, I heard him.

'Burns! You and Cox! Bring your drums!'

He ran back towards the crest, nearly tripping over his sword, where he rejoined Hare and the other 27th officers. Heart pounding, I slung on my drum. Reggie did the same and together we ran after him. And what a different view we beheld.

The sweeping valley and the ridge beyond were almost totally obscured with thick smoke that drifted in great palls, almost hiding the Grand Battery from view. Only the occasional flash was visible through the small gaps that appeared in the dense clouds. Just below us, the Dutch troops holding that part of the line had been almost destroyed by artillery grapeshot, the huddles of prone, blue-uniformed bodies dotting the slope. By the rate of fire coming from the farmhouse itself and the orchard beyond it, it was obvious that the King's German Legion was putting up a stiff resistance. Sporadic shooting was also coming from the sandpit opposite, where the 95th Rifles were holding out. I hoped Tanner, Jarvis and Craven were still alive in spite of the numbers of blue-coated infantry that were swarming all around. The battalions nearby had been battered furiously. There was little sense of organisation among the surviving clusters of shaken soldiers wandering aimlessly on the slope as most of their officers had been killed or injured by sniping voltigeurs, light infantry who specialised in skirmishing.

The sound of the cannon on that side of the ridge was deafening, with crack following crack, splitting the air. Being in an exposed position now, Reggie and I instinctively bobbed, the redcoat word for getting your head down, although a group of senior officers who had dismounted to observe the enemy's progress didn't. Because of their rank, they were expected to set an example of courage to the men by standing unflinchingly in the face of whatever came their way, be it cannonball, shell or musket fire. And so they acted as if they were oblivious to the enemy fire. As for the common soldier, or even a newly-fledged corporal like me, it was acceptable to bob when being shot at. We weren't gentlemen, and right glad I was of that, too.

'They're shooting at us,' roared Reggie, as if it were sudden news to him. Crouching over, we scurried the short distance to Captain Hare. He was with a green-jacketed officer who smiled a welcome at us and said something in accented English. We straightened up and remembered to salute despite the noise and confusion. Hare had to shout to make himself heard.

'Corporal, the Hanoverians have lost their drummers so you two are being temporarily reassigned. Go with the Lieutenant.'

36

'La Haye Sainte,' the Lieutenant shouted, as we ran the short distance along the battered ridge to the crossroads above the farmhouse. 'That's where we're going but first we must get to the battalion.'

My mind was in turmoil, not from the thought of going into action at last but because we would be doing it with foreign troops whom we didn't know. The Lieutenant was German, from a Hanoverian Light Battalion on the right flank of the exposed slope taking sporadic shots from the Grand Battery. As we headed over to it, we caught glimpses of the French infantry still grinding their way up towards us through the smoke rolling up the valley. Fanned out in front of them were their voltigeurs, running ahead of the column; all smaller men, it was their job to disrupt our lines by picking off our officers and NCOs who were easily identifiable by their distinctive uniforms and bright sashes on the battlefield.

A bullet whistled past my head as we ran beside the Lieutenant and I bobbed again instinctively. The skirmishers had obviously spotted him and were trying to hit him. Then it dawned on me. I was a target too. McNeilis was right. He said that drummers were the peacocks of the battlefield but there was a price to be paid for the fancy uniform. I ducked lower beside Reggie as we ran and quickly completed the distance to the Hanoverians.

They had suffered several casualties already including their drummers whose broken bodies and shattered instruments we stepped over. They both looked younger than me, their lives ended before they even got started. Probably, like me, all they wanted to do was play the drum but the hold they had on life was as fragile as the instruments they played. However, there was no time to dwell on that. The Hanoverians had lost their drummers and Reggie and I would have step into their place. We'd beat for them. We'd take them where they had to go. We were Skins. I stopped bobbing then.

Their NCOs were busy forming the rest of the green-jacketed soldiers into line in preparation for advancing. I scowled at their captain when we met him, making no attempt at hiding my displeasure at being detached from the 27th. He greeted us in German first, then immediately switched to English when he heard we were Inniskillings. Shaking our hands warmly, he cupped his hands and shouted to us that he had once been stationed in Tullamore in 1806 and he hoped to survive the day to go back there and maybe we'd talk after the battle. He then indicated where he wanted us to stand in his assault line. We took up our positions and readied our drums.

On the exposed side of the slope where we stood, the air continued to crack with the thunderous roar of artillery, both ours and theirs, hurting our ears and making our legs shake. Through sporadic gaps in the smoke, the sharp-eyed French artillerymen had spotted the long, inviting line of exposed Hanoverians readying to advance because they aimed a few more ranging shots at our position. Their gunners then began to skim roundshot on the incline so that they would bounce and smash straight into the Hanoverian lines. A single shell fizzed right over our heads and exploded beyond the crest. Then a section of the Grand Battery opened up on us. Nobody could doubt the courage of the young Germans as they stood in the face of such murderous fire both from the cannon opposite and from the voltigeurs who had advanced along the side of La Haye Sainte and approached within effective range of our position. Yet another ball whistled out of the smoke, bounced forward and cut a file of five men in half. The soldiers on either side drew back at first, a natural reaction, then closed ranks over the bodies of the dead, hiding them.

A great roar came from deep within the body of men, building up as the whole battalion joined in, like a giant animal straining at the leash, waiting to be let loose. Still, they held their line. Reggie and I stood poised to drum them forward but the captain didn't give the order to advance. So we waited and took some more casualties. A troop of Hussars suddenly charged into sight and made straight for the voltigeurs who scattered before them. There was a brief lull as the Hussars withdrew.

During that short delay, Wellington himself appeared below us, further down the slope, trying to get a better view of the French advance. He had gone through a gap in a tall hedgerow accompanied by a few of his senior staff, when a few of the voltigeurs reappeared and spotted him.

They rushed forward and opened fire. Turning swiftly, the Duke and his small party barely managed to escape unscathed back through the same tight hole in the hedge. The last officer through had his horse shot from under him but managed to bolt on foot, leaving the wounded animal behind. The skirmishers broke through the hedgerow in pursuit of the retreating Duke. Just one lucky shot, they must have thought, and the battle would be over. Seeing the danger to Wellington, a company of the King's German Legion across from our position advanced down the slope at a swift pace, their officer charging ahead on horseback. The skirmishers again scattered at their approach, escaping through any small gaps they could find. That's when I noticed the French drummer for the first time.

He had accompanied the voltigeurs forward and, on seeing the KGL charge, had turned with his fellows and tried to escape. He jumped over a shallow ditch and then, swivelling his drum around onto his back, tried to scramble through a clump of thick brambles. Impeded by the bulk of his drum, he was held fast. I felt a pang of concern for him possibly because, as a drummer, he was a sort of kindred spirit, like the dead German drummers whose places we were taking. I watched with interest to see what would happen. The KGL officer spotted him and spurred his horse on. The French drummer tried to squirm free but the brambles were like so many talons holding him fast. Just as the KGL officer leaned over to grab hold of him, a Cuirassier burst through the hedge and struck him on the head with the flat of his heavy sword. The German fell off his horse, either unconscious or dead. The

Cuirassier then slashed at the brambles until the French drummer shrugged himself free. Then, hugging his instrument, he ran beside the cavalryman back towards his own lines, holding on to the stirrup, until I lost sight of him in the confusion. Meanwhile, the Duke cantered back up the slope, unflustered by his near escape. The rest of the KGL infantry returned to their position in the line, bringing their unconscious officer with them, fortunate to have survived the skirmishers. The whole episode had taken maybe sixty seconds.

Suddenly, the Hanoverian captain was shouting at us, 'Drummers, sound The Advance!' My heart hammered louder than ever before. Finally, the moment had come.

'Good luck,' Reggie mouthed at me, touching his forehead with his stick. I returned the salute and we started to drum.

Just two hundred metres to march to La Haye Sainte.

The long ranks of green uniforms moved forward as one, setting out at Ordinary Time, seventy-five paces to the minute, exactly as we had practised countless times while drilling with the 27th on the lush fields of Fermanagh. How extraordinary to think that two Irishmen were drumming a Hanoverian battalion across Belgian fields to join the King's German Legion fighting the French.

That thought only lasted a second. There's nothing like the sound of a 12- or 9-pounder cannonball flying over your head to keep you focused. With shot of that size, you can actually see them coming at you, a tiny black dot travelling so quickly that it has passed you even before you hear the hissing sound they make. The eye also conspires against you, fooling you into thinking that every one of them is heading straight for you. It takes a brave man not to flinch under fire, and I tried to stand tall. Added to that, when you're in line, shoulder to shoulder with the man on either side of you, with the next rank following in close order one pace behind, you can't slow down or the soldier coming hard on your heels would give you the butt of his musket or a prod of his bayonet. You just had to keep going. This is the kind of determination that Ned Kennedy had built into us. Now, going into battle, the relentless beating of our drums called upon those young Hanoverians to follow us. And they did, to a man. They were courageous, I give them that. They advanced in an ominous silence, their earlier roar of defiance replaced by an implacable desire to get at their tormentors and make them pay.

We marched in the front rank beside the officers, keeping perfect time for the Hanoverians, advancing at a regular, mechanical pace, slithering and skidding our way at an angle down the slope heading towards La Haye Sainte. I prayed that our unhurried descent wouldn't result in too many casualties. My uniform clung to my body as cold sweat seeped from every pore. With a huge effort of will, I controlled my terror and concentrated on my drum, feeling the familiar spring in the calfskin with each beat, letting the vibrations go up my arm, doing it over and over, blanking everything else out.

One hundred metres to go.

It seemed like time was standing still. But already we were half way there. There was so much smoke around us it was impossible to see what exactly was happening at La

Haye Sainte but nothing was going to prevent us from getting there. Bullets sought us out, hitting and felling a man every few seconds. Then the awful shouts came time and again from the sergeants. 'Close up! Close up!' For every man that dropped out of the line, another would instantly step forward from the rank behind to take his place. Each gap had to be closed, and fast. The green wall stayed firm. And still we drummed. There was no stopping for any reason. Every French bastard artilleryman was aiming at us, blasting at us. And every cursed voltigeur was shooting at me. But we just kept those brave Hanoverians marching. Our training had taken over. We were mechanical men keeping a steady beat, exactly seventy-five steps to the minute, Reggie and I controlling the advance, our heads empty of all thought other than to beat that drum, making Ned Kennedy proud of us, every tap on the calfskin taking us closer to the enemy. Our progress was relentless, like clockwork, our sticks doing the tick-tocking.

Fifty metres to go.

The Hanoverian captain signalled to us and we changed instantly to Quick March, upping the tempo to one hundred and eight paces to the minute, the soft ground and collapsed crop deadening the tramp of stamping feet, our drumsticks a blur in our aching hands, the sweat that we couldn't wipe streaming down our faces. We stepped over bodies. On bodies. Dead, dying, wounded, it didn't matter. Just get there alive. The sergeants were hoarse by then, still calling out for the ranks to 'Close up', their voices nearly lost in the great din of the fighting around the walled farmhouse that we were approaching.

Suddenly, Reggie skipped a beat. So unlike him to do that. I glanced sideways to tell him to keep with me and, oh, Sweet God, his left arm was gone from the shoulder down. I can still see him drumming one-handed. What little jagged bone he had left protruded from his torn sleeve, a tangle of shredded muscle swayed and his ruptured veins dripped blood. My uniform was sprayed with shards of his bone and blood too. He never screamed, not a sound, just gritted his teeth and clenched up his body. He never looked at me either. He just marched on, hitting his drum with the one remaining stick. Two steps. Three steps. Five steps, he managed. Then he twirled slowly and I lost sight of him as he fell and the green wall walked over him and swallowed him up and he was gone. I had to keep moving. My stomach heaved and I nearly vomited all over the drum that was gently rising and falling on my knee with every step I took. And I beat that calfskin for all I was worth. You fucking savage, Burns, keep going, I screamed to myself. Just keep the fucking Hanoverians moving.

'Close up!' the sergeant bawled again.

But there was no one to step up to take Reggie's place. I drummed on alone, taking those men to Hell.

37

We were almost at La Haye Sainte by the time the Hanoverian captain finally signalled the charge. Oh, the blessed relief of that moment, and the freedom to move without restriction that it brought. A howling, green-jacketed horde of men, crazed with pent-up frustration and bloodlust, their bayonets to the fore, rapidly overtook me. My drum had done its job. It had brought them to the point of battle and could do no more. It must have been just then that a bullet tugged at my sleeve and, almost at the same moment, I felt a jolt in my left heel. I hobbled, and lost my balance. A green jacket grabbed me by my shoulder, saving me from falling. He pulled me along for a few steps, my drum awkward on my hip, until I got going again. 'I'm okay,' I said, steadying myself. He seemed to have understood as he let me go and raced on with other quarry in mind. I limped the next few steps and the fog and chaos embraced me. Looming high in front of me were the walls of La Haye Sainte.

The Hanoverians had maintained their mad charge, taking the French at the front of the farm by surprise. Their attention had been on firing up at the loopholes in the wall as we arrived and the Germans were on them before they realised what was happening, savagely cutting them down. A few survivors bolted, trying to escape by running around the side walls but the Hanoverians chased them quickly, veering both left and right, smashing into the French who also swarmed there. The fight was short and brutal as the green jackets tore into them and, with renewed firing coming from the defenders on the walls, the French were forced to give way. Slowly, they fell back with the Hanoverians continuing after them, harrying them as far as the orchard. I hobbled along, lurching in their wake, their momentum carrying me with them.

Through a clearing in the smoke, I noticed a pocket of green-jacketed soldiers already there, firing frantically at the French from the far side of the perimeter hedge. The enemy, caught in a blistering crossfire, turned on their pursuers in large numbers, jabbing with their bayonets and swords, cutting, slashing and stabbing. The attack didn't last long as the second wave of the Hanoverian battalion arrived, forcing the French to retreat and leaving us in charge of the orchard. The firing died down and at last we could draw breath. The KGL defenders from within and the Hanoverians outside raised a great cheer at their success, calling out in derision to their enemy. But the cheers died away as the smoke briefly lifted and bodies could be seen everywhere, lying in the contorted positions of sudden death. Any blue uniform that still moved was quickly dispatched with a bayonet. One green-jacketed soldier systematically moved among the prone figures on the ground, prodding each French body in turn with his bayonet, making sure that none was trying to escape by pretending to be dead. The Germans had taken horrendous punishment while standing on the ridge; now it was time for retribution, and they exacted it with vengeance.

The lull didn't last long as the next assault began. Drums announced the arrival of another French infantry column coming straight out of the smoke, heading for La Haye Sainte. Most of the Hanoverians raced for the cover of the orchard hedge and prepared to defend it. I dithered, wondering where to go. Then, through all the noise and chaos, I heard my name being called. A green jacket, darker than that of the Germans, was waving at me from behind a low wall across the road from the orchard. It was Tanner of the 95th Rifles. Awkwardly, I ran across the corpse-strewn road and cleared the wall, landing in a heap with my drum. He pulled me up with a cheery grin but there was no time to talk. The French were almost upon us again.

The remaining Hanoverians jumped over the wall as well, scattering among the 95th, eager to join in the fight. The shooting began immediately, and there was no shortage of targets. I slouched beside Tanner in the middle of a row of riflemen, panting. He gave a wild yell and punched me by way of saying hello. His face was blackened with gunpowder and streaked with sweat, his braided jacket was filthy but he was unhurt. He pointed to his bugle and gave me a thumbs up. It was dented where it had stopped a bullet. He had been lucky. Maybe Jarvis and Craven hadn't been so fortunate. There was no time to ask. I quickly examined my foot. No sign of an injury. Just the heel of my boot had been shot off, the cause of my hobbling. Tanner saw me eyeing my ruined footwear.

'Damn,' I shouted at him, 'they were a good pair.' The incongruity of being concerned only for my boots while in the thick of a vicious fight never struck me. Tanner frantically continued reloading for a 95th Rifleman beside him.

He shouted back. 'You'll find another pair soon,' and he indicated over the wall. The Rifleman grabbed the reloaded weapon and threw Tanner the one he had just fired. Someone flung himself down beside me and gave me a thump. It was another Rifleman with a crazed look on his face. He pointed. I understood. Crawling quickly over to a dead green jacket, I retrieved his rifle and cartridge pouch and desperately began to reload it.

I paired with that soldier as Tanner did with his, me reloading and him firing, our heads lost in a pall of dirty, grey smoke every time he pulled the trigger. We worked together until that cartridge pouch was empty. Then Tanner threw me another. I sat in the shelter of that wall and kept reloading until my finger tips were raw and bleeding from handling the hot metal of the rifles. I thought I would have to do it forever. I peeked over once or twice to scan what was happening beyond. The French column had nearly passed us by heading for our ridge. They were tormented all the way by a deadly hail of bullets sniping into its flank from the combined defenders of the orchard and the farm. The huge mass of the column was an unmissable and irresistible target. Only the flank infantry facing us were able to shoot back but, once they had fired, they couldn't reload due to the press of ranks coming on behind. They doggedly kept going, absorbing our fire with terrible casualties. When the huge phalanx of men had eventually gone by, they left a long trail of dead and wounded in their wake. The 95th marksmen were expert with the Baker Rifle and it seemed that the Hanoverians were fairly handy too.

A lull came in the action at last and we breathed a sigh of relief at still being alive. In that brief interlude the screams of men in agony could be heard. There was nothing we could do for them. My broken boot was annoying me so I nudged Tanner and indicated my intent. He nodded as he slugged from his canteen, baring teeth blackened from continuous biting on cartridges, and again gave me the thumbs up.

'Jarvis? Craven?' I asked, not having the energy to formulate a sentence.

'Gone,' he replied. There was no emotion in his voice. 'Reggie?' he asked.

I shook my head; no words would come. He said nothing either, just put his hand on my shoulder in commiseration. I squirmed up and slithered over the wall and saw that I wasn't the only one intent on looting the dead and wounded. Some green jackets were already kneeling over fallen Frenchmen, going through their pockets as well as feeling their cuffs and hems, knowing that coins or small valuables could be hidden there. They weren't wasting any time either, flitting among the bodies. A few times, I saw the flash of a knife and turned away. All I was interested in was a pair of boots so I continued ducking from corpse to corpse examining their footwear.

It seems unthinkable that I would consider plundering the dead with such ease at a time like that but I was beyond human feeling by then. I continued my search until I found what I wanted, a fine pair of almost-new, leather boots, caked in drying mud. As I deftly removed them, I avoided looking directly at the bloodied face of my dead benefactor or at his almost-severed arm but I did pat his shoulder by way of saying 'thank you'. I scurried back to the protection of the low wall and rolled over it.

No sooner had I pulled on my new boots than sporadic firing began again from the direction of the French lines. The volume of musketry quickly increased as a fresh column of blue-uniformed infantry approached intending to give us a wide berth. With wild enthusiasm, a large number of Hanoverians leapt from the cover of the orchard hedge and formed a skirmishing line, firing as they ran. Within seconds, through gaps in the dense smoke, I saw another full column of enemy infantry advancing directly on our position, with a screen of voltigeurs out in front. The French seemed determined on taking the orchard and La Haye Sainte with the numbers they were committing. Through the haze, I spotted cannon and artillerymen as well. Quickly, they sited the guns and set to loading. We were going to be obliterated. Suddenly, shards of jagged stone and hot metal flew through the air as canister shot was poured in upon us.

The Hanoverians who had left the cover of the orchard wall were so engrossed in chasing the French column and firing at its rear ranks that they hadn't noticed this new threat even when the cannon opened fire. They were in danger of being cut off and annihilated. But their captain had also spotted their predicament. He suddenly appeared beside me out of the smoke, shouting, 'Corporal, get over there and beat The Withdraw. Quick, man, before they're slaughtered.'

I dropped the rifle I was reloading, slung on my drum and raced off, bent almost double. I got to the corner of the orchard and, thinking that my drumming wouldn't be heard with all the noise, I hopped up on a large pile of firewood in order to be seen as well. Oblivious to the risk I was running, I frantically began to drum. As if in response, to my absolute surprise, the sounds of battle ebbed away and the French attack evaporated. I peered through the smoke but the entire advancing column had disappeared as had the artillery. For the first time since the action started, I could actually hear my own drumming clearly as all the other sounds of battle receded into the distance. The Hanoverians had ceased firing and stood up, as puzzled by the vanishing French as I was.

Something made me glance towards the enemy lines just as a break came in the smoke.

From my more elevated position, I saw the wide tranche of trampled corn, flattened by the feet of the French columns as they had passed. Beyond that, dropping into a slight dip in the ground, the corn crop was still standing proud, as yet, untouched, for no column had marched that way. It wasn't the corn, though, that made me gasp. It was the sight of approaching cavalry, hundreds of them, their horses gliding silently through the tall stalks as if they were floating on a sea of green. I could see no movement of the horses' legs, just their steady, silent, dreamlike advance, with only the head and upper portion of each horse and rider visible. The sun shone down on burnished helmets with trailing black horse-hair plumes, matching the glistening silver of their breast armour and the striking blue of their uniforms. Cuirassiers! I stared in awe at the extraordinary sight, my hands suspended over the drum. As I beheld them, the troopers spurred their horses from walk to trot, closing on the still unsuspecting Hanoverians. Although the advancing horsemen wouldn't see them until they came out of the hollow, they were about to find what every cavalryman dreamed of, infantry caught in the open.

I snapped out of my trance and found my voice. I roared a warning. There was no longer any point in beating The Withdraw. Only one formation would save them. Infantry under attack by cavalry should defend themselves by forming square. Once formed in square in four ranks deep, with the bayonets effectively creating a porcupine defence, it would be virtually impregnable to everything except artillery. But even as I started to drum Form Square, it was already too late. The pile of wood on which I was standing started to crumble with the thunder of mighty hooves as the big horses eased into a canter, building up speed. The exposed Hanoverians felt it too and looked around, alarmed, my drumming unheard. Suddenly, a bow wave of armoured Cuirassiers burst from the field of standing corn, rose out of the dip, building up speed all the time and, at last, the Hanoverians saw the danger they were in.

Nothing is as frightening to scattered infantry as a charge by heavy cavalry yelling in full voice. Knee to knee, the Cuirassiers urged their huge mounts on, drawing their long, straight swords as they did so. The young soldiers panicked, then broke and ran, making for the safety of the walls of La Haye Sainte. It was the wrong decision. Had they heard my drumming and formed square, maybe more of them might have survived but the deafening sound of the charging hooves drowned out everything, including their own fearful screams. The Hanoverians' only chance of survival was gone.

38

Only a few brave men stood and fired their muskets before turning to run, obviously hoping to make it back to the ridge. The Cuirassiers charged down the fleeing soldiers, using the heavy bodies of their horses to bowl them over before slicing down at them as they lay on the ground. It was impossible for Hanoverians to avoid injury by throwing themselves flat as the heavy cavalry swords were long enough to reach them. Men screamed as the Cuirassiers stomped around in the grey smoke seeking new victims for their broad blades. No wounded man was left alive that I could see, the French showing no mercy to any green jacket they came across. How they missed seeing me I'll never know. I had hopped down off the wood pile as the cavalry broke into their charge and crouched behind some scraggy bushes, my arms wrapped around my drum as if to protect it, or it to protect me, I don't know which. I watched as the brave Hanoverian captain tried to rally some stragglers into a hive, the small circle with outward-pointing bayonets that would offer some hope of being able to resist, but to no avail. Even raw and unseasoned recruits might be able to fend off cavalry if they could hive in time but the young green jackets were in a sheer panic, incapable of any defensive organisation. Most of them were cut down by the prancing cavalry, their bodies trampled in the melee.

The captain managed to fend off a Cuirassier, stabbing him in the thigh with his sword, and broke loose with a few survivors. They started the long run back towards the ridge, heading past La Haye Sainte, closely pursued by yelling horsemen. The defenders within the farm fired from the walls, managing to bring down a few cavalrymen but the bulk of the Cuirassiers continued their charge. They slashed at the fleeing Hanoverians all the way up the slope to our lines until the few surviving green jackets, including their captain, slid in under the bayonets of a KGL battalion that had formed square. The KGL volley-fired, bringing down some of the horsemen. The rest quickly withdrew.

I must have been in a state of shock while this was going on but when the French artillery resumed their business in our direction, I came to my senses. I was all alone in a dangerous position and, as the Hanoverian battalion had been all but destroyed, I needed either to get inside La Haye Sainte or else make it back to the ridge and rejoin the 27th. Neither prospect offered any hope but I certainly couldn't remain where I was.

I eased up and moved away from the scrub that had hidden me. I hadn't gone far when there was a loud snort behind me. I turned in fright. A French Lancer! He had appeared as if from nowhere. With a triumphant yell, he lowered his lance. His horse reared and leapt into a charge. I was frozen to the spot, caught in the open. Suddenly, a volley of musket fire thundered from the smoke-obscured walls of La Haye Sainte. Lancer and horse were bowled over as several, well-aimed shots struck home. There was a loud cheer as horse and man hit the ground. I ran over but the enemy was already dead, the side of his head shattered where a well-aimed musket ball had hit him. His horse lay twitching, its flank a mass of gaping wounds. I pulled one of the Lancer's pistols from its saddle holster, checked that it was loaded, and stuffed it into my belt, thinking it might be of use should I meet another cavalryman. The smoke cleared sufficiently and I saw the KGL soldiers who had saved me. I saluted them in gratitude. They called out to me, pointing to a large loophole cut in the wall. I thought I could manage to reach it by standing on the pile of corpses directly under it.

As I was gauging my chances of squeezing through unscathed, a bullet flew past my head. Then another. I spun around to see a line of voltigeurs approaching. I ran for my life, the drum bouncing at my side, trying to dodge their best efforts. I headed away from La Haye Sainte and the orchard, seeking the cover of the tall crops. More bullets whistled around me. The KGL opened fire on the voltigeurs, distracting them. I kept going, leaping over the slashed bodies of the dead Hanoverians until I was at the edge of the hollow from which the Cuirassiers had emerged. I glanced back, panting. La Haye Sainte had disappeared again in a cloud of smoke under a renewed assault. All hope of finding sanctuary there was gone.

I moved further into the tall corn in search of better shelter. I proceeded cautiously, knowing that enemy cavalry or infantry could pass back that way as they retreated from the attack on our lines. It would take just one more trooper to spot me and I wouldn't have a chance. I crouched down among the corn and, after some time, turned what I thought was a half-circle and headed back towards our lines. How I wished I had Reggie with me. With him, I knew I'd have a better chance of survival.

All this time, I had been ignoring the cannonballs that streaked overhead in both directions. They were no threat to me as long as I stayed in the middle of the battlefield, the lowest part of the valley. I ran on, alert for any danger, my drum thumping awkwardly against my thigh. I thought I heard voices approaching so I paused for a few seconds to hear who they were. Then a horse whinnied and someone called out in French. There was a burst of laughter. I scurried away, praying that they hadn't seen me for I knew only too well that I could expect no mercy if they found me. I crept stealthily through the stalks of corn until I was beyond the cavalry. Only then did I sit down to take a short rest. Being parched, I reached for my canteen and, forgetting it contained brandy, had swallowed a mouthful before realising it wasn't water. The neat spirit made me gag but luckily there was nobody near enough to hear me over the din. I stayed hunkered down wondering what to do next.

The booming of artillery was coming from every side so I really had no idea in which direction I should go. Totally disorientated and driven mad by the noise of the guns, I cowered in terror. But things got worse for me then. Over the roar of the cannon came the sound of bugles and trumpets. Then massed drums joined in. The *Pas de Charges*! And even louder than the din of battle came the sound of thousands of voices shouting *'Vive l'Empereur!'* The French were coming again and were bound to discover me. They'd crush me underfoot without having to fire a shot. Coughing and choking, I made off in a blind panic. I'm not ashamed to admit it. I ran, terrified out of my wits, and I didn't stop until I came to a small clearing in the corn and descended into a hollow. Immediately my boots sank into the muddy slime at the bottom slowing me down. That short delay dragging myself through the sludge led to my undoing but things that initially seem trivial can have unexpected consequences. Had I cleared the hollow a few seconds earlier, I'd have been long gone and none of the things that happened after that would ever have occurred.

As I rose out of the dip, I glanced around quickly. Nothing stirred in the tall corn but the rattle of musketry some distance away and the cheers of the oncoming French continued unabated. No sooner had I taken my first step than something sizzled past my right leg and disappeared on to scythe a narrow line in the thick corn stalks. There was an instant smell of burning cloth as my leg suddenly gave under me, and I crumpled.

Fuck! I'd been hit. The pain was instant and fierce, worse than anything I had ever felt before. I clutched at my drum as I fell, rolling back down almost to the bottom of the hollow. I lay still for a few moments, looking up at the sky, as the shock drove home. I tried to stay focused but the pain drove me mad and I screamed. It felt as if someone had taken hold of my right leg above the ankle and twisted it back behind the knee and left it there. I panted for breath as tears blurred my vision. Then I leaned over and puked. I must have blacked out for a while because I remember coming to, wondering where I was and what had happened. The pain in my leg was excruciating, I stank of vomit and the back of my uniform was wet under me. For a split second, I thought I was lying in my own blood but when I felt with my fingers, I saw that they were merely wet. I was relieved at that but I knew I had to move. I raised myself on my elbows and painstakingly hauled myself on my back out of the wettest part of the dip, pushing with my left leg until I felt more solid ground underneath. The pain was piercing but I gritted my teeth and stuck at it, dragging the drum with me until the back of my head hit something solid. It was a low, moss-covered stump. Gathering myself for one last effort, I pushed back once more and managed to prop myself up using the stump as a support. This took the last bit of strength out of me. There I lay with my canteen half under my torso and my short sword doubled-back poking into my shoulder, the Lancer's pistol still snagged in my belt and my drum on its side. I had to think how to make my position more comfortable.

I shifted the sword first, then lifted the canteen out, taking a tiny swig of the brandy as I did so, the burning taste welcome this time. The pistol had mud on the barrel so I didn't know if it would fire or not. I placed it on the grass at my side. Gritting my teeth against the pain, I propped the drum on my chest and turned it around, examining it. It was a sorry-looking instrument by then. I wiped the regimental crest with my cuff and tapped the calfskin top. Miraculously it had survived being damaged but I was in a much worse state. I looked down at my sore leg and saw that the cloth had been singed on the outside of my shin exactly where my leg hurt. I looked away quickly. Sweat dripped into my eyes so I took my shako off. It had a dent on one side and the cords at the front had come loose. I scuffed dirt off the badge and the sight of the castle reminded me of how far away from Enniskillen I was at that moment. An image of my mother flashed into my head but I banished it straight away thinking that she wouldn't want to see me in this sorry state. I didn't feel much like a soldier then.

Rolling the drum to one side, I felt for the sticks on my cross belt. Both were intact. The fall hadn't broken them. I looked around in desperation, straining to hear if there was anybody nearby who could come and help me. Unbelievably, I had managed the impossible. With all the thousands of men around me in the middle of a great battlefield, I had found a place to be quite alone.

In spite of the agony, I remember a feeling of calm coming over me when the first sense of panic had worn off and I began to take stock of my situation. The sound of the guns resumed again, both artillery and musketry, as thick, acrid smoke spiralled around above the hollow, drifting down to where I lay, stinging my eyes. I knew the injury to my leg was severe and I feared for my life. When Felton had taken Patrick Magee's leg off, the shock of the amputation killed him. I wondered if the same fate lay in store for me, if I ever got as far as a surgeon's table. At any rate, when I looked again, it was a relief to see two boots. Whatever injury I had suffered, I still had both my lower limbs even if they were lying at a slightly unusual angle to each other.

After resting for a bit, I reached forward and felt as far as my knee. All was intact. I tried to move my injured leg but was pulled up short by a stab of hot pain. I reached down and lifted a flap of torn material out of the way. There was a swelling below the knee, and a bit of bruising, but there was no soggy feel of blood and still no stain of red on the grey trousers. That was a good sign. At least I wasn't going to bleed to death. I leaned back to think what I should do. Biting my lip to fight the pain, I backed up more against the tree stump. The effort exhausted me but I was more in command of my situation then. I must have lost consciousness again, for how long I don't know.

When I opened my eyes I became aware of movement at the top of the hollow across from me. A soldier became visible in the grey smoke framed by the tall corn behind him, a drummer by the elaborate cut of his uniform. It had to be Reggie, come to find me. Good old Reggie!

39

Of course it wasn't Reggie. How could it have been? Hadn't I seen him lose an arm and then fall on the way down to La Haye Sainte. My mind was just playing tricks on me. I closed my eyes and breathed deeply before looking at the figure again. The light was behind him so I couldn't determine whether he was friend or foe. He stood there for a while and I knew he was observing me.

He may have been confused by my mud-spattered jacket as to what side I was on so I didn't move. There was nothing I could do to defend myself anyway. If I reached for the pistol, he'd be on me before I could lift it, pull back the cock, aim and shoot. Even then, it mightn't fire. I groaned as a sudden stab of pain hit me and I closed my eyes for a few seconds. Maybe that's what made him decide it was safe to approach me for I heard him slither down the slope and cautiously come nearer. I opened my eyes slightly to see if I could recognise the colour of his coat but my sight was blurred with a mixture of tears and sweat.

The newcomer straightened up, taking stock of me all the while, then drew something from his belt. He crept towards me, wary like an animal, with blackened face and taut lips. I blinked a couple of times and my vision cleared. The first thing I saw was the tip of a sword pointing towards me, held in an unwavering hand. Then, I looked beyond the sword to the uniform of the soldier who stood over me. Through the dirt and grime of battle, I saw that it was blue. Jesus, I was done for, I thought – he was French. I have no recollection of being afraid at that moment, just of accepting that, as I couldn't defend myself, I was going to die at this man's hand. With the combination of shock and pain that was taking its toll on my body, I was incapable of moving so I feigned unconsciousness, hoping that he'd leave me alone. My ruse didn't work. His sword nicked my neck, drawing blood. I wasn't going to die with my eyes closed so I opened them. The Frenchman was standing over me. He saw I was no threat to him and moved his sword to my throat. I didn't care. The pain in my leg was excruciating so let him kill me. That would end it.

'Stand up!'

I only half heard him at first so the words didn't register with me initially, nor did the fact that he was speaking in English. 'I said stand up,' he repeated. 'I challenge you to a duel.'

'I can't stand,' I wheezed. 'I think my leg is broken.'

'Then surrender. You are my prisoner.'

The Frenchman was crouching slightly, his sword held in front of him in a defensive stance. To my surprise, he wasn't much older than I was. I spotted the sticks in their slots on his broad belt, the same as where I carried mine.

'You're a drummer,' I said, my voice coming out in a sort of croak. He nodded. I tried to lever myself up on my elbows, the hard stump now uncomfortable at the back of my neck.

'Your English is good,' I said.

'I spoke English before I learned French,' he retorted. 'But that's not important. You heard me, do you surrender?'

'Of course I don't bloody surrender,' I replied with as much indignation as I could muster.

He reached down. Thinking he wanted to take my drum as a trophy, I tried to lean over and wrap my arms around it protectively.

'No, you French bastard,' I shouted, panting for breath. 'You can't have my drum.'

He laughed but there was no humour in it. 'I don't want your drum, English,' he said. 'I want to take you prisoner. Give me your sword.'

'No,' I said defiantly.

'Then you must accept the consequences. I have to prove myself to my captain so I either bring you in as a prisoner or I kill you here here and now.'

'Are you blind? You see I can't walk.' He looked frustrated at that. 'Why do you have to prove yourself anyway?' I asked curiously, thinking that a bit strange.

'Because I was nearly caught by your cavalry earlier,' he replied angrily, 'and I didn't fight back.'

An image flashed into my mind. 'It was you,' I blurted out, seeing again the French drummer caught in the hedge.

'What?'

'In the hedge. That KGL officer had you except the Cuirassier arrived to save you.'

'You saw me?' His face flushed with sudden anger. 'The whole battalion laughed at me when I came back. Called me a coward. Well, they won't laugh when they see that I can kill as well as they can.'

He straightened up and stuck his sword in the ground. His had a short blade, similar to my own. Then I noticed that he had his drum behind him. He took his drum belt off over his head and laid the instrument carefully on its base on a dry patch of ground. His regiment's number, the 55e *d'Infanterie de Ligne* and the eagle crest were prominently visible. He picked up his sword again and held it against my throat. Again I felt a dribble on my skin. For an instant, I saw Curley in front of me, his bayonet jabbing into my skin and his voice jeering me in the same manner.

'For the last time, Englishman, will you surrender?' I recall his arrogance as he said that. All kinds of thoughts raced through my head. Surrender? To a Frenchman? Since joining the Inniskillings, it had been impressed upon us that the 27th never backed down, no matter what. Giving up without a fight just wasn't an option. But what can you do when you're lying on your back with a fractured limb and an enemy standing over you with a short sword at your throat demanding your surrender? Suddenly, I was shouting. 'I accept your challenge, you bastard. And I'm fucking Irish, not English.'

The French drummer stepped back in surprise. 'I thought you weren't able to fight?' he asked, giving a mocking laugh. 'Okay, let's do it. Of course, you have choice of weapon. What will it be? Swords? Pistols?' He continued to chuckle at the stupidity of my acceptance.

But I wasn't stopping to think.

'Drums!' I shouted back at him. 'I choose drums.'

He looked at me blankly, and took a step back. 'That's ridiculous,' he retorted.

'No, it's not. You challenged me to a duel and I have accepted. I choose drums.'

'You're serious?' he asked incredulously.

'Yes, we'll drum in turns, you and me. The better drummer wins.'

'Okay, mad Irish. I accept but when we finish, I'm going to kill you anyway,' and he laughed. Obviously the notion amused him. 'Now, how will we do this since you cannot stand?'

It was easy to see why he sounded so confident but I had to continue with what I had started. I hadn't quite thought that far when I shouted out my acceptance. Maybe I should have. I began to regret my rash words but I couldn't let him see that.

40

'Help me up against the stump,' I said. 'I'll drum between my knees.'

That was another suggestion I regretted as soon as I had made it. I was little prepared for what came next. The absolute agony I felt as soon as he put his hands under my arms to haul me upright made me yell when my bad leg dragged on the grass. But at least I was at a better angle. He then unstrapped his knapsack and placed it under the broken limb, supporting it. The pain was excruciating at first, then it settled to a dull throb. I touched the tender spot but there was no feeling, just a severe swelling. I prayed that the break was a clean one and that I would somehow end up in Mostyn's hands for I had confidence in him to save my leg. But first I had to deal with the French drummer.

'If I'm going to fight you, we should at least exchange names,' I said.

'Christophe,' he replied. 'Yours?'

'James,' I said, then added, 'Look, let's agree to play fair. We'll both know which of us is the better drummer by the time we finish. Muted drums, agreed?'

'Agreed,' said the French drummer.

I scraped out a little of the soft ground between my legs to give myself a better playing angle. Christophe then placed my drum between my knees. I removed the sticks from my cross belt, took a deep breath, and I was as ready to drum-fight as I ever would be. The sounds of the great battle taking place beyond our little duelling arena faded away as I tapped a few muted beats to loosen up. He did likewise. It was our way of taking ten steps away from an opponent.

'I'll start,' he said.

The Frenchman began with a flourish, playing a medley of cadences that I presumed to be the French Order of the Day, their version of our Regulatory Calls. He warmed to his task, staring at me all the while, as his drumming increased in speed. He had learned the art well, I had to allow, but there is a difference in playing the drum as a musical instrument and playing the drum as if it's part of your body. I let him drum for a spell, listening to him carefully, watching his wrist and arm movements, assessing his ability. Had we been duelling for real, I imagined myself lowering my pistol and aiming, taking the measure of my opponent before opening fire. Abruptly he stopped, inviting me to pick up, and I began to drum. I didn't hurry myself. I eased into it slowly letting the muted rolls and paradiddles come out in a natural sequence while I hummed the tunes in my head. I imagined Ned Kennedy talking to me back at the drum school in the depot, urging me on. 'Fingers, wrists and elbows, lad. Love your drum. Every touch is a caress.' And I let myself go.

Christophe was impressed, I could see, but that simply

encouraged him to greater effort and, when he slipped in after a while and overlapped with me, his playing had dramatically improved. He began to stomp in a wide circle around me, exhaling loudly while he moved, pausing to glare angrily at me every now and then, as if every beat he played was a hard punch landing on my body. By then, I was so absorbed in our duel that I was oblivious to the pain in my leg and the great battle going on around us. Had Napoleon himself fired all of his Grand Battery just beyond the hollow, I doubt that I would have heard it. All I wanted to do was to destroy my enemy with my skill on the drum.

Then it was my turn to overlap and I took him through a lot of the music that Ned Kennedy had spent so much time teaching us. I pounded the calfskin, not just knocking down the walls of Jericho, but tearing that French drummer apart, there in that hollow. I became the savage drummer, the one that Hicks back in the depot always wanted me to be, the one that marched the Hanoverians to their deaths, hitting the dead centre of the calfskin every time, throwing in dramatic flourishes with my hands at such a speed that my movements were all a blur.

Not wanting to be outdone, Christophe took over again and produced a performance that showed how good a drummer he was. I began to admire his playing as his face contorted with the effort of concentration. Although I recognised some of his tunes from the rhythms he was producing, I let him drum on his own for a while. Then, to unnerve him, I began to hum the tunes he was playing, moving my hands as if conducting him. He didn't like that. I could see I had rattled him so, when he suddenly reverted to playing Old Trousers, our mocking name for the *Pas de Charge*, I knew he was working himself up to attack me when our little charade of a duel was over.

To frustrate him, I started to play Old Trousers on my drum too. So there we were, two mortal enemies, one an Irishman in the British Army and the other a Frenchman, both playing the *Pas de Charge* in perfect unison, every beat, every click, mirrored from one to the other. I don't think I ever beat my drum with more skill and, yes, more venom, than on that single occasion. I played for my mother and her sad life. For the father I never knew. For the honour of the regiment. For myself. Staring fiercely into each other's eyes, our mutual hatred was mirrored. But he, like me, was just a drummer. There was no time then to wonder at the sheer animosity that could be projected through the playing of an instrument. Yet I certainly felt it because I was drumming for my life and I was simply not going to give in. I was the devil himself on that drum, pouring every ounce of energy in my damaged body, every drop of blood in my veins, every beat of my heart, onto that calfskin.

It was Christophe who cracked first. He dropped a beat. He knew I had spotted it so I gave him a little mocking nod in acknowledgement. This enraged him even more. Abruptly, I changed tack, switching to some of the more formal, ceremonial tunes just to vary things. Christophe matched this change in tempo but, as I was now leading, I took him through a series of numbers we called the Sunrise Reveille. In effect, it was like playing a short concert and then throwing in a couple of rousing encores for good measure. I could see he was tiring quickly, and he lost the beat again. I had kept with him but he couldn't keep with me. I knew I had him. Christophe paused suddenly, sticks held in the air, timing his re-entry while I drummed magnificently on my own. He stayed with his sticks in the air as I increased the tempo still further. It must have hurt him to stop but he did, while I played on, gloriously, wishing Corporal Ned Kennedy and Drum Major Edward Hicks could see my triumph.

Christophe's hands dropped to his side as the sweat poured down his face and onto his chin. Then he abruptly crossed his sticks in front of me and lowered them. The French drummer conceded. I had won. However, the honour of the Inniskillings demanded that I finish with a grand display of my skills so I played The Drummer's Call, ending it with a dramatic, sustained roll before I, too, lowered my sticks. I was utterly exhausted from my exertions, far too tired even to enjoy my victory. Christophe stared at me, panting, his face and eyes blank, devoid of any emotion. I must have looked the same, breathless, and utterly spent. It was a long time before he spoke.

'All right, Irish,' Christophe said, eventually. 'It's over. You win.'

'Yes,' I agreed, 'I win. You can kill me now but you'll always know that I was the better drummer.'

He laid his drum on the grass and slowly stepped towards me, drawing his sword from its scabbard.

I placed my sticks carefully back in the slots on my belt and, for the first time since the Frenchman entered the hollow, I allowed myself to relax. I closed my eyes, feeling absolutely drained of all energy. Let him do whatever he wants, I thought. At least I hadn't surrendered. I had fought him the only way I could.

I tensed my body, waiting for the feel of the cold steel and the warm flow of blood, just as Curley must have done when I stabbed him.

41

But the blade didn't come. I opened my eyes to see Christophe still standing over me. There was no longer any trace of animosity in his expression. It's hard to explain after all these years but it was like two warriors who had exhausted themselves trying to kill each other only then to discover that they are like two sides of the same coin. In that moment, a spark of mutual respect was kindled. He was no longer my enemy. He was simply a drummer who happened to be on a different side.

I tried to move but my legs had stiffened during the drum duel. The dull pain returned, making me wince. Christophe edged closer to me, the sword still in his hand. I was sure he was going to kill me but instead he went down on one knee and started to slit my breeches from the ankle. I breathed more easily. Then, I watched in dismay as he cut through the leather sides of my new boot and flattened it out. He saw my expression of annoyance.

'I need to get at the break,' he said. 'I can fix it.' With his fingertips, he began to press along the swollen area. 'How did it happen?'

When I had calmed down a bit, I described to him how I had been about to leave the hollow when a cannonball flew by and my leg folded under me. As I talked, he continued to prod gingerly.

'Hold steady,' he said, 'this will hurt a bit.' I leaned back and stuffed the cuff of my tunic in my mouth to stop the scream. Feverishly, I panted for air but he didn't stop, just kept pressing and pressing. I know I cursed at him non-stop, calling him every name I could think of but that didn't deter him. 'Stay still,' he snapped again, as he continued to manipulate the two broken ends of bone back into alignment. Sweat rolled off my face as pain darted through me. I thought he'd never stop but at last he did.

'Good,' he said, leaning back. 'That part's done. Keep very still. I need splints and dressings, neither of which I have. You don't have anything, do you?'

'No,' I replied, thinking of McNeilis sagely telling me to buy lint and bandages back in Ghent, and I hadn't. 'I've nothing that would be useful.'

'Then we'll have to make do.'

Christophe picked up his sword again and quickly cut the calfskin top off his own drum. He had it done before I could say anything. Without a second thought, he had reduced his beautiful instrument to a useless, hollow shell. He saw my expression.

'Don't worry,' he said. 'I can get it fixed when the battle's over.' He untied the drum cords and cut them into lengths, then pulled the calfskin tight around the fracture and told me to hold it. Using his drumsticks as splints, he wound the lengths of rope around my leg and knotted them. It was a perfect example of medical improvisation on the battlefield. Christophe leaned back and admired his handiwork. I doubted even assistant surgeon Mostyn could do as good a job. He then loosely tied up the flaps of my ruined boot.

'There! That'll do until they get you to the surgeon,' he said.

'Thank you,' I said, grimacing with pain. I held out my canteen to him.

'It's okay, I have my own,' he said, reaching back for his flask.

'It's brandy,' I explained. 'French!'

He smiled. 'Well, in that case,' he said, taking a swig. He wiped his lips. 'That's good.'

'You ruined your drum,' I said.

'It was out of tune,' he replied, with a grin.

I took a small mouthful of the brandy. The spirit took the dull edge off the pain. Christophe leaned back as he took the canteen from me and glugged another mouthful.

'How does it feel now?'

'Like I could walk with Wellington to Paris.'

'It's not going to happen,' Christophe said. 'We're going to win here. You'll be walking to Brussels as a prisoner. It's only a matter of time before we break your line and then you'll lose. At least you'll go home alive, though,' he added.

'That's more than can be said for Reggie,' I retorted, quietly.

'Who's Reggie?'

'My friend, another drummer. He's dead.' And I found myself telling a total stranger about the day at The White Star crossroads when Reggie had first made me play a drum, only for it all to end on the way down to La Haye Sainte. He listened patiently, saying nothing. There was nothing he could say.

But our interlude was soon cut short as, beyond our hollow, the lull in the great battle ended and the brutal sound of the guns rose again. The sudden thunder of horses' hooves told us that cavalry were involved so we listened to the bugle calls.

'Ours,' declared Christophe. 'I have to go now,' and he reached back for his now-useless husk of a drum. He turned to me for a moment. 'No matter who wins this, we've all lost today,' he said.

At that moment, I realised the sheer pointlessness of it all. He was my enemy and we had sworn to kill each other simply because he wore a different uniform to mine yet, he had tended to me as meticulously as Mostyn would have done. It didn't make sense.

'You did a good job, Christophe,' I said. 'I still have my leg. Thank you.'

As he strapped on his knapsack, my curiosity returned and I felt compelled to ask him. 'Where did you learn to speak English?'

'From my father,' he replied. 'He was from Donegal.' Christophe saw my surprise. 'After 1798, my father came to Paris and joined the French army. He met my mother, stayed, and here I am.'

I was silent at that for a few moments, thinking of the extraordinary series of unpredictable events that had befallen both of us that day, struck by how different things could have been except that fate, or some other benign providence, had taken a hand. Christophe carefully fixed his useless instrument over his head and made ready to leave.

'How will you explain your drum?' I asked.

'I'll just tell the truth,' he replied simply. 'I won't be in the army forever. I want to be a surgeon.'

'I think you'll make a great one,' I said. 'If you ever come looking for your father's people, you'll find me in Enniskillen. I owe you.'

'I'll do that. Good luck, Irish,' he said, saluting.

'And good luck to you too, Half-Irish,' I replied.

Christophe nodded, then headed up the incline. At the rise he turned and saluted.

Just as the musket exploded behind me, deafening me.

42

The India Pattern Musket, the Brown Bess, has a thirty-nine inch barrel that fires a one-ounce lead ball over a nominally effective range of one-hundred yards. However, at that distance, three times out of four the average soldier will miss the target but, at twenty yards, he is almost guaranteed a devastating hit. That was roughly how far the ball had to travel from the muzzle of the firelock until it hit Christophe in the lower chest. He doubled over with the impact, a look of astonishment on his face, then crumpled to the ground and rolled halfway back down the hollow.

With a tremendous yell, a blue-uniformed soldier charged past me, bayonet extended at the end of his still-smoking musket. Christophe twisted awkwardly onto his back, impeded by his knapsack, his chest exposed, arms flung back. With a vicious downward lunge, the soldier's bayonet went right through the drummer's stomach, penetrating as far as the socket. He twisted it back and forth. I can still hear Christophe's screams as he gripped the barrel of the musket, trying to stop the torture. The suddenness and ferocity of the attack took me by such total surprise that, for a moment, I thought it was

Frenchman killing Frenchman, a terrible battlefield mistake. But then I noticed that it was the lighter blue uniform of the Dutch-Belgian militia, our allies.

'No!' I screamed, from where I lay, helpless to intervene. 'Don't do it!' But it was too late. The soldier put his muddy boot on Christophe's blood-soaked body and the bayonet came free. He gave another savage roar of triumph and then turned to me. I didn't recognise him at first, with his blackened, sweat-streaked face and his wild-eyed, exultant expression. But the voice was unchanged, coming at me through a waft of thick smoke.

'Hello again, Burns, you shit,' snarled ex-Captain George Benedict Baxter. 'So, we meet again.'

Stunned by his sudden reappearance, and by the brutal killing of Christophe, I was speechless for a moment before the rage kicked in.

'Bastard,' I shouted at him with every ounce of strength I could muster. I wanted to shred him for what he had just done. 'You didn't have to do that, you fucking murderer.'

'And what about you, Burns. Aren't you a fucking murderer too? I heard about Curley. That was you, I'm wagering. You've got away with everything so far, even got your stripes out of it too, but the piper has to be paid in the end, and this piper wants to be paid now.'

Baxter drew nearer to me as he said that, the musket held out threateningly, Christophe's blood dripping from the bayonet. My heart started to pound. Once again, I imagined the feel of the cold steel entering my body and, this time, it was really going to happen. Baxter wouldn't hold back, certainly not now.

'I saw the 27th arrive this morning and you with them. Since then, I've been following you, hoping to get you alone but I lost sight of you back at the orchard, when that Lancer missed his chance. And then there was all that cavalry charging back and forth, so I thought I'd never find you. But now, here you are.'

Baxter stood over me, brandishing the tip of the bayonet in my face. A drop of blood landed on my cheek.

'I was barred from joining another British regiment so I had to enlist in a useless Dutch-Belgian militia. It was either that or starve. All on account of you.' He spat at me. His boot pressed on my broken leg, the one that Christophe had so carefully tended. I screamed with agony and Baxter just smiled. In desperation, I felt for the Lancer's pistol but it wasn't there. My other hand was behind me, resting on the handle of my sword but there was no point in trying to use it. Baxter would have me skewered in a second.

'I'm enjoying this, Burns,' he said, 'aren't you?' He pressed harder on my leg. I gritted my teeth and a low moan escaped.

'That's the sound your father made too,' Baxter said, 'right before he died. You sounded exactly like him just then.'

For a moment I thought I had misheard. But he continued. 'Yes, Burns, the last face your father saw before he went to eternity was mine. And now it's going to be the same with you. Extraordinary coincidence, what? Like father, like son.'

He was relishing things now, toying with me before finishing me off. My mind was in consternation with what he had said. More than anything else, I wanted to know the truth about the allegation Baxter had made all those months ago about my father being a coward but I wasn't going to give him the satisfaction of asking. As it turned out, I didn't have to, Baxter wanted me to know.

'You thought I sent Curley after you for planting the watch on me. Well now, that was only a small part of it. You see, your father did something to me too. He took my woman, your mother. From me, an officer, and him just a bog-trotting private. Made me the laughing stock of the battalion. She never wanted me after she met him. So I waited my chance and got him in Flanders; gave it to him in the back. He died like a stuck pig. I made it look like he had been running away. That ruined his reputation in the regiment. But when I came home, even then your whore of a mother wouldn't have me. Instead she left the depot, taking you with her. And years later, to my great surprise, who's waiting for me when I return to the 27th? You! It amused me to let Curley make your life a misery. I'd still be enjoying it only you outsmarted me with the watch. But we'll put that to rights here and now, Burns. Maybe your mother'll be glad to have me when she finds out she has no brat to mind her in her old age, and that he died a coward's death as well.'

'Do your worst, you bastard,' I yelled, and stared him in the eyes. 'She'll never have you.'

Baxter raised the musket in a tight grip right over me. The bayonet, a triangular spike of iron, was poised to pierce my heart. From where I lay, the small point of the tip looked enormous. I prayed it would be quick. I tensed myself in terrible anticipation.

The sound of a sudden gunshot filled the hollow again. Baxter's mouth opened in shock. A choking gurgle came from him as blood dribbled down his chin. At the same time, a dark stain slowly spread on his blue jacket. The heavy musket fell from his grasp as his hands slowly went to his chest, his eyes boring into mine. I pulled my sword free and squirmed quickly to one side. Baxter's eyes glazed as he stiffened, then slowly pitched forward. I rammed the base of the handle into the ground with the blade directed upwards. Baxter landed straight on the point, the blade going right through him. I heard it click past his spine before protruding through the back of his uniform. Blood trickled from his mouth as he tried to prop himself on his hands but, instead, he rolled slowly to his side and lay facing me. His eyes were still open but I doubt that he could see anything. He grasped the handle with both hands and tried to pull it out but he had no strength. His throat rattled a few times as the spasms of approaching death passed through his body. He exhaled quietly once or twice and then he was still.

I propped myself up. Christophe was on his knees across from me, his head lolling, my Lancer's pistol still smoking in his hand. He slowly crumpled to one side and drew his legs up into his chest like a baby going to sleep.

'Christophe,' I shouted, and I started to crawl over to him. The agony in my leg was excruciating but I kept it stiff and straight and avoided putting any pressure on it. It took ages but I eventually got to him and managed to roll him on his back and then, it was my turn to tend to him. With one hand, I opened his tunic, unbuttoned his shirt and revealed his wounds. The musket ball had done ferocious damage to his chest, shattering the bone and tearing his insides apart. From the amount of blood underneath him, it must have passed right through him, leaving a gaping hole at his back. That wound alone would have finished him without the ferocious bayonet thrust to the stomach which had ripped his intestines open. His combined injuries were devastating. How he was still alive was beyond comprehension.

'Christophe,' I said again, not knowing if he heard me or not. He opened his eyes.

'Did I get him?' he asked.

'Yes,' I replied, my voice shaking, 'you got him. He landed on my sword. Shot and skewered.'

He put his hands on his stomach. 'Is it bad? I can't feel anything.'

'Yes,' I said, 'he got you rightly.'

Christophe shivered. 'I'm cold,' he said, his voice very low.

'I knew that bastard,' I said. 'His name was Baxter. It was me he was after, not you. He just couldn't resist an easy target first.'

Christophe tried a smile. 'Well, it was your pistol that got him,' he whispered. 'I took it from you. Didn't want you using it on me.'

'Actually, it was a Red Lancer's pistol. I thought it might come in useful, and it did.'

He tried to smile, then a sudden spasm wracked through his body. 'James, I think I'm dying,' he said, his voice fading.

'Yes, Christophe, I think you are,' I said. There was no point in lying.

'You saved my life,' I said. 'How can I thank you?'

'You can drum for me,' he wheezed.

'What?' I said, not comprehending what he wanted.

'Drum for me till I'm gone.' His voice was so low I could barely hear it, his eyes almost closed.

'Okay,' I choked, my soul in torment that I didn't get to do that for Reggie. Ignoring the pain, I crawled back to the stump, snagged my drum on my good leg and dragged it laboriously all the way back across to where Christophe lay. It took ages to do that short return journey, taking more out of me than the whole trip from the depot to Waterloo. I prayed every time I dug my elbows into the ground that he would be alive when I got back. Eventually I hauled myself alongside him and put my ear to his mouth. I was rewarded with the faintest rasp of his breathing. I thanked God he was still alive.

'I'm here, Christophe,' I said. 'Hold on a bit longer.' I slid the sticks from my belt, fighting back the choking sobs. For Reggie. For Christophe. For the father I never knew. I swallowed hard.

'Christophe,' I said, trying to rouse him.

His eyes flickered and he gave the faintest smile. 'I let you win,' he breathed.

'Rubbish!' I said, smiling back at him. 'I've kept my best drumming for now.'

I was still playing when they found me.

43

'He's dead, laddie. You can stop,' the Highlander kept saying but I didn't hear him at first. It wasn't until he caught me by the wrist and stayed my hand that I quit. How long I drummed for, I have no idea but I must have played every rhythm I knew, and then repeated them.

Slowly, my senses returned to me like one who was awakening from a long dream. My body was sore and stiff, my arms ached, my fingers were numb, my leg was throbbing and the tears had dried in my eyes.

'No point in drumming now, Corporal,' the Scot repeated. 'He can't hear you.'

I wiped my face with the back of my hand and took stock of who was talking to me. It was a sergeant from the 92nd Gordons, a couple of battle-weary, kilted Highlanders with him. I recollected myself and became a soldier again. I saluted and, momentarily forgetting about my leg, tried to stand but he held me down.

'Stay there, Corporal,' he said. 'Your leg is broken but you've been tended to, I see.'

I had to think for a moment. 'Yes, he fixed me,' I said, pointing. Remarkably, Christophe's features were peaceful now in spite of the brutal nature of his passing.

'He was a drummer.'

'And who's that?' the sergeant asked, pointing at Baxter's waxen body.

'No idea,' I lied. 'Some bastard Dutch-Belgian militia who was running away.'

'Useless scum,' said the sergeant.

'Is it over yet?' I asked, noticing that the noise of battle had almost ceased.

'Yes, but it was a close-run thing. Blücher's Prussians are here and the day is won. Our lads are advancing and the French are in full retreat.' He handed me a loaded pistol, then stuck Christophe's sword into my hand. 'The scavengers will be around as soon as it's dark. You'll need these to ward them off. Good luck, lad.'

I thanked the sergeant and they left. Slowly, the rattle of musket fire grew more sporadic with only the distant boom of an odd cannon reaching me every now and then. It wasn't until much later that I heard about the vengeful pursuit of the French by the Prussians but I had seen enough of killing that day. Long after darkness had fallen, I heard the last shot at Waterloo being fired and then an eerie silence descended. The chilly night air was heavy with the sickly scent of blood and the more earthy perfume of crushed vegetation now that the acrid smoke of battle had cleared away.

But the silence didn't last long. Other heart-breaking sounds rose all around me, reaching into my little sanctuary. The anguished sobs of wounded and dying men lying on the battlefield, calling for help in languages as varied as their once-magnificent uniforms, mingled with the horrific squeals of mutilated horses in their death agony. The constant sound of such distress from all around was torture to me and I tried in vain to block it out. What was left of the brandy numbed the pain in my leg but, lying in that God-forsaken place in Belgium, there was nothing that could numb my mind to the horrors of that day and night.

I was roused from my torpor by whispering voices just as dawn was about to break. Two spectral figures were outlined at the rim of the hollow carrying a glowing lantern. They were not soldiers, that much I knew straight away. I raised the pistol and shouted at them. They must have seen I was capable of resistance as they immediately withdrew in search of easier prey. And there was no shortage of it on the battlefield, I was sure.

When dawn came, a unit of 18th Hussars trotted by at the top of the hollow and I called out to them. A couple of troopers dismounted and came down to me. After that, events happened quickly. They alerted some tired redcoats from the 40th Regiment who were returning from their all-night pursuit of the French. Recognising my 27th Inniskillings uniform, they kindly agreed to carry me over to the ruins of La Haye Sainte. Next to a regiment's colours, the drum is its most valuable, symbolic representation so, when I asked the redcoats to carry Christophe's ruined 55*e* shell for me as a trophy, they willingly obliged. I bade a silent farewell to the French drummer as the redcoats carried me out of the hollow but I didn't even bestow a glance at Baxter's corpse. I was glad to leave that place of torment but the world into which I emerged was a vision of hell.

The havoc and destruction all around defied

description. Bodies lay everywhere, both injured and dead, animal and human, strewn across the rolling farmland as far as the eye could see. Many of them had already been stripped naked by looters during the night as they lay unguarded on the ground, their mouths gaping open with mutilated jaws devoid of teeth. I heard every imaginable sound humanly possible coming from the battlefield. The despairing cries for water of the wounded were interspersed with loud shouts of jubilation as men, hoarse from fighting, turned to hurrahing and cheering when they discovered a comrade who was still alive. Ambulance wagons loaded with wounded, their wheels rolling over the corpses, were trying to make their way off the battlefield. Women were there too, searching for a loved one, their pitiable cries becoming inconsolable when their quest ended with the discovery of a shattered body. Farriers stepped among the carnage, dispatching the wounded horses, a heart-breaking task for men who loved these wonderful animals. Some poor, stricken beasts were struggling to rise on broken hind legs or with gaping wounds to their bodies, but a blow of a farrier's hammer soon ended their agony. As far as I could see, all was utter desolation. Never had a butcher's bill been so high.

It was a struggle for the 40th redcoats to carry me, tripping and stumbling over the bodies, as far the smouldering farmhouse but they managed it somehow. I was beyond feeling any pain at that point, the nightmare world we occupied being more than enough to banish all human feeling. Among the heaped corpses of French and Allied infantry that lay around the walls of the ruined farm, I could see the scattered bodies of fallen

Hanoverians and 95th Riflemen, their green jackets almost black now as the dye had run out of them with the rain. Somewhere in that pile lay Craven and Jarvis, and maybe Tanner too because La Haye Sainte had fallen late in the afternoon. The cobbled road leading back up to the crossroads was invisible under the wreckage of French gun carriages and supply wagons, the corpses lying thick in the grotesque positions of violent death, the mangled bodies of horses trapped between the shafts of their gun limbers, and discarded backpacks, breastplates and broken weapons strewn everywhere. It was a pitiful, hellish sight.

The redcoats had initially thought to leave me at La Haye Sainte but they took pity on me and decided to carry me up to the crossroads, not far from where I had set out with the Hanoverians. Everywhere, soldiers wandered around, all of them in a daze, their faces blackened, seeking what was left of their units. At the crossroads, officers were busy organising more work parties and wagons to collect the wounded and bring them to the hospital tents. There were so many casualties that the surgeons must have been overwhelmed. I spotted assistant surgeon Mostyn, his arms bloodied up to the elbows and his shirt stained crimson, near a makeshift tent beyond the sunken road. My rescuers carried me over to him.

Mostyn was leaning over a cavalry officer who had lost an arm and a leg. The man was clearly dying but the assistant surgeon still laboured to give him comfort. The redcoats put me down gently beside a broken wagon wheel, my drums beside me. Leaning back against the wheel, I thanked them profusely for their kind-hearted generosity. They patted me on the back, wished me luck, and headed off, their good deed done. Mostyn spotted me and saluted in greeting. A few minutes later, he stepped over the line of wounded men and came across to me.

'You been seen to, Burns?' he asked. I was in severe pain after the uncomfortable journey all the way from the hollow, but the sight of the bloodied, shattered bodies awaiting his attention had humbled me.

'Yes, Sir, my leg has been attended to already.'

'Good! Otherwise you'd have to wait. It's officers first and you've only got two stripes. That last one's gone, I'm afraid but there's plenty more waiting. Most won't see dawn tomorrow. You can stay here so long as you keep out of the way.'

'Thank you, Sir.'

From then on, I tried to keep my eyes averted but a battlefield after the fighting has stopped has a way of assaulting every sense that the body possesses. It cannot be blocked out. Nor could the grinding of Mostyn's saw and the moans and cries of unfortunate men who needed him. Those sounds live on in my memory.

Along with the scavengers who had descended on the place like a plague of locusts from midnight, groups of citizens from Brussels and other nearby towns also arrived. At first, they loitered on the fringes of the battlefield gawping at the horrific scene. Then they moved in among the bodies with the other ghouls, picking up broken weapons and discarded military equipment, trying on Cuirassier and Dragoon helmets, and even cutting buttons off the jackets of the uniforms, especially from the Old Guard. The intrusion of these interlopers onto the battlefield was nothing short of sacrilegious but not a single thing could stop them. I eventually closed my eyes and leaned back. I had seen enough. Then, someone called my name.

44

I recognised the voice as if from a previous life, it was The Fox Maguire with Nosey McNeilis beside him. Maguire had a bloodied bandage around his head but, other than that, they seemed uninjured. They made their way over to me, walking on the corpses and the debris of battle that covered the ground.

'Where's Reggie?' asked Nosey, straightaway.

All I could do by way of reply was shake my head. The words wouldn't come out. How could I describe what had happened to him? McNeilis sat down beside me and bowed his head. The Fox Maguire kicked at the ground, aimlessly. I took a few deep breaths to collect myself.

'Where's the rest of the regiment?' I finally managed to ask.

'Over there,' The Fox said. 'We'll show you. Nice drum, by the way,' he added, noticing the shell of Christophe's once-fine instrument.

They helped me up and, leaning on their shoulders, I hobbled as far as the knoll, passed the remains of the elm tree, crossed the sunken road and beheld the devastation. My beloved regiment, the 27th Foot, the Inniskillings, had been butchered. Bodies still lay heaped together in the most undignified of poses, some minus their heads or limbs, their torsos shattered, bloodied all over, struck down in the most brutal fashion. A few shaken survivors were staggering among the corpses, seeking out any wounded soldier lucky enough not to have bled out. From the way they lay, the regiment had formed square and had remained steadfast in that position. They had been slaughtered where they stood. The regimental colours, shredded to pieces, flapped gently in the warm breeze, the wounded heaped around the poles. Welter and Reihill were with them, muddied and blood-stained. There was no sign of Astwith or the company captains.

'The French hit us hard,' McNeilis went on, 'again and again. When the Cuirassiers didn't get into the square, they brought horse artillery up to within three hundred metres and poured canister and grapeshot into us at close range. We kept closing ranks and firing back as best we could even though the square kept shrinking.' His voice choked for a few moments. 'Their voltigeurs cut us down from there,' he said, pointing to the knoll. 'We had little enough to shoot back with for most of the time but we wouldn't budge. Wellington had told us to hold the line no matter what, so that's what we did. We kept pulling the wounded into the middle of the square and throwing out the dead, then we'd close up ranks again. The dead bodies were piled up as barricades. When we ran out of ammunition, we called for more but none could get through to us because of the damned French cavalry. Someone had the bright idea of taking the cartridge pouches from the dead as they had no more need of them, so that's how we held out.'

McNeilis' description was just too awful to contemplate.

'And the others?' I asked, meaning the drummers.

'Crooks and Gallagher were wounded but they'll both live,' he added. 'They've been taken to the hospital at the rear already. Many of the officers were either killed or wounded. Logue and Grant are dead, so too is McGreel. Captain Dunne and Drum Major Hicks were wounded. Captain Hare is still in command.'

'Lieutenant Astwith?' I asked, remembering what he had made me promise.

'One of the first to fall,' said Maguire. 'Shot in the gut. No hope. He was found late last night among a pile of corpses by a priest and a doctor. After confessing, the priest gave him absolution and then the doctor cut his throat. It was an act of mercy as he was otherwise going to lie there in agony for days until gangrene took him. He pleaded with them to do it, saying that you were no longer there to carry out your promise. So that's what the priest and the doctor spent the rest of the night doing, giving absolution and then slitting throats, God help us.'

Maguire fell silent. I slowly let all of this sink in, thinking what a sorry state we had come to if that was the kind of ministry a priest and a doctor had to dispense. At least, though, I was spared having to keep my promise. Poor Astwith, his premonition had been correct, after all. Maybe mercy comes in many forms. Who was I to judge?

'We have to go, James,' said McNeilis, 'to help Mostyn. Will you be all right? We'll come back in a while when we find something for you to eat.'

I nodded. 'You go on,' I said.

They propped me against an empty cartridge box, placed my drums beside me and headed off. I watched them as they joined with other survivors, searching for the wounded among the dead, using a greatcoat with two muskets through the sleeves as a stretcher.

Sitting there on my own, I contemplated the extraordinary scene around me, the lifeless Inniskillings in the embrace of violent death and the living engaged in recovering the wounded. I tried to visualise my father lying in the middle of such carnage once, having fallen to a coward's dastardly blow. Baxter not only took my father's life; he also took his reputation, my mother's happiness and my chance to know a good man. All the veterans knew my father had been killed by a bayonet wound in the back. They must have assumed he had turned to run and had been cut down. Nobody in the 27th does that. At last, I had found out the truth. My father was no coward.

I would see to it that Baxter was exposed and my father's reputation restored. I'd go home to my mother and tell her all. Then maybe she'd tell me about the man she once knew. Did Drum Major Hicks suspect something, for he always stood up for me? Maybe he couldn't prove my father wasn't a coward, just as nobody would ever be able to prove I killed Curley. The only other witness to that was dead.

Reggie was lying somewhere in that pile of corpses out there, stripped of his uniform now like all the others, his dead body lacking an arm, a cruel fate for a drummer. He had drummed every step of the way with me from Enniskillen and I'd lost him. But Christophe had come

313

upon me. Who could ever believe that he and I had fought with our drums, that our duel had the same deadly intent as if we had used swords or pistols? He had saved my life at the cost of his own. Reggie and Christophe, drummers both, two men to whom I owed everything.

With that, the relieving tears came to me at last and I mourned for them both as I sat there, and for all those lost on that field whose bodies lay strewn among the crushed grass and the ruined summer crops. I stroked Christophe's drum, the eagle crest and the regimental number, 55*e*, and resolved what I was going to do. At that moment, horses approached from behind and a shadow fell across the drum.

'The 27th, Sir,' a voice said, 'and, by God, the report was correct. They are lying dead in square.'

A Brigadier General rode forward into my line of sight and stayed astride his horse. I was collected enough to salute him from my reclined position.

'A French drum, Corporal,' the Brigadier General said, dismounting. 'A worthy trophy, and I see you've put the skin and sticks to good use. Has the surgeon seen to you already?'

'No, Sir. It was the French drummer who fixed my leg.'

'Well then, I hope he's saved you from the surgeon's saw because I'd say it must be blunt by now.'

Other horsemen dismounted behind me. I heard them removing their hats as they observed the Inniskillings in silence. One of them stepped beside me, where I could see him. The assured face from yesterday was now pained and drawn.

'Drum for them, Corporal,' the Duke of Wellington said. 'Drum for my brave boys of the 27th, like you did for me yesterday, for they deserve it now more than I.'

So I put my drum between my legs, as I had done in the hollow, and started to beat The Retreat, the traditional soldier's call at dusk. The Duke would have known that this was the drum roll to mark the end of a day's battle, and no battle could ever be greater than the one just fought at Waterloo.

From somewhere not far away, another drum joined in, then a third, and from further across the battlefield, yet more. I can't tell now how many played, all of us drumming mournfully together, the soldier's final farewell to all fallen comrades. When the last, sad beat of my drum had died away, and the echoes of the others had faded, the Duke acknowledged me with his hat.

'Thank you, Drummer,' he said quietly. 'The 27th Inniskillings will be remembered. They saved my line, they saved the battle.' Then he remounted his horse, Copenhagen, and slowly walked off, his hat held in his hand, his staff close behind him.

I stayed for a long time on that ridge, me and my melancholy thoughts. McNeilis and Maguire came back a few times to check on me, as did other survivors from the regiment. Some of them kept shaking their heads in disbelief, incapable of speech, such was the effect of that day. We were indeed a sorry gathering. But we were proud.

****

I envy people who have never seen a battlefield after the guns fall silent. Human eyes should never have to behold such devastation. At Waterloo, there were no tidy rows of corpses waiting to embrace the soil. Instead, it was an abattoir, a charnel house, a clutter of torsos, limbs and heads, sprayed with guts and blood, the remains of horse and man entangled in ugly death. No matter where I turned, I beheld death, misery, mutilation and destruction, and yet, I had sufficient reason to thank God that I was alive. I spent one long day and one long night at Waterloo but it seemed that a lifetime, no, I must correct myself, several lifetimes had passed in the space of those horrific hours. And I have spent decades since then trying to make sense of it all.

Drum Major Edward Hicks was right. The drum is a savage instrument. In my hands it had drilled men into a machine of war and had then drummed them to their deaths. The results of this folly were all around me. For those of us who were there, we have all since buried our memories of Waterloo with the mutilated bodies of the dead and started life again, for that is what the soldier does when he survives and his comrades die.

Taking a final look across the valley, I patted the soft calfskin on my drum, then played The Retreat once more. I muted my drum because this time the tribute to my fallen comrades was from me alone. As on that day at the crossroads, when I touched a drum for the first time, I let the sound wash over me and take hold of me. It possessed me for the last time. And then I let it all go. When I finished, I put my drum aside, laying it carefully on the ground. I wiped the regimental crest as best I could with a torn piece of my shirt before placing the ticken cover carefully over the calfskin top. Then I took the drumsticks in my hand and broke each in turn and pressed the ends deep into the soft, blood-soaked ground of that Belgian field. I felt a great weight lifting off my shoulders as the last piece of wood disappeared into the clay. The 27th Regiment of Foot, the Inniskillings, would never again march to the beat of my savage drum.

SIXTY-FOUR YEARS LATER

Obituary Notice, *Ulster Medical Gazette,* March, 1879.

The death has recently taken place of renowned Surgeon James Anthony Burns, formerly a drummer in the 27th (Inniskilling) Regiment of Foot and a Waterloo veteran. Deeply affected by the lack of medical provision for wounded soldiers after the battle, Burns retrained as an assistant surgeon and went on to give a lifetime of dedicated service to the enhancement of care for soldiers injured or maimed in war.

Although Burns refused to talk about his period in the army, it is known that, at Waterloo, his life was saved by Christophe Molloy, a drummer of Irish extraction in the French 55*e d'Infanterie de Ligne* who, unfortunately, was himself killed later on that day. On recovering from injuries sustained during the battle, Burns visited Molloy's mother in Saint-Marc-le-Blanc, Brittany, and presented her with the restored regimental drum her son had played so valiantly at Waterloo. It is now known that he supported Madame Molloy financially for the rest of her life.

It is ironic that Burns himself died without ever being able to establish the whereabouts of his own beloved mother whose fate remains a mystery. Being an only child, he has no known kin. A manuscript of his experiences with the 27th is believed to exist and is in the hands of his solicitors.

ACKNOWLEDGEMENTS

My sincere thanks to Tom Reilly and Eugene O'Connor for reading the story in its original draft; their comments and observations were of great assistance in the development of the narrative, as was their continuing interest and enthusiasm.

My deep appreciation to Deirdre Devine at Choice Publishing in Drogheda who, from our first meeting, offered me every assistance possible and ensured that everything to do with this publication was done to the highest professional standard. A particular thank you to Tess Purcell whose brilliant, eye-catching cover design graces this book.

I wish to offer a special word of gratitude to The Inniskillings Museum, The Castle, Enniskillen, for providing me with resource material on drummers of the 27th Foot. My thanks also to the Management of Ardgillan Castle, Co Dublin, for permission to photograph the Napoleonic era drum which Tess featured on the cover of the book.

And to my long-suffering friends who patiently listened to me obsess about drummers and Waterloo over the last year or two (probably longer, if the truth be told).

My family were invaluable – Amy and Brian as constant motivators and supports, Amy especially in the role of editor of the book; and Anne Marie for putting up with me while I was writing it, for painstakingly reading it in its various drafts, for her unflagging assistance and her unerring eye to detail.

I save the last word of acknowledgement for my mother, Mai Burns Herron, who was born and reared in Enniskillen and, although she lived most of her life in Dublin, remained a proud Fermanagh woman to the end. I think she would have enjoyed reading this book.

HISTORICAL NOTE ON THE 27TH
(INNISKILLING) REGIMENT OF FOOT

The 27th (Inniskilling) Regiment of Foot was first raised in 1689 as a local militia at Enniskillen, Co Fermanagh, by Colonel Zachariah Tiffin, taking the Williamite side against James II. Due to their performance at the Battle of Newtownbutler, they fought as a regular infantry regiment at the Battle of the Boyne in 1690. Since that year, their list of engagements includes Falkirk and Culloden (1746), Maida (1806), Siege of Badajoz (1812), Salamanca (1812), Toulouse (1814) and Waterloo (1815).

During the Seven Years' War (1756-1763), the regiment served in North America and the West Indies fighting against the French, and later took part in the American War of Independence. When the French Revolutionary Wars broke out, the 27th found itself back in Europe and participated in the Flanders Campaign of 1793. It went on to serve during the Napoleonic Wars starting in Egypt where it was with Sir Ralph Abercrombie's force at the Battle of Alexandria in 1801. After that, separate battalions of the regiment went on to fight with distinction in most of the battles that took place on the Iberian Peninsula.

With Napoleon's return from exile, the 1st Battalion

joined Sir John Lambert's 10th Brigade as described in *To the Beat of a Savage Drum*, and marched to Waterloo where it was initially held in reserve. At around 6.30pm on June 18th, 1815, the French advanced to within 270 metres of their position in the line and found the 27th deployed 'in square'. French artillery opened a devastating fire on the exposed Inniskillings resulting in the highest percentage casualty rate of any Allied unit on that day. Out of 698 men mustered, the Inniskillings lost 105 killed and 373 wounded, a total of 478 casualties, or 69%. After the battle, the battalion was described as 'lying dead in square'. Wellington later accredited the 27th with having saved his line.

After Waterloo, the regiment served in South Africa from 1837 to 1847, proceeding to India during the Indian Mutiny where it later served for a period on the North-West Frontier. In 1881, due to reforms in the British Army, the 27th became the 1st Battalion, Royal Inniskilling Fusiliers, joining with the 108th (Madras Infantry) Regiment of Foot as the 2nd Battalion.

ABOUT THE AUTHOR

Aidan J Herron – A winner of the Irish Writers Centre 2015 Novel Fair

Since retiring as a primary school principal, Aidan is fortunate to have more time to devote to writing fiction. All of his previous publications were in the field of education. He combines his passion for history and military research with voluntary tour-guiding in Ardgillan Castle. The Napoleonic era drum featured on the cover and a marching scene from the film, *Barry Lyndon*, were the main inspirations for *To the Beat of a Savage Drum*. By happy coincidence, Aidan's mother was from Enniskillen, the home town of the 27th Regiment of Foot, The Inniskillings.